KILLER
IN THE
KITCHEN

KILLER
IN THE
KITCHEN

A Chesapeake Bay Mystery

Judy L. Murray

LEVEL
BEST BOOKS

First published by Level Best Books 2022

Author Photo Credit: Malgorzata Baker Photography

First edition

ISBN: 978-1-68512-192-1

Cover art by Level Best Designs

This book was professionally typeset on Reedsy.
Find out more at reedsy.com

To family and friends and shared special times.

"It's important, you know, that wickedness shouldn't triumph."

—Miss Jane Marple, A Pocket Full of Rye

Praise for Judy L Murray and Her Chesapeake Bay Mystery Series

"…plenty of romance, surprises, and a climax that's quite the cliffhanger." —*Kirkus Reviews*

"Engaging & Entertaining!" —*Kings River Life Magazine*

"A masterful job." —*Writers Who Kill Review*

"A well-layered mystery…a little romance along with suspenseful story-telling." —*Books To The Ceiling Review*

"A 'couldn't put it down' mystery with an entertaining writing style, diverse characters, and a complex investigation to challenge my own inner Miss Marple." —*Kings River Life Magazine*

"…if you are an avid reader of mysteries…you'll want to get your hands on a copy of her first novel, *Murder in the Master*." —*APG Chesapeake Newspapers*

"Fans of traditional mysteries will cheer." —Colleen Shogan, Washington Whodunit Mysteries

Chapter One

Real Estate Rule #2: How to sell a house—Offer a drop-dead kitchen.

"Darn! Darn, darn, darn!" Helen stood up, pulled off her gardening gloves, and tossed them onto the driveway. She pushed her short swing of dark hair out of her green eyes and glared down at the nubs of leaves barely poking out of her flower bed. "Those darn deer! They eat everything!"

"Mom! Are you talking to yourself again?" Her daughter Lizzie poked her platinum head outside a window and looked down at her.

"I'm cursing at the deer. I've been trying to grow these Hostas ever since I moved out of Port Anne four years ago. I would think since I live in a state park, the deer could find plenty to eat other than my plants."

"For heaven's sake. Just because Dad's gone doesn't mean you've become the expert gardener. Since when did you grow a green thumb? It's the end of August. Why don't you just let them go? Besides, I've got a hot lead for you on a great house to sell. Come sit on the deck, and I'll bring you a tall glass of iced tea. Interested?" Lizzie wiggled her dramatic eyebrows.

"Yes, to the iced tea. And maybe yes to the hot lead." Helen dusted off the mulch stuck to her knees and picked up her trowel. She stepped back and squinted up at her daughter, her real estate agent antenna up and working. "Where's the house? Remember the last goose chase you sent me on? I couldn't decide which was worse, the pervy owner or his house that needed to be torched. He couldn't understand why buyers didn't want to see his tighty-whities drying on his oven handle."

Her daughter laughed as she ducked her head back inside.

Helen walked around the house and onto her deck, the broad expanse of blue Chesapeake Bay and woods her back yard. She leaned against the rail that ran the length of her house and spotted an American eagle perusing the water for dinner. She could still hear her daughter chuckling from the kitchen. "Don't be such a smarty pants. You knew a lead on a new client would suck me in. What's the story?"

Lizzie handed her a glass before sprawling across the closest navy canvas chaise. "Do you remember *Cooking with Roberto*, the cooking show I host on ShopTV twice a week?"

Helen gave a cautious shrug. "I watch you as often as I can, but I really haven't noticed your guest chef. Should I? You know I'm not into cooking shows."

"Mom." Lizzie gave her a condescending stare with her bright blue eyes. "Everyone's heard of Roberto Barto. He just got named Best Chef Mid-Atlantic by *Gourmet Magazine*. He has three of the hottest restaurants on the East Coast. One's on the Rittenhouse in Philadelphia. One's right on the Baltimore Inner Harbor. One's here in Port Anne. People wait months for a reservation."

"They must get awfully hungry."

Lizzie let out an exasperated groan. "You don't have to be a saucier to hear about Roberto. He's the bay's answer to Gordon Ramsay. He's got everyone feasting on his 'Taste the Chesapeake' recipes. Blue crabs, oysters, and rockfish with Italian pastas." Lizzie's bright red fingernails made little quote marks in the air. "Three years ago, no one ever thought of Old Bay seasoned crab on top of angel hair pasta. He's reinvented Chesapeake staples into five-star dining. His cookbooks are international bestsellers."

Helen regarded her daughter's frown. Lizzie was an expert in juggling famous guests to attract shopaholics at home. It made her a celebrity in her own right. "I realize being a Host on the biggest shopping channel means sell, sell, sell."

"ShopTV has tripled its business since it bought out the BTB station."

Helen took a sip of her iced tea and tilted her face toward the sun. "That still doesn't mean I remember anything about him."

"I never thought you would be so completely uninformed about a local restaurant. You may not like to cook, but you love to eat. He converted the old steakhouse right here in Port Anne to the Water Street Bistro ten months ago."

"Okay, I admit I've heard his name. I never connected him to the bistro. That's definitely the new hot spot," Helen mused. "I treated Susan and Tammi there for their birthdays. We loved it."

Lizzie gave another groan. "I even gave you one of Roberto's custom Flying Pans we were selling last Christmas."

"Was that his?" Helen furrowed her brows.

"It was my fruitless attempt at encouraging you to cook something for yourself besides Special K."

Helen grinned. "I did like the color, eggplant."

"Since when does Special K come in purple?"

"Very funny." Helen sat down and kicked off her muddy orange Crocs.

"Laugh if you will, but his cookware is selling like hotcakes—pardon the pun. His partner, Adrian, invented a non-stick surface that's threatening to put major brands out of business. Their coating is completely organic. No chemical compounds whatsoever, so all the foodies and health fanatics are crazy about their pans. I had a show with Roberto just this week. We sold 10,000 sets in less than thirty minutes. Right now, ShopTV thinks he's a god."

"Are you telling me this because he's the one who wants to sell his house? I'm assuming there's a connection. Now I'm interested."

"Yup." Lizzie followed her mother into the kitchen. Helen's two cats, Trixie and Watson, trailed hopefully behind her.

Her mother poked around in the refrigerator. She came out with a squished triangle of cheddar, a bruised apple, and a can of cat food.

"Mom, his place is stunning. He bought it before he opened up the bistro.

3

It's right off Riding Cross, but you can't see it from the road."

Helen's face brightened. "Riding Cross is a breathtaking spot. Horse farms on the water. I would think it's pretty safe to assume that this famous chef has a kitchen to die for. Have you seen inside?"

"I did. He had a big party last night. I thought I told you I was going. His house is massive, totally renovated. A classic Southern colonial with gobs of extras. Not exactly Little House on the Prairie." She waved her arms. "The kitchen has miles and miles of white marble, black soapstone, and Sub-Zero appliances. He's got a huge Wolf range and every gadget you can imagine. There's an outdoor kitchen off the patio near a gorgeous custom inground pool. It's a fabulous place for a party."

Helen scooped two dry food servings of cat food into blue bowls and placed them on the floor to silence the yowling at her feet. She pulled out a paring knife. "How's the decorating?"

"No expense spared. A bit heavy on the black and silver, but beautiful." Lizzie started to dig through Helen's wine rack.

Helen gave a little chuckle. "Are you sure the house wasn't financed by the Mob? They love the restaurant business."

Lizzie pulled out a wine bottle. "You're impossible. Not everyone who owns restaurants needs a loan shark. You read too many mysteries."

"No one can read too many mysteries. *That's* not possible. Why wasn't I invited to this little get together?" She took a big slice of the questionable apple and offered the plate to Lizzie. She wrinkled her nose and opted for the mangled cheese.

"Sorry, only our studio muckety-mucks were invited. He mentioned that he wanted to sell. I told him you're the best real estate agent in Kent County."

"Only Kent County? Why not the entire state of Maryland?" Helen stretched her tanned arms around her taller daughter and gave her a squeeze. "I may hate to cook, but I sure know how to sell a kitchen and the house that comes with it. When do I get to meet the Chesapeake's answer to Ramsay?"

"I told him you'd stop by the studio after our 10 am show tomorrow. I'll introduce you. Does that work?" Lizzie's pretty face beamed.

"Works for me. Who wouldn't like to mix shopping with making money?

Did I ever tell you how you light up when you're trying to convince me of something?" Helen reached for a wine glass.

"The apple doesn't fall far from the tree. I'm one of the reasons the network has eight million viewers." Her daughter popped the last piece of cheese into her mouth. She twisted her fit band. "I've got to go. Jason swore he'd leave his office in time for dinner together. That's an event I can't miss."

Helen wrinkled her brow. "How *is* Jason?"

Lizzie slung a huge dusty pink canvas bag over her shoulder and kissed her mother. "Another time, Mom. See you!"

"Doesn't a mother have the right to ask?"

"Not unless you're going to tell me what's happening with Joe McAlister, your favorite detective." She pointed to her dad's wedding band hanging from a silver chain on her mother's neck.

"Humph. Hey, what's Barto's home address? I want to do a little homework."

"It's on your To Do pad on the counter," Lizzie called back as she headed out the front door.

Helen picked up the pad and squinted at her daughter's messy scrawl. *Roberto Barto. Internationally known chef, creator of The Flying Pan. Yes, people actually buy cookware and use it! House is at 2 Riding Cross Lane, Port Anne. Be at the studio by 9:45 am Monday. I'll meet you at security in the lobby.*

Helen drew a circle around Roberto Barto and muttered aloud. "What is a saucier, anyway? And why's he selling his house so soon after spending all that money on it?" After years in the real estate business, she had a hunch there was more to this decision than what they knew. She gave another little shrug, rummaged through a kitchen cabinet, and spotted a lonely can of clam chowder. Maybe she should start watching some cooking shows so she could actually invite a man home for dinner. Even Joe brought his own pizza when he visited. She decided to upgrade her dinner tonight and pushed the soup aside. "I swear I've got a box of granola somewhere," she said to her cats. Two pairs of large eyes, one green, the other blue, blinked back with indifference. They knew her too well.

Chapter Two

The next morning Helen drove through the ShopTV corporate entrance and down a mile-long private road through the complex toward the main building. She followed signs for guest parking. Tracing a winding path led her toward a broad tier of steps, under the giant ShopTV sign, and through a set of eight double doors to the security desk. A friendly guard checked her name against his computer screen of expected visitors, called Lizzie, and then handed her a badge with her name printed on it. A minute later, Lizzie opened the double doors behind the guard's station and greeted her. She already wore a full face of makeup with inch-long false eyelashes.

"You timed it perfectly. Roberto and I are going on air in about ten minutes. I'll take you into the green room, and you can watch the show from there. I'll introduce you after the show's over." She stopped to study her mother up and down. "You look terrific. Love the khaki jacket and the orange bag. Not too Realtor serious."

Helen smiled at her daughter. "Just following your fashion advice." She pursed her lips and mimicked her. "Wear a great bag and shoes, and you'll turn an old pair of jeans into a look. Besides, you know orange is my favorite color."

"Got that right," Lizzie retorted. She pushed open another set of double doors. She turned back. "Why are you wearing Dad's wedding ring more lately?"

Helen pulled on the long silver chain around her neck. "I decided it was my lucky charm, my talisman." Her daughter smiled.

Minutes later, Helen watched her get wired up with a portable mic at the Operations Desk. An OPS technician gave it a quick test to check the volume. Lizzie winked at her mother and disappeared through another door into the set. Helen headed into the green room. It buzzed with nervous guests waiting to go on air and their vendors fussing over product displays. Eight small flatscreens strung high along the walls displayed the live show. Six computer monitors flashed the latest products just aired. Their sales numbers hopped across the screens like the New York Stock Exchange. Two vendors were giving each other a high five as the numbers kept climbing for a designer handbag.

She grabbed a cup of coffee and settled into an L-shaped sofa to watch the introduction of *Cooking with Roberto*. She was loving the "let's get it sold" atmosphere of a company generating twelve billion dollars in revenue every year.

Helen spotted her daughter's face on the screen as Lizzie welcomed viewers into the show and introduced Roberto as chef. Most products had three to eight minutes of precious, expensive live airtime. *Cooking with Roberto* ran a half hour and was projected from a full-sized kitchen with all the latest, top-of-the-line gadgets. I guess if you're named Best Chef by *Gourmet Magazine*, you can demand a studio kitchen better than most magazine covers, Helen thought.

Roberto was tall, a little beefy, easily six foot two with a curly mop of thick black hair, and dressed in a pure white chef's jacket. His name was embroidered in red and black across the breast pocket. She could understand why he was causing such a buzz with the women. A natural in front of the camera, he leaned over and took Lizzie's hand as he planted a kiss on her cheek. He beamed a wide grin accented by two deep dimples at the camera and introduced a new recipe from his latest cookbook. Lizzie launched into a review of his cookware collection, elaborating on the technical details of the organic, non-stick surface and how it made his recipes so easy to make. Roberto, after searing a flank steak and smothering it with red peppers, wiped the pan clean with a dramatic swish of a paper towel.

It was mostly light banter interspersed with live calls from the viewers, obviously all adoring fans. His quips delivered with a warm demeanor created bonding moments. One caller from North Dakota talked about her dinner party. Her friends had oohed and ahhed over Roberto's recipes made in her set of Flying Plan cookware.

"Hi Darlin', delighted you discovered my cookware," the chef wooed. "You'll need to use it to make my Chesapeake with a Twang Crab Stew from my newest cookbook. So easy for a crowd, and no clean-up. You'll love it."

A male fan with a strong Boston accent called in to discuss the merits of using Roberto's spicy croutons on crab chowder at his pre-season Patriots party. Always going for the sell, Roberto pointed out a deep Flying Pan soup pot as part of his collection. Lizzie kept the callers moving, adept at wrapping up their conversations without them feeling shuttled off the air.

"Only four minutes left to our *Cooking with Roberto* show." Lizzie mugged a disappointed frown toward the camera. "We have less than eight hundred sets in the navy. Just five hundred remaining in the extremely popular eggplant. Black is sold out. Remember, free shipping is only for today!" Lizzie and Roberto gave a friendly wave to the viewers, and the camera moved away. Another host with the next product came onto the television screen.

After Roberto's show, Lizzie pulled Helen from the green room. They weaved in between huge wall dividers on casters that separated one set from another. Orange and yellow electrical cords crisscrossed the floors like giant balls of yarn. Set assistants were positioning the next product in line while crews shifted huge robotic cameras on wheels into focus.

Lizzie flagged Roberto as he turned toward his private green room, a rare perk no matter how famous the celebrity. He unbuttoned his chef's coat and ran his fingers through his hair as he reached out to shake Helen's hand.

"So nice to meet my favorite host's mother. Thanks so much for coming to the show. I really appreciate it."

"My pleasure. You've got quite a fan club, including my daughter."

He gave a self-deprecating glance to Lizzie. "It's been a great ride, that's for sure. Who would have thought my Flying Pans would make such a hit?"

"I don't think your cooking skills hurt," Helen offered.

"Hopefully not." Another modest smile.

"I gather you're thinking about selling your house."

"I am. In fact, I'd like to get it on the market as soon as I can. According to Lizzie, you're the best agent around." Roberto raised thick dark eyebrows. "I checked you out. You've got a reputation for getting the job done.'

"Thank you very much. You may have also heard that I'll never be a threat to your culinary skills." She paused. "Tell me, why are you moving?"

Roberto gave a quick glance around the set and spotted a small group of women on a tour. He sent them a big smile, then turned back. "For now," he said in a low, firm voice. "Let's just say that with the expansion of my third restaurant scheduled for late fall, I need to make traveling up and down the East Coast easier. I've already lined up a townhouse on the Baltimore Inner Harbor."

"Lizzie tells me your property is gorgeous and your kitchen amazing. How old is the house?"

"It was built in the 1890s, but I totally renovated it about a year after I bought it. I'm very proud of the result, but with all this travel, the house isn't used enough." He examined his neatly manicured nails.

"Can you bear to leave your kitchen?" Helen probed for more motivation.

"Actually, I'm really not leaving it. This studio kitchen is a replica. I required it as part of my contract."

Lizzie gave her mother a quick nod.

"Clearly, the network thought you well worth the investment." Helen waved toward the sea of stainless-steel appliances. "When shall we meet? I could see the house tomorrow afternoon if that works for you." She pulled out her iPhone to check her calendar.

"That sounds fine. Give my assistant Adrian a call to check my schedule." Roberto gave Lizzie an affectionate squeeze and, with a wave, hustled off the set.

"Well, he's certainly a whirlwind," Helen commented. "He seems to know how to charm you while he sticks to his own agenda."

"Oh, no doubt. He hasn't turned into a multi-million-dollar sensation without knowing how to control his viewers. Come on, let's find Adrian. By the way, he's Roberto's business partner, not his assistant."

"Then why did Roberto say that?"

Lizzie's eyes swept the room. "That's a little ego game Roberto plays if Adrian isn't around."

Helen quick-stepped behind her daughter's longer strides, weaving in between another half dozen sets and down a maze of hallways lined with racks and racks of merchandise samples.

"Why is all this stuff hanging out here?" A row of black, yellow, and white sweaters hung next to three metal shelves overflowing with cosmetics. A giant piece of white cardboard with the number eighteen hung on the racks.

"Those are products in the queue to go on air later today." Lizzie tossed back as she rounded another corner. "There's Adrian. I was hoping he was still in the building." She gave a little wave to a slight man wearing a headset around his neck, chatting with a model. She was sporting a heavy wool sweater even though it was mid-August.

Barely even with Helen's 5'6", with thinning hair pulled back into a ponytail, Roberto's partner was as unremarkable as the chef was a standout. His washed-out Army green Under Armour t-shirt was tucked into worn jeans held up by a brown leather belt buckled beyond three worn holes. A pair of scuffed designer moccasins and no socks finished his deliberate scruffy style.

"Adrian, I want you to meet my mother, Helen Morrisey." Lizzie turned to her. "Mom, this is Adrian Stanton, Roberto's business partner, and all-around brilliant problem solver."

Adrian shifted an iPad from right to left and shook her hand. "Good to meet you, Lizzie's mother." He offered a thin-lipped smile without showing any teeth. "I hear you may be selling Riding Cross. I hope you're used to dealing with a...." He stopped, glanced at Lizzie, then finished. "Personality." His sharp brown eyes through round, tortoiseshell glasses met Helen's green ones.

Helen had the feeling prima donna was his first word choice. She returned the comment with a little smile. "Oh, I've worked with my fair share of artists. I'm not afraid of dealing with a little drama."

He nodded a slow approval. "Then you won't be disappointed. When does our chef king want you to see the house?"

"Does three tomorrow work for you? I'll walk through the house, take some measurements, and then discuss pricing."

Adrian flipped open the iPad's black leather cover and ran his index finger across his calendar. "That works. Roberto will want to give you the White House tour. I'll need to be part of the pricing discussion. We've already met with two other Realtors. Is there anything you need at this point?"

Helen didn't wince at the news of competition. "He mentioned that he did a lot of renovations. Given the size, would you have a floor plan I can borrow?"

"You're the first person to ask for one." Hesitating, Adrian offered another polite, meager smile. "I think we may have one on hand. I'll see what I can do." He headed off.

"He's definitely the opposite personality," muttered Helen.

"He's the chemist and financial brains behind Barto Enterprises. Roberto is the frontman. He's nice enough to me, but he's certainly not Roberto."

"I've had a lot of experience with partners," Helen considered. "I've come to realize that the dull ones can be just as important to their company's success as the flashy ones. Makes me appreciate them."

"He has some kind of ownership interest in Riding Cross."

"The deed has Barto Enterprises Corporation as owner. Does Adrian live there with Roberto?"

"I never asked, but someone mentioned it at the party Sunday. Sounds like Adrian has his own separate wing. They're not a couple, if that's what you're wondering."

Helen paused and watched Adrian's quick retreat. "I'm wondering about a lot of things."

Chapter Three

Helen decided to head into Port Anne and Safe Harbor Realty. It was time to do some homework before she met with Roberto tomorrow. She liked to walk into a property prepared with a market value in mind. This one was going to be a challenge. Her little bay town was enjoying a hot market with waterfront properties in even more demand. Still, property in the two-to-three-million-dollar price range was a rarity.

August was the height of the boating season for the Chesapeake and Port Anne. Shopkeepers depended on the influx of visitors. According to Lizzie, Roberto's bistro was helping draw in the crowds. She pointed her four-seater blue MiniCooper over the narrow, two-lane bridge into town past the navy and gold "Welcome to Port Anne – Top of the Chesapeake" sign that greeted the tourists. The big American flag next to it barely moved in the light breeze. The Chesapeake in August was usually hot and sticky. Good for power boaters wanting flat water. Not so good for sailors praying for steady wind. It was a quirky little town with its lifetime locals playing tug of war with new residents and vacationers and their influx of money and upscale tastes. She understood why some felt cast out. Yet, she honestly believed this new wave brought opportunities for everyone. She gave a quick smile at the shop windows. Besides, who doesn't love trendy clothes?

She grabbed a parking spot in front of Jean's Coffee Pot. Jean greeted her over the whine of a grinder. The shop was quiet, with just a few people in need of a mid-morning shot of caffeine.

"Usually see you earlier." Jean smiled. At least a dozen plastic coffee pot pins danced merrily across the bright yellow apron covering her ample bosom.

"I decided I needed a pick-me-up."

"I guess you heard about the real estate agent attacked last night in Far Hill?"

Helen set her bag down on the counter with a thud. "No, I haven't. Do you know who it was?"

"Paula Brezow. She's a regular customer of mine."

"What happened?"

"Police are working on it. Stole her new Land Rover. Knocked her unconscious and stuffed her in a bedroom closet. The homeowner came home from work and found her. Lucky she's alive." Jean tsked, tsked as she poured cream into a pitcher.

"That's terrifying. Our board sent out a warning a few weeks ago. Forty-nine agents killed in one year across the country. We're easy targets. Meet too many strangers in houses alone." Helen dug into her wallet.

"You need to be careful."

"I will, don't worry." She switched the subject to lighten the mood. "You're the Water Street maven when it comes to all the happenings around town. I've got some homework to do on a property." She hesitated. "How much do you know about Chef Roberto Barto? I just learned he owns Water Street Bistro. I gather he's doing well." She stuck her hand into a jar and pulled out two fresh biscotti wrapped in tissue.

The older woman raised her heavily penciled eyebrows at his name. "Seems like Chef Barto has got the touch. The parking lot is always packed. My sister and I ate dinner there last week. The food was delicious. The tab was definitely harder on our wallets than our local crab houses, but we loved it."

"Know anything about him personally? Sounds like he's got a lot of balls up in the air between his cooking show and three restaurants."

Jean funneled fresh ground coffee into a brown paper sack and gave the top a quick twist with a red tag. "Other than his food, I haven't heard much." Jean stopped. "I did hear he's making plans to open a fourth in Palm Beach.

You know Dottie, who owns Taylor Lumber, don't you?"

Helen squinted. "Of course, Andy and I bought most of our materials from her when we were restoring our Victorian. I would kid her that Taylor Lumber was actually our second mortgage. We liked giving her the business over the big box stores. Why?"

"I overheard her talking on her cell last time she stopped in for coffee. Got the idea our chef was more than a little slow in paying suppliers." Jean handed her an extra-large latte.

"That's an interesting tidbit."

The older woman chuckled as she brushed back her short gray bangs. "Are you suggesting I like to gossip?"

Helen crunched on the biscotti. "You know what Agatha Christie's Jane Marple would say? She'd consider gossip as a healthy interest in human nature."

"Now, don't you go there. Whenever you start quoting one of your mythical detective friends, I know your curiosity is going into overdrive."

"Why, whatever do you mean?" She gave her eyes an exaggerated roll and picked up her packages. "Just keep me in mind if you hear anything interesting." The shop's bell tinkled behind her as she put her back to the door and maneuvered her way out.

* * *

Promptly at three the next day, Helen drove through iron gates and up a long drive to pull into a cobblestoned parking circle in front of Roberto and Adrian's mansion. Lizzie pulled in beside her.

"You certainly weren't exaggerating about this house," Helen commented under her breath. "Kent County tax records say it's over 10,000 square feet on twelve acres."

"Pretty amazing," Lizzie studied the elaborate roofline. "How much is waterfront?"

"That's the best part. It's about a thousand feet along the bay. I think it could even be subdividable if the land percs for septic." She adjusted her leather tote over her shoulder as she reached for the doorbell.

Adrian opened a carved mahogany door and offered them a polite welcome. "Let's head right back to the terrace. Roberto and I just finished a late lunch." He led them through the massive foyer, tiled in black and white, straight through onto a blue-stoned patio. A sparkling blue edgeless pool and cabana were positioned for swimming while admiring the bay beyond it.

Helen reached out to Roberto and shook his hand. "Hello again. Lizzie told me your location was special. No Google map of the location could prepare me for this," she exclaimed, stretching her arms in front of her.

Roberto rose and beamed with pleasure. "It is definitely a treasure. I will miss it."

She gestured at her daughter. "I hope you don't mind that I invited Lizzie. I thought she could be of help with photographs. I hire a professional photographer, but if a house is this large, I use my own snapshots as early reference."

"I'm delighted," Roberto said, gesturing for them to sit down. "She has great marketing instincts. I'm sure she'll be an asset."

Lizzie gave the two men an appreciative grin. "Well, thank you very much. I think you'll see where I inherited those instincts."

Roberto's cell phone gave a little beep. He sighed. "I suggest we get started. I need to leave for Philadelphia by five. Follow us."

Helen's eyes lit up as she entered the enormous kitchen. "Gentlemen. *This* is what I call a drop dead kitchen !" She walked from one end to the other, running her hands over thick white marble countertops and opening each gleaming appliance. Copper handles accented dark wood cabinets. Sunshine from six skylights reflected off the island. A stone pizza oven was banked in one corner of the room with seating nearby. A complete latte and espresso bar she knew cost easily three thousand dollars flanked the opposite corner. She'd seen a lot of beautiful houses. This was unreal.

"Maybe this will help inspire you to cook," Lizzie piped up as she started to click off photos.

Roberto rocked back on his heels and chuckled.

Helen caught his expression and laughed. "I'm afraid this completely intimidates me." She turned to Adrian. "How do you stay thin with a chef like this as your business partner?"

He grunted. "Only someone who doesn't know the life of a restauranteur would say that. When most people are relaxing, he's supervising kitchens up and down the coastline. I usually eat alone." His tone inferred it was a touchy subject.

"Let's hope you get great leftovers. Shall we keep moving through the house? I'll take initial notes. When you're ready to set a marketing date, I'll come back in with a recorder and add to them."

About four-thirty, they all returned to the kitchen island. Adrian unrolled a cardboard tube filled with floor plans. Helen asked for more details on the original condition of the house and Roberto's renovations over the past two years. Clearly, they'd sunk a ton of money into the property. Ka-ching. Ka-ching.

"Can you clarify who owns the property? I need to be sure any paperwork is signed by the rightful people since your deed and title list Barto Enterprises."

Adrian adjusted his glasses. "Roberto and I are equal partners and purchased the house as a corporate asset. You'll need both our signatures."

Helen jotted down a few notes.

"What's your price assessment," Roberto asked.

"I'll be upfront with you," she offered, choosing her words carefully. "You've done an incredible job of updating this property. I wish I could be sure you'll be able to recoup all your investment given you've been here a short amount of time." She looked from one man to the other. "Does that surprise you?"

Roberto ran his hands across the diagrams. "I've gotten a couple price opinions. You're the first one who's been so blunt. You don't sound optimistic." He leaned back and crossed his arms.

Never a good reaction.

Helen didn't flinch. "Choosing a marketing price that's more realistic will have a huge effect upon finding a strong buyer. Buyers with multi-million-dollar pocketbooks are rare, especially in the mid-Atlantic region. This isn't Manhattan or L.A.. If you want to free up your money for restaurant expansions, you'll need to decide what's most important to you, time or money. Too often I've seen sellers who overpriced end up losing both in the end." She took in the two men's reactions. She knew she might be blowing her chance to get hired. She also knew she'd take on a lot of work with little guarantee she'd get compensated. No point in wasting everyone's time.

"Give us a few days to discuss this. I appreciate your directness, although I'm disappointed in your prediction." He eyed Adrian, who gave a nod of agreement.

She rolled up the floor plans and tipped them back into the cardboard tube. "I'd love to work with both of you. I can't guarantee you a certain price. I can guarantee that I'll represent you well."

Minutes later, Adrian walked her and Lizzie to the door. They followed each other back down the drive. Helen wondered if it was the first and last time.

Chapter Four

Wednesday mid-morning, she called her daughter's cell number on the way into Port Anne and her office. "Lizzie! Adrian called me early this morning. Roberto still isn't sure of the price, but he wants me to put his property on the market ASAP."

"That's great! Congratulations. What's next?"

"He wants me to stop by the studio after his airing this afternoon, about four-thirty. Do you want to meet me? We could go out for a drink afterwards. Tomorrow, I'm meeting Adrian at the house so I can start writing up all the details."

"That's perfect. I'm hosting. I'll have someone at the OPS Desk meet you at security and walk you back. You can watch from the wings. This is so much fun. Listing a famous chef's house. And he hired you over other agents. I thought you might have blown it when you told him he'd likely take a loss."

"You and me both." Helen laughed. "I am excited. Let's see if he actually takes my advice."

"We can celebrate afterwards. Got to go for now. Great job, Mom. See you about four!" Lizzie clicked off.

* * *

At four-twenty, a thin, freckled face surrounded by bright, curly red hair tied into two long braids poked out between the double doors at ShopTV security. A gangly, tall Pippi Longstocking form in a long pink and yellow cotton sweater and pink flowered pants followed. "Hi! Are you Lizzie's mom? I'm Mariah Manley. I'm the food stylist here. She asked me to walk you back from security." She stuck out a thin hand. "Sign in, and we'll head over to Roberto's set. They're just wrapping up their show."

Helen returned the friendly handshake, grabbed her temporary pass, and scooted through the doors. "Nice to meet you. Lizzie mentions you often." She tucked the tube of floor plans and paperwork under her arm and tried to keep pace with Mariah's long legs in Birkenstocks. "Sounds like an interesting job. How'd you get into styling food?"

The redhead scrunched her nose for a split second. "When I finished culinary school, restaurants were struggling, and the competition for good jobs was brutal. I decided to get my certification in food styling three years ago. I do miss cooking. I was tops in my class."

"Is there enough work in it?"

"The network's cooking shows are super popular. It's not the most glamorous job, but it also doesn't have the crazy hours working in a restaurant requires. Do you know Dana Moore?"

"I've heard her name. Isn't she a chef from California? I'm not a cook, so she's not on my radar."

Mariah waved her hand. "She's another celebrity with her own private company like Roberto. She's had a contract with ShopTV for years and her *Dana's Delights* was always number one. I style her set for demos too."

"How does she feel about Roberto's popularity?"

Mariah glanced behind her and leaned in. "She's not happy about it. She loved being queen of cooking here. Roberto gets contracted with the network, and they've been neck and neck with ratings ever since." She shrugged her shoulders. "I don't mind because I'm busy working back and forth between the two shows."

Helen laughed. "Dueling chefs. That must be interesting?"

Strands of Mariah's red, corkscrew curls bounced across her forehead. "No shortage of egos there. Especially if one thinks I'm doing a better job for the other."

The OPS Desk pointed them toward Roberto's set. They squeezed in between a production crew adjusting cameras. Weaving down narrow hallways, they stopped to allow two techs to maneuver equipment through a doorway and on down the hall. Mariah slowed, pressing her index finger to her lips as they approached. They could overhear voices from a live presentation starting nearby. Passing three sets, they rounded another corner and reached the kitchen. Stepping from behind a large row of cabinets, they spotted Roberto, Lizzie, and a cameraman. Lizzie cried out, "Help! Someone help!"

The Flying Pan chef was leaning over his center island, his back to Mariah and Helen. Lizzie was gasping, pressing her left hand to her chest while her right arm was wrapped around his waist. The camera operator was struggling to prop up the big man. She focused on the two women, her face white and her blue eyes wide.

"Mom, thank God!"

Roberto's thick black hair draped over his face and touched the counter. Blood dribbled across his souffle onto the island and trailed down the cabinet. Too heavy for them, he began to slide to his knees, his right arm dragging the dish off the counter. It crashed in pieces onto the concrete floor as Helen and Mariah rushed forward. "Lizzie! What's going on? Is he sick?"

"Oh, my God!" Lizzie's face scrunched into a cry, and she sank to the floor. Helen gasped.

They tried to cushion him from the fall. Roberto's brown eyes stared up, unseeing. His teeth and jaw formed a bizarre grin. The blood from his mouth drained scarlet down his immaculate white jacket.

Helen dropped to her knees next to the chef. She pressed her index finger against his neck. "No pulse!"

"Mariah, call 911!" Helen spotted the entry. "No! Run to the OPS Desk. Ask for Security. Tell them we need an ambulance and the Sheriff's Office!"

Trembling and wide-eyed, Mariah stared down in shock at the chef, her sandals glued to the floor.

Helen stood up and gave her a shake. "Go on! Quickly! Run." The stylist's pigtails shook. She nodded, then bolted toward the hall.

Sinking back down on her knees, Helen reached over to press her fingers against the big man's neck again. Nothing. She pivoted to her daughter, forcing her to sit up, her head between her knees.

"Lizzie, are you sick too? What happened?"

"Roberto. He acted weird all through the show. He got worse and worse. I was fine until he offered me a bite at the end." Lizzie's breathing slowed. Her eyes were tearing.

Helen pressed her shaking fingers to Lizzie's forehead, then rose to her feet and scanned the room. The kitchen appeared in order. Only bits of souffle and an apron were on the counter. The kitchen cabinets formed the rear of the set. Moveable room dividers on casters flanked both left and right. She tried to control her own breathing. 'Come on, Helen. Think. What happened here?'

In less than a minute, she and Lizzie heard running footsteps approaching the set opening. Two men in security uniforms ran towards her with Mariah right behind.

"Stop!" she shouted, her hands up, palms forward. "Don't step onto the set! Don't come any farther. This might be a crime scene. We can't disturb anything!"

Lizzie inhaled a sob between coughs. "You can't be serious! We have to help him."

"There's nothing we can do for him. We have to wait for the police and the medics." Her tone told them not to argue. She'd been here once before.

Chapter Five

Five minutes later, two medics arrived. Tossing down their equipment, they reached for their patient. One raised his eyes at their anxious faces and shook his head. "He's gone."

Helen pointed to Lizzie. "Please, check her! They both might have been poisoned." The medics helped her onto a nearby stool and started taking her vitals. Lizzie seemed to be stable, but very shaken. Seconds later, three uniformed Sheriff's Office deputies and two plain-clothed detectives followed. Helen spotted her on-again, off-again date before he saw her and tried not to groan out loud.

Detective Joe McAlister, dressed in a grey suit, pushed through the gathering onlookers. McAlister was tall, mid-fifties, and built like a Marine. He leaned over the chef, then spotted her. He drew his arms across his chest, his dark brows pulled close, his lips a tight straight line.

Helen inhaled. Oh boy, she thought. I'm in hot water. I'm the last person he wants to see at the scene of a murder. She crossed her arms across her own chest and mirrored his stance.

"Good grief! If it isn't Nancy Drew. Or is it Jessica Fletcher? What are *you* doing here?"

His partner, Rick Lauer, stepped out from behind him. "What's happened?" He spotted Helen. "What in the world?" He took one look at the two of them exchanging daggers and backed away.

Helen gestured toward her daughter.

"Is she all right?" Joe leaned over Lizzie and turned to the medics. They nodded.

"Lizzie was just finishing an airing with Roberto," Helen declared. "I had an appointment to see him afterwards. I'm putting his house on the market. Or I was."

Joe studied Lizzie, white-faced under her streaked makeup. Mariah stood with her hands covering her face.

"When Mom walked in, I was choking and trying to keep him from falling. He was acting erratic during the program." She took another breath. "Then he collapsed." She buried her face in her hands. Her mother squeezed her arms around her shoulders.

"Unbelievable." He stared at Helen with disbelief. "You find dead bodies like cats find mice. Has anyone been in here since you found him?"

"No. I know better. I told everyone to stay off the set." Shivering, she pulled her light jacket across her chest. "We're lucky Lizzie's alive."

Rick turned toward the curious crowd and displayed his badge. "I'm going to ask everyone here to leave. Security, please move these people into a nearby room where they can wait to be interviewed. Take down all names. Close off all corridors and outside access. I'll be there shortly. No one can leave. No exceptions." He turned to the three uniforms. "Deputies, we need to cordon off the entire area. Call the coroner and our crime scene techs."

Joe pulled over another stool. The two women sat next to each other like kids in the principal's office. He pulled a pad from his suit jacket pocket.

Warily, he pointed at Helen. "What time did you arrive?"

She checked her watch. "It was just about four-twenty. Mariah met me at security. We walked down the main hallway together. We worked our way down the side hall that passes each set until we came to this one. Their show had just ended."

"How did you know it ended?"

Lizzie pointed at a huge digital clock near the set with a shaky hand. "All sells are timed. Each one starts and ends exactly as scheduled. Ours ended at four thirty." The stunned camera operator nodded agreement.

Helen turned toward Mariah. "We saw them on air as we passed a tv monitor in the hallway. We started toward his set as soon as the cameras pulled away from them and started filming the next promo."

23

"How long did it take you to walk from the monitor to his set?"

The two women eyed each other. "I'd say about four or five minutes," Helen said.

"That long?" he quizzed. "Can't be a couple hundred feet."

Mariah took a hesitant step forward and spoke up. "One of the production crews was moving video equipment in front of us. We had to wait until they maneuvered it out of the walkway."

"You are?"

"Mariah Manley. I'm the food stylist. Lizzie asked me to bring her mother back after the show."

"Tell me about this guy. Who is he?"

Lizzie averted her reddened eyes from the contorted chef's face. Her voice quivered. "His name is Roberto Barto. He's a famous chef. ShopTV carries his cookware. He holds a cooking class for our viewers twice a week and sells his products at the same time. He's a huge star. Cookbooks, three restaurants, awards. He's the owner of Water Street Bistro right on Water Street in Port Anne. People are crazy about him." She stared over at the gruesome scene and swallowed. "At least, they were. This is terrible news for his fans."

Two more uniforms and a small, round man carrying a medical kit rushed in. Joe glanced at the women and sighed. Reaching into his pocket, the detective handed them paper booties. "Here. Put these on. I want you to tell me exactly what you saw. Mariah, can you please wait over there?" He pointed to a chair a few steps away.

He covered his shoes, and they followed. "Don't dare touch anything."

The coroner was examining Roberto, careful not to shift him, while an officer took photos.

"Craig, this is Mrs. Helen Morrisey and her daughter."

The coroner raised his eyes at the two.

"According to these ladies, he finished a live show at four-thirty pm, then collapsed," Joe commented, turning toward Helen. "Where was Mr. Barto when you arrived?"

She gestured toward the island. "Mariah and I came in behind him from the back of the set. I walked around the front of the island to say hello. He was leaning over the island. I heard Lizzie choking. She was trying to hold him up. His head was down, and he started to slide to the floor. All of us tried to lay him down, but he was so big and heavy. As soon as I spotted all the blood, I sent Mariah to get help. I couldn't find his pulse."

Craig touched the concrete floor. "That's the reason for the small bump on the back of his head."

Joe flipped to his notepad and nodded. "According to security, they got the request for police at four thirty-four. Could his death be natural causes, or is this something bigger?"

The coroner spoke into a small recording device, rattling off vital signs. He reached over and used practiced fingers to palpitate the inside of Roberto's mouth. "I can't tell you much until the autopsy and blood tests. Was he feeling okay?"

"That's the odd thing," Lizzie shuddered. "We had a thirty-minute show. He seemed like himself at the beginning, but as he cooked, he started to forget his points and slur his words. I thought he wasn't feeling well or had been drinking. I tried to cover for him. I couldn't wait until we wrapped up his demo and got off the air."

"Has he ever been drunk on the show before?"

"No, never. He's always professional. I couldn't figure out why he was so off cue. Right after his program, he started spitting blood and gasping. I grabbed him."

"When did you start to feel sick?"

Lizzie paused. "Not until the last couple minutes of the show. I hadn't tasted the dish until Roberto offered me a bite. I can't digest coconut, so I barely touched it. Just enough for the cameras."

Joe turned to the doctor. "What do you think?"

"Their description of his actions could mean some kind of seizure. But that doesn't match with his tongue. It's discolored, and the inner lining of his mouth is stained and swollen." He shoved thick black eyeglasses back onto the bridge of his nose. "It could be stroke, but I don't think so. His lips are pulled back, and his teeth are clamped together. He's got Ricket's Grin which is usually a sign of poisoning." All three women shuddered.

Joe studied the chef. "Was he eating the dish during the show?"

"When he began blending together his ingredients, he kept tasting his sauce," Lizzie replied.

Craig signaled to the medics for a stretcher. "He was either highly allergic or poisoned. This young woman is lucky."

"Could he have accidentally poisoned himself?"

"Seems unlikely. He *is* a chef."

Lizzie gulped. "If it was in any other recipe, I would have sampled it." She turned to her mother. "I could have been poisoned too!"

"Let's not get ahead of ourselves," Joe interrupted.

"She's right. This was an awfully close call." Craig gave a stern headshake.

"Do poisons work this quickly? Maybe he ingested it before the show started," Joe pursued.

The coroner pulled off his gloves. "Depends upon the poison. I won't know until I complete his autopsy."

Helen spotted a television monitor on a stand nearby. "I wonder if you can get a copy of his show. Watch his progression?"

Joe raised his eyes from a note he was making. "Seriously? Do you plan to run this investigation?" He crossed his arms and sighed. "Are you planning on putting together your Detection Club again? Let's remember they're fictional sleuths, and this may be a real crime."

She winced, and her face flushed red. "Sorry. The idea popped into my head. You know I'm not good at holding back. I'm definitely not holding back when my daughter could have been a second victim." She returned a stubborn glare.

Joe sighed. "Don't bring your detective buddies into this. I refuse to get sucked in again."

"My detective buddies helped before, didn't they?" Helen caught Rick examining the ceiling, a small grin fighting to get out.

Lizzie's eyes moved from one to the other then to Rick. "This is uncomfortable. You two will need to sort out your working relationship issues. Mom's got a good idea. The network records each show. They post previous airings online so viewers can watch later and place more orders."

"Who usually comes in after the demo? Anyone do cleanup?"

"I do." Mariah raised a tenuous hand. "I come in and put away anything he's left out, so he's ready for the next show."

The detective walked around the kitchen. "Do you see anything out of place?"

Mariah shook her head.

Joe turned again to his squad. "Let's wrap up every ingredient in this kitchen. Make sure you scrape up any bits of this broken dish. Send all of it to forensics."

"Who would we notify about his death," Joe asked. "Does he have family? Is he married?"

"I'm not sure about family. He's single. I heard there was an ex-wife somewhere. He's originally from right here in Kent County. His business partner, Adrian Stanton, is the one to contact. They've worked together for years." Lizzie rubbed her arms. "If Roberto had any health issues, Adrian would know. They're together every day."

"Anything I should know about that relationship?"

"Hard to say. It seemed kind of testy lately. Little digs and snide remarks. I haven't any idea if it was more than that."

"Any chance they're a couple?"

Lizzie lifted her eyes. "I've never heard it, and it's pretty hard to keep secrets around here. Roberto liked to flirt with the ladies."

Helen piped in. "They do live in the same house. 2 Riding Cross, Port Anne."

Joe turned to her. "You said you were about to put his house on the market. Why was he selling? Any money problems there?"

"I've only been with him twice. He told me he wanted to use the house proceeds to acquire another restaurant. With all his businesses, he had to be stretched pretty thin. I expect Adrian would know. That's not based on fact. Just my conjecture. I heard a rumor in town that he was a slow payer."

The detective's dark brown eyes looked up at her through thickly drawn brows. "Of course, you did." He sighed.

Helen put her right hand on her hip. "I was just doing a little research, hoping he would hire me."

"Is that what you call it now, research?" He couldn't help eking out a reluctant smile.

"Well, I don't interrogate like you do." Her green eyes sparked. "Do you think we can go now? This is horrible."

"Definitely horrible. I'll give you a call later in case something else comes to mind. Mariah, we'll be contacting you again in the morning."

Joe turned to the medics and pointed to Lizzie. "Is she okay to go?" They checked her heart rate and temperature again, then gave him another nod.

Helen picked up her tote. Lizzie grabbed her arm. Her voice wavered. "I can't imagine who would do this."

He took the women's elbows and guided them toward the doorway. "Do me a favor. Start imagining."

"Wait. What?" Helen stopped short. "I thought you didn't want me to get involved."

He grimaced. "You're right. I don't. Forget I said that. I forgot I was talking to your imaginary Detection Club. By the way, I assume dinner tonight is out."

Lizzie shot a glance at both of them and clamped her mouth shut.

Smart move, Helen thought.

Chapter Six

Helen and Lizzie stepped outside the lobby entrance and into the lowering sun. They both shivered.

"I can't believe this happened. It's so sad and so sudden. He was larger than life. Full of energy." Lizzie stroked away tears with the back of her hands.

"It's such a shock. Who would want to kill him? I can't even guess." Helen reached up and pushed her daughter's light hair back off her swollen cheeks and wrapped her into her arms. "Thank God you didn't eat his food. You could have died." Her voice quivered. They hugged on the sidewalk. "Are you sure you're okay?"

Lizzie's hands shook as she dug into her purse. "My stomach is a little queasy, that's all. I wonder how Adrian will react to this news. Their entire business was built around Roberto and his fan base. The network just signed them up for another new product line."

"I'm sure there are a lot of people affected. Your execs will be going nuts trying to deal with the negative press."

"We're talking millions here. Our viewers are family oriented. I'll bet the first call from the Operations Desk went to Greg Waldron, our VP in charge of talent."

"Do you think the studio and Adrian will be stigmatized if they keep selling Roberto's Flying Pans?"

Her daughter tugged out her keys. "It's hard to predict. Remember when Joan Rivers died? Fans went wild for anything that had her name tied to it. They couldn't get enough of her. Could happen here."

Together, they gaped at the entrance to the parking lot, choked with police cars. Already, local press was storming the lobby. Two reporters were giving live updates on camera in front of the building with the gigantic studio sign lit up behind them for backdrop.

"Let's go back to my house," Helen suggested. "We can try to talk this out."

"Sounds good. I sure don't want to be home alone. Jason's working." She gave her mother a little smile. "Give me a second to text Jason so he knows I'm with you. Is there any wine in my future? I could use it."

Her mother squeezed her arm. "I've got a bottle with your name on it. Follow me."

Helen pulled out of the lot and turned toward Port Anne. In twenty minutes, the little shops and restaurants came into view. It was a sweltering summer night, and locals and visitors wandered about, gift bags under some hands, ice cream cones in others. The water town felt like any other day, without murder. It was close to six o'clock, and people were filling the local restaurants, including Roberto's bistro. She passed Safe Harbor Realty, its lot empty except for a few cars. An American flag and a large Welcome flag hung from the second floor of the yellow-painted Victorian. Someone would pull them in for the night. She recognized her personal assistant Tammi's silver Prius. She was probably wondering why Helen hadn't checked in with her.

She wound south about five miles from Port Anne on a narrow two-lane road into Osprey Point State Park and the peninsula. Her Mini twisted along the road, cutting through the woods with bits of blue water peeking from both sides of the road as the point narrowed. A unique community of houses, built over the past thirty or so years, peeked out among the trees. They felt a part of the park woods. A historic lighthouse at the southern point stood sturdy at the top of the bay. Its flashing white light marked the shoreline for boaters traveling north from Baltimore Inner Harbor up to the C&D Canal toward Philadelphia and its shipyards.

In this quiet, her mind usually slowed. This evening, it raced through the gruesome scene she'd just left behind of the handsome chef's macabre expression glued on his face. She was glad Joe McAlister was in charge tonight. "I'll stick to being an amateur," she uttered to herself.

Home, she unlocked her front door, and Lizzie followed behind. Silently, they headed to separate bedrooms to change.

Her daughter's face, scrubbed of TV makeup, was stark. She let out a huge sigh as she filled a tea kettle with water. "How does someone decide they hate Roberto so much they want to kill him? He was so smiley, so personable. I can't even wrap my head around all this." Her blue eyes teared again, her voice trembling.

"Let's not get ahead of ourselves. We don't know how he was poisoned. Maybe it was a terrible mistake. Here, let's have some Red Rose tea first. It was your grandmother's favorite." Helen gave her daughter an encouraging smile, picked up a mug, and padded into the living room.

Open to the kitchen, a big, native blue-stone fireplace divided it from the dining room behind. Sliders on the opposite side opened to the deck and the now dark bay. A large bookcase crammed with books covered the third wall. Helen sat on the couch, tucking her feet under her, and wrapped a fluffy teal Afghan across her knees. Watson hopped up next to her and nestled in, his white milk face lifting for a chin scratch. "Obviously, he ingested something he didn't realize was dangerous."

"Roberto's not you. You forget when you add salt instead of sugar. He's a professional and very particular."

"Good point. I actually spoiled a cherry cobbler by doing that. Never tried again," She smiled ruefully.

"Whatever the poison, it was very well hidden."

"Maybe it was accidental. Maybe he had an allergy. Or maybe this is about love, not hate."

Her daughter tossed an orange floor pillow onto the carpet and plopped down. "Love! It's a terrible way to show it. Do you think he had a relationship that went sour? Or a fanatical fan?"

"I heard rumors his company owed people money. Did our chef have too many fingers in too many pies? Did someone want him to pay up? Did Adrian ever comment on their investments?"

Her daughter twisted a strand of hair between her fingers. "No, not that I know. But I'm not likely to be involved in such a personal conversation."

"Could they be lovers that weren't getting along? Is it possible Roberto had a new love interest? Adrian might have been afraid he would be replaced."

"Mom, that's total spin. You're saying that based on nothing."

She shrugged. "I wonder, should I call Adrian tomorrow morning to check on him? See if he's willing to meet me. After all, now he really needs to sell that house. I'm guessing their business might be depending on it."

"Seems awfully callous to approach him the day after his partner died." Lizzie pulled on her lower lip. "Besides, Joe will freak if he finds out you're talking to him. I can't say I'd blame him." She wrinkled her nose. "How are things going with you two, anyway?"

Helen sighed. "I'm not sure. I'm still wavering between head over heels and no way, no how. He's probably frustrated because I'm such a slow mover."

"Well, I think he's terrific. He's smart and good-looking and obviously interested. I would think you two would have a lot in common, especially after solving the Capelli case together." She considered the chain around her mother's neck. "We all know there'll never be another Dad. It's been almost four years since he died. It's time to let someone new into your life. I know Shawn thinks so."

"Stop with the counseling. Just because you're twins doesn't mean you and your brother can gang up on me. I'm in no hurry. I don't see Shawn jumping into any serious relationship. You've been with Jason for ages. Is he ever going to put a ring on your finger?"

Lizzie regarded her hand and grimaced. "Let's get back to Roberto." Her eyes traveled up to her mother's rows and rows of books, mostly mysteries with worn covers. "You're the amateur detective. Who else would want him dead?"

"One case hardly makes me a detective, amateur or not."

"You're good at it. You know how to get people to open up. Why don't you ask your Detection Club ladies?"

"Let's not forget they're only my favorite fictional sleuths, and I refer to them for advice. If we're not careful, people will think I talk to imaginary friends and have gone delusional."

Her daughter laughed. "But, you kind of are! Besides, if you were a shrink, you'd call on Freud."

"Stop," protested Helen.

Her daughter clamped her lips together and gave them a little wiggle. "Remind me again who's in your squad?"

Helen counted on her fingers. "Jane Marple. She's my wise sage who studies people. Jessica Fletcher is my practical thinker. Nora Charles knows how to blend into the social set to dig out answers. Agatha Raisin is brazen and stubborn. Nancy Drew is gutsy. She's not intimidated by authority. They give me great advice, contrary to Joe's opinion."

Lizzie pursed her lips. "That's quite a powerhouse of talent. Seems a shame to keep them on the sidelines."

"Given you were almost the second victim, it's tempting." She leaned back against the couch and groaned. "That would definitely doom my relationship with Joe. You heard his warning. He thought dealing with my club was a one-and-done scenario." She stared up at the ceiling and muttered. "On the other hand, why should I take a backseat? My daughter almost got killed."

"His advice hasn't stopped you before." Her daughter rubbed her forehead. "Of course, my brother would totally agree with him. As a district attorney, he'd tell you to leave it to the professionals."

"Those two are cut from the same cloth." She tapped her fingers across her lips. "If I were Jessica Fletcher, I'd ask who else had opportunity? Seems like half of ShopTV could have entered that kitchen and gone back out again."

Lizzie reached for her mug "The only person I think might benefit is Dana Moore. She couldn't stand him, even though she tried to pretend they got along. She's been the biggest contracted guest name for the network the past ten or twelve years. She's got a gazillion Facebook and Instagram followers. Viewers are obsessed with her. She resented sharing the spotlight with him."

"Would she know how to mix a poison into his ingredients without him noticing?"

"Mom, she's a trained chef. Roberto came on the scene eighteen months ago and carved into her numbers big time. Her sweet veneer was wearing thin under the pressure."

"Did they argue?"

"When the network built that custom kitchen for him, she was beyond furious. Threatened to leave for another shopping network, although I don't think any of the execs believed her."

"How'd the execs calm her down? More money?"

Lizzie shrugged. "Probably. I know they increased her budget for promotion."

"How much work does Mariah do for Dana?" Helen pulled her legs up against her chest and leaned her chin on them.

"A lot. She came on board soon after Roberto. He introduced her to ShopTV. She does food styling for online blogs and commercial videos too. It surprised me he and Dana were willing to use the same stylist. I like her. We've gone out for drinks together a couple times. It just took me a little while to get used to her outfits." Her daughter chuckled. "She dresses like she's on her way to a Woodstock concert. I get the idea she's good at her job. If she messes up her food styling, our chefs' demos turn into on-air disasters. They really depend on her."

"Ever see her get chewed out by one of them?" Helen studied her mug. "Is she good enough to choose a poison and bury it in a recipe?"

"That's not funny."

"It wasn't meant to be."

"I've overheard a few tense moments. Dana jumped all over Mariah after one of her *Dana's Delights* segments tanked. Blamed her for the poor sales numbers because the food displays appeared washed out on camera. I felt bad for her. Typical Dana, she wasn't going to blame herself."

Helen studied her daughter. "Could you put on Nancy's hat for me and get Mariah to open up? Find out how often it happened." She sighed. "In the meantime, I need to get to bed. I'm meeting a buyer tomorrow at nine-thirty. You won't believe who it is."

"Tell me."

Her mother smiled. "Ms. Cantor."

"Our Ms. Cantor? From Port Anne High School? No way!" Lizzie sat up. "I can't wait to hear how she keeps you in line."

"Thanks for that. She is a one and only."

34

Lizzie leaned over to kiss her mother. "Goodnight. Thanks for taking me in. I need to stop thinking about the close call I had today. Knowing Roberto is gone is bad enough. You really should get Miss Marple and her buddies working on this. Ignore Joe and Shawn."

Helen tossed her Afghan aside. Watson gave her a baleful eye and marched toward her bedroom. Trixie jumped down from the hearth and followed. Her daughter climbed the stairs to her room, then turned.

"Whoever killed Roberto also didn't care about me. That was evil. There's no other word to describe it. I know I'm lucky to be here." Her voice quivered.

Helen paused at the bottom and leaned on the newel post, listening to Lizzie rummaging around her bedroom until her light flicked off. She shuddered, then turned, and, pulling open the sliders, stepped onto her deck. She stood in the dark, taking in the sound of water hitting the dock below and a hoot owl in his nearby tree. 'I miss you, Andy, especially in times like these. What do you think I should do? Should I call in my experts?'

A soft, firm voice whispered in the dark. Helen stopped, alert. She swore it was Jane Marple. 'I hear you, Jane,' she uttered. 'You do not like evil beings who do evil things. Nor do I.' She turned off the porch light. Watson and Trixie were waiting.

Chapter Seven

Her name was Olivia Cantor, although Helen would never dare call her Olivia. It was Ms. Cantor to Helen and three generations of Port Anne students. After all, she had been principal of the local high school for twenty-eight years and had ruled with an unwavering eye and a devoted heart. Tiny, with a full face, her gray and silver hair was cut short and neatly swooped back. She was a pro at staring down recalcitrant, acne-faced basketball players as they towered above her. No one messed with the determined Ms. Cantor.

The two shook hands in Safe Harbor Realty's little lobby the following morning. Love this woman, she mused. They don't make principals like her anymore. Her style probably wouldn't fly today with all our helicopter parents, but their kids would certainly learn.

"Ms. Cantor, this is such a pleasure. I am so delighted you called me. The last time we were together was at Shawn and Lizzie's graduation. Hard to believe that was twelve years ago."

The teacher's hazel eyes brightened. She smiled with thin lips that seemed to reach up to her ears like the original smiley face. Her straight-as-an-arrow reputation didn't quite align with her cheerful expression. "Your twins gave me a run for my money. I remember when Lizzie ran Shawn's campaign for class president. After he won, the class pilfered the mascot from our gym and strung it from the top of our flagpole. The school board was furious."

Helen laughed. "Andy and I were furious. They were grounded for a month."

Gesturing toward a conference room, she turned to the educator. "When we talked on the phone, you said you wanted to sell your house and find an over fifty-five community. I've made appointments at two locations. Shall we see them first, or would you rather go over my numbers assessing your house?"

"I'd rather see my choices first. See if I like them."

"Then let's get on the road." Helen grabbed her cell and an iPad.

The two women settled into the Mini and buzzed out of the lot. Ms. Cantor showed Helen her wide grin and reached for her grab handle. "Tell me, how is Lizzie doing? I watch her all the time. When she was a student, she'd poke her head into my office. I knew she had a new scheme her classmates put her up to. Looks like she put that power of persuasion to good use." She chuckled.

Helen slowed as they approached a private drive and an elegant white and aqua sign with *Seasons for Living* in script. "My daughter definitely knows how to converse with viewers. She can sell ice to polar bears. Shawn's just like her. He just applies it to the law."

"Did you hear about that handsome, young chef dying yesterday? Right after his show. So awful. I enjoyed him. Even have one of his autographed cookbooks."

Helen gripped the wheel. "Believe it or not, Lizzie was with him, and I walked in as he collapsed. He was meeting me to discuss selling his house."

"I hear he may have been poisoned."

Helen slowed her car. "News travels fast. It seems likely. It's a miracle Lizzie wasn't poisoned too. She usually tastes his recipes."

"My goodness! I never would have dreamed." She paused. "Will this affect anyone else at the network? There are quite a few Port Anne graduates working there."

"As shocking as his death is, ShopTV is a mega-company. They'll try to smooth it over pretty quickly, although that will be tougher if one of their employees killed him."

The principal tapped on her teeth with a neat pink nail and made no further comment. They pulled into the community guest parking at the entrance.

"So, shall we check this out?" Helen deliberately injected a little extra cheer into her voice.

* * *

By noon, the roadster cruised back into Port Anne, followed by a red truck pulling a power boat. Ms. Cantor adjusted her wire glasses and wiped them with a silk cloth from a copious tapestry handbag. "I'm very pleased. I definitely liked the cottages and club workout facilities."

Helen chuckled. "Ms. Cantor, you are a marvel. Why don't you review the floor plans? We can meet at their model and arrange your deposit if you decide to move ahead. I'd like to know your contract is secure before we put your house on the market. Something tells me it's in great shape."

"I do keep a tidy house." The older woman pulled out a small spiral-bound notebook and pen. "I'll call you no later than Wednesday to set up a meeting. Thank you. As one professional to another, it's been a pleasure. By the way, I prefer you call me Olivia."

She snapped her bag together and deftly climbed out of the Mini. With a smart wave, she marched across the lot toward her red Subaru 4x4.

Helen yanked on the tall Victorian oak door to Safe Harbor, still smiling from her time with the principal. 'I think I just got an A plus!' A brass captain's bell jangled overhead as she stepped inside. A young receptionist sat behind a wide front desk, a throwback to its old hotel days. She scooted past her and down the narrow hallway.

Tammi, her personal Marine sergeant, and maintainer of sanity, was on the phone. She wiggled her long, sparkly green nails and wrapped up her call. Following her into her office, a coffee mug in hand, she sank into a large leather chair across from Helen's desk.

"Where have you been? I texted you three times this morning." The young woman's curly dark Afro was trimmed close round her smooth brown face. Large green and silver starfish hung down from her ears. She always wore jewelry that reflected her mood. Helen marveled at her endless array of choices.

"Why? What's going on? I was tied up showing property. Something wrong?"

"Going on!" Tammi's brows drew together. "Everyone is buzzing about Chef Roberto dying after his show. I thought for sure your daughter filled you in."

Helen sighed as she tossed her tote behind her desk. "Worse than that, she had just finished the airing with him. I walked onto the set to discuss listing his house and found her propping him up. He was already dead. The coroner thinks he was poisoned."

"Oh, my, God." Tammi's dark eyes widened.

Helen tapped a pen up and down on her desk. "It was a miracle Lizzie wasn't poisoned." Her voice wavered as the words came out.

"Who's investigating the case?"

Helen raised her eyes. "Who do you think?"

"Not Joe McAlister? I'll bet he was thrilled to see you on the scene." Tammi couldn't help injecting a little sarcasm.

"Not thrilled was an understatement. I believe his exact words were 'you find dead bodies like cats find mice.'"

Her assistant coughed on her coffee. "Now, that's funny. I can picture his face. Second time in one year. You do seem to have a talent for it. Have you heard from him today?"

"I got a text early this morning asking about Lizzie. He said he'd stop by."

"Probably wants to pick your brain." Tammi's colorful nails pointed to her forehead.

Helen placed her chin in her hands. "Don't dare tell him that. The male ego gets easily bruised."

"He seems to handle your input pretty well."

"Maybe not this time." She tapped open her phone. "Anything going on here I should know? I want to check in with Roberto's partner, but I don't want to act like an ambulance chaser. On the other hand, I feel like I have to express my condolences." She pursed her lips.

"A huh. That's it? After working with you seven years, I know one thing. You'll work your way into this case somehow. You're never going to stand back and watch, especially when your own daughter was almost a victim. If someone tried to hurt my little Kayla, I'd be after blood." Tammi picked up her cup and flashed knowing eyes as she reached for the door. "Good luck with your call."

Helen stuck out her tongue. She pulled up Adrian's number and dialed. On the fourth ring, he answered, his voice low.

"Adrian, it's Helen Morrisey. I'm calling to check on you. Lizzie and I are so deeply sorry about Roberto. I really don't know what to say." She paused.

A sharp inhale came across the line. "Thank you. It's an incredible shock. I'm at a loss. I've got a business I have to keep going. A lot of people depend on it."

"It's a terrible position to be in. Needing to grieve and yet, keep going."

"Our front driveway is already lined with flowers and notes from his fans. And the press keeps ringing and texting. It's all too much." He released a big sigh. "How is Lizzie? The police told me she barely escaped herself."

"It was a close call. Thank you for asking."

"Of course. I'd feel terrible if she were hurt too." He sounded tired.

"Is there anything we can do to help? Is there anything you need?"

"Thank you. Our secretary arrived about eight am. She's covering our company phone lines. We can't do anything about services until the coroner releases his body." His voice quivered again. "I'm overwhelmed with people asking me to make business decisions. I could care less right now. All I can think about is Roberto. I've lost my best friend."

"Did Roberto have family that could help you?"

"Not really. He wasn't close to his parents. They're gone now. He doesn't have anyone else. I was his family."

"Would you like Lizzie and me to stop over later this afternoon? I don't want to intrude, but I feel badly you're on your own."

"Thanks for the offer, but I need time to be alone. I appreciate your call."

"Let us know." She clicked off. Minutes later, her cell rang.

"Mom, you won't believe what's all over the news. Go online and look." Lizzie's voice echoed.

"I'm here at my desk. Give me a second. Where are you right now?" Her fingers flew across the keyboard.

"I'm at work. Greg told all of us the show must go on. I've been on air since noon. It feels so unreal."

"I'm sorry, hon. That has to be hard." A few more taps and Helen inhaled. "I inputted Roberto's name, and my entire screen is flooded with headlines. Celebrity Chef Roberto Barto Dies in Arms of ShopTV Host! There's photos of him and you with scenes from his cooking show. Here's another news post. Police Suspect Chef Poisoned." She picked up her phone and walked over to her window. Kids were climbing down off a bus at the corner. "Is the press calling you?"

"Calling me? My cell started ringing at six am. I didn't want to wake you up before I slipped out of the house. They were haunting my driveway as I pulled in at home. I had to turn off the ringer." She stopped. "Hang on a second. It's Joe calling me." Thirty seconds later, she was back on. "He needs to meet with us. If I take a guess, he wants to be sure we keep our mouths shut. It's almost four now. Can we meet at six? I have another hour of airings."

"Sounds good, but why didn't he call me?" Helen bit her lower lip.

"For heaven's sake. I am the one who was with Roberto."

"You're right, you're right."

"He suggested we meet for dinner at The Blue Crab."

"I'll see you there." She clicked off.

Chapter Eight

Three minutes after six, Helen followed a greeter through the crowded bar and into the dining room. Lizzie gave her a little wave from a rear booth reset with brown paper and square cardboard coasters. This time they advertised Blue Moon, one of her favorites.

Joe stood up, and she squeezed in beside him. He shot her an upside-down smile.

"This is cozy." She gazed about the room. "Trying to hide us away? Two observers of the crime?"

Joe grunted. "Two women this good-looking tend to attract attention. With Lizzie's photo plastered on the internet today, I hoped to get some time alone with you without everyone leaning in to listen. And I'm starving. Haven't eaten all day." He tugged off his tie, loosened his shirt collar, and rolled up his sleeves. "What are you hearing? Anything worthwhile?"

Lizzie reached into a big basket of unshelled peanuts in the center of the table. "The network execs are buzzing all around the building. Greg is apparently making plans to assign another chef to demo Roberto's Flying Pan."

Joe stopped her. "Who's Greg?"

"Greg Waldron. He's our VP in charge of talent assignments. He's got everyone jockeying for position while pretending to be heartbroken over Roberto. It's all so phony. The only person honest about it is Dana Moore. She acts like she's the only logical choice, which she probably is."

Mary Lou, the head of wait staff, bustled over to their table and offered menus. "Hi, Joe. Hi Helen. Good to see you." She nodded at Lizzie. "Can I get you a drink?" She looked at Joe. "I'm guessing you want a lager?"

"Sounds like you know me. How about some Old Bay wings to help us get started?" He turned to the ladies. Helen ordered a pint of Blue Moon with a slice of orange, and Lizzie ordered a cabernet. "Would you mind if we order now?" he asked. Mary Lou jotted down their requests and headed for the kitchen.

Turning back to Lizzie, he studied her face. "Is it that big a deal to take over his products?"

Lizzie raised her eyes. "If you follow the restaurant business, you know that chefs today are like rock stars. Getting on air with your own cooking show and your own product line is the motherlode."

"What makes you consider Dana a suspect," Joe asked. "She already has *Dana's Delights* and her own private company."

She sipped again. "Dana was our top chef of the kitchen shows before Roberto showed up and stole her thunder. She's been feeling the pressure. Her sales were dropping – a lot. With his restaurants expanding and his designer cookware a hit, he was the buzz, and the network was making the most of it. She was green with envy. She hated being old news. She couldn't squeeze out a nice thing to say about him. Until he died." Lizzie mumbled around the wings. "Sorry. I'm starving too."

Helen smiled at Joe. "You can see she's got her appetite back. Morrisey women like to eat. Only she can cook. Don't ask me where she got that ability."

He raised an eyebrow. "Certainly not from her mother."

He watched Lizzie chew away. "I would think you have as good a chance as anyone to take over selling his products."

"Thanks for your loyalty, but that's not how it works. My position on-air won't change. *Cooking with Roberto* started as a product demonstration and grew into a cooking show. Greg's likely to pick another celebrity chef to be on air with me. The obvious choice is Dana. Greg will be inundated with applications from top chefs around the world. They'd love the public exposure."

Helen studied her glass. "I assume Adrian would have a say in who's chosen.

Anyone know if he takes over complete ownership of the business?" She turned to her daughter. "You told me he was the brains behind the invention of the organic coating for the Flying Pans."

"There's a motive for murder." He stopped as Mary Lou approached with their order.

"True," Lizzie lowered her voice. "But it's a huge risk to eliminate your partner who had all the name recognition and star power. Why would he do that?"

"Good point." Helen reached into her bag and pulled out a yellow legal pad. She clicked open a pen. "Actually, my Detection Club has already begun working on some pros and cons." She lifted up her head and thrust out her chin, knowing his reaction.

"No, freaking way." Joe gulped his beer.

"Jessica Fletcher taught me to start with a list." Ignoring Joe, her mother pointed at the pad's vertical lines running from top to bottom and steamrolled forward. "Across the top, we've got Suspect, Relationship to Roberto, Pros, Cons, Motivations. Down the side, I've got Adrian, Dana Moore, and lots of blanks."

Lizzie giggled. "You sure know how to time things, Mom."

Joe turned to her daughter. "Nancy Drew here pulled this the last time when I was working on the Capelli murder. Fortunately, I was smart enough not to put her on any official payroll."

She tasted her cabernet and smiled. "If I remember, Detective, my mother and her Detection Club turned out to be a particularly good investment for you. Even if she operates a little off the grid."

Helen batted her eyelashes at him. "They *do* come in handy."

Joe cleared his throat. "You once told me your Jane Marple warned against real murder versus fiction. I also recall your list of suspects was a lot longer. This list is pretty scant." He dug back into his steak.

"That's because this time, we have Lizzie's inside track. Besides, it's early. I think we should add Mariah Manley onto this list." Helen swallowed a bite.

"Mariah! She can't possibly have a reason for killing Roberto. He was a major account for her," her daughter protested.

Joe interrupted. "Mariah's a food stylist. She certainly had opportunity and advance notice of what he'd be cooking. Right now, she's near the top of *my* list. I just don't know her motivation yet."

"Which came first, the chicken or the egg? Jessica would ask if it was the motive or the opportunity?" Helen scribbled Mariah's name on her list. "She also has the cooking skills. She told me she graduated from culinary school. Was she jealous of his success?"

"Lots of people have opportunity. That doesn't make them murderers." Lizzie pushed back. "Even I had opportunity."

"Agatha Raisin might agree with me regarding Mariah. She deals with young people who work for her detective agency. She knows how unstable and over-emotional they can be." Helen mused. "Come to think of it, Agatha's not exactly Miss Calm either. Kind of like the pot calling the kettle black."

Joe set his knife down with a clatter. "Agatha Raisin is not real. Her agency is not real. Your Detection Club is not real. Get a grip."

The dark-haired Realtor pointed her fork at him. "Don't insult my women. Millions of people visit Sherlock Holmes' house in London every year. Agatha is just as real."

He cleared his throat. "We're getting off track. Tell me, who else is involved in his business?"

Lizzie swallowed. "The company had a lot riding on Roberto. I can't imagine why anyone there would want him gone. I heard a rumor there was a new product line coming out. They were likely to launch it under his name but bring in a new chef to partner on-air with him."

"Anyone in particular involved in the setup? Bonuses? Stock options? Promotions?" Joe stopped.

Lizzie sat back and stared at the ceiling, then back at the two. "If I had to pick, I'd say Greg. Getting Roberto to sign an exclusive contract with this network was a huge deal. He went from mid-level to executive overnight. From Ford wagon to BMW luxury sedan. But I can't picture him wanting to poison his golden goose?"

"Unless the golden goose demanded more. Sounds like we need to nose around, don't you think?" She studied her daughter. "Are you ready to be my George if I'm your Nancy?"

Lizzie examined her manicure. "I'd rather be Nora Charles, if you don't mind."

Joe signed their check with a quick, frustrated flourish. He turned, stood up and eyed the Morrisey women. "No. No Nora, no Nancy, no Jane, no Jessica. No Detection Club chums. Have I missed anyone?"

Helen rolled her eyes. "Agatha, Trixie?"

He glanced over his shoulder, then leaned on the table. "This is murder we're talking about," he said in a hushed tone.

Helen rose to her feet and crossed her arms over her chest. "Yes, this is murder," she said between her teeth. "A murder that, for the grace of God and dislike of coconut, would have made my daughter the second victim. Nancy Drew would tell you that delivering justice is a duty. Have you known me to back off?"

Joe raised his hands. "Unfortunately, no. Not even when it's good for you. I asked you two to dinner to get the background on ShopTV. It wasn't an invitation to get more involved. You have a propensity to want to fix things, and it gets you in trouble. You are bullheaded. If you hear something, tell me. Otherwise, stay out of this. You too, Lizzie. I don't want you hurt."

Lizzie watched the big man weave between tables and shove open the entrance door. "Well," she said. "That's one way to shake up a relationship."

Helen pulled on her jacket. "Do I really have a propensity to fix things?"

Lizzie stopped, lowered her chin, and stared at her mother.

"Yes. Yes, Mom, you do. And sometimes it's really annoying, even when you mean well."

"Huh."

* * *

It was growing dark as Helen walked Lizzie to her car. She headed down Water Street toward Roberto's bistro and Safe Harbor Realty to get her car from its lot. She passed Jean's Coffee Pot, then slowed. Except for two glowing lantern lights at its entrance, the restaurant was in complete darkness two stores beyond. She stopped, almost tripping over candles, note cards, and bouquets of flowers cramming the sidewalk. She watched as a car pulled up along the sidewalk. Someone jumped out and tucked a stuffed bear among the flowers. They hopped back into the car and moved on.

Helen stepped into the street, around the display, and back on the sidewalk. The memorial was sad, lonely, and dead quiet. The bistro's usual noisy bustle flickered across her mind. Twenty feet beyond, she approached a narrow driveway between the row of frame and brick buildings and glanced up and down. The town's iron streetlamps cast a dim view down the drive. Hesitating, she turned on her cell's flashlight and darted down a shortcut behind the old buildings and a narrow, gravel alleyway used for deliveries. The rear of the bistro was hidden in darkness. Only a faint light from a gift shop next door cast a dim shadow toward the café's door.

Silence broke as tires started to crunch over the gravel behind her, and headlights from a sleek black Lincoln Town Car swept down the alley from the opposite entrance. Its driver stopped and parked behind the bistro.

She jumped back behind a dumpster and pressed against its side. She clicked off her light, silenced her ring, and slowly peeked out. Her heart raced. Darn! Who was that? She waited, her heels sinking into the stones.

A large man in a dark, pin-striped suit, his hat pulled over his eyes, hoisted himself out of the sedan, and glanced up and down the alley. Quickly, he approached the restaurant's rear entrance. A glint of metal slivers wiggled in between his meaty fingers. In seconds, the door lock popped open, and he slipped inside.

Frozen, she waited to see a light flick on. Instead, she spotted a cylinder of light running across the windows and up the interior walls. 'Well, Agatha Raisin. You've been in these spots before. What would you do? Call the police? What the heck is he hunting for in Roberto's restaurant?'

Slowly she pulled out her cell phone, dropping her tote to the ground. Knees bent, shoulders hunched, she tiptoed closer to the car. Opening her camera app, she pressed her index finger for one snap of the license plate. New Jersey plate. Then, edging to the far side of the car, she kept her eye on the entrance, praying the man hadn't noticed her phone flash. Kneeling, she turned her back and dialed Joe's cell. It rang five times and went to voice mail. 'Darn! We'll lose him!' Jessica Fletcher muttered into her ear.

Turning, she tiptoed back across the gap between the Lincoln and the dumpster and kneeled down on the gravel to wait. **I'm behind the bistro. Someone broke in. Come quick.** Helen hit send on her text box and waited again. She could hear little Saint Mary's Church clock tower toll nine o'clock a few blocks away. Voices from late diners wafted down from Water Street. She drew in her breath and tried to calm her pounding heart. She was sure the intruder could hear it.

A minute or so later, she heard footsteps crunching across the gravel. The car door opened and shut. She peeked from the dumpster, hoping she would see the intruder's face under the dome light. Damn. Too much shadow. She could only see a rough beard. Light skin. The big sedan turned around and pulled down the lane. Its taillights disappeared.

Her cell buzzed in her hand.

"Joe," she whispered.

"Where are you?" He sounded furious.

"I'm in the alley behind Roberto's bistro. Someone broke in, but he's gone."

"Holy crap. What were you doing there in the first place? Don't dare tell me one of your detective friends told you to do it."

Ignoring him, she stood up and brushed off her knees. "I was walking back to my car. Agatha told me to take a peek at the back of the restaurant. I came around the corner of the building. A black Lincoln Town Car pulled in the alley and up to the door. I hid behind a dumpster to watch. I took a photo of his license plate. It's kind of blurry but I'll send it to you now."

"Can you walk to your car, or should I come get you?"

"Don't be silly. I'm only a block away," she whispered.

He muttered under his breath. "Promise me you'll lock your car doors and drive directly home. I'll put out an APB with the state police to see if they can pick this guy up. I'll talk to you first thing tomorrow. I swear to

God, Helen, you and your imaginary friends drive me crazy." He hung up.

She stared at the blank phone. 'Huh. What do you think of that, chums?'

Chapter Nine

Her cell rang at eight-thirty the next morning. She was trying to get through a second cup of coffee after being up half the night pacing.

"Helen, this is Adrian. I'd like to meet today to discuss putting Riding Cross on the market if you're available. Given our need to maintain company stability, I think it's important to move forward with our original plans."

"Are you sure you want to make this decision right now? It's a lot to deal with at once." She tried to control the surprise in her tone.

He dismissed her comment. "I'm quite sure. Roberto would have wanted it."

"I can meet you at noon. I'm tied up later this afternoon."

"That's fine. I'll see you here at the house. Thanks. I appreciate it." He clicked off.

She stared at her phone and then out toward the water. Why would a man want to sell his partner's house three days after his poisoning? What's the rush?

* * *

Forty minutes later, she ran into Jean's to pick up two coffees. She was bustling back and forth behind the counter between three pots and a foam machine. She beamed as Helen stepped forward. "Good morning. I thought I might see you."

Helen smiled. "Why's that?"

The shop owner squinted at her. "Rumors are flying. I've known you since I first opened this shop. Your mother used to stop in with you tailing behind. Always poking around, getting into mischief. There's no way you're not doing your own investigation into Roberto's murder." She handed her the first foaming cup. Helen took a sip and added more sugar.

"You do know me. Did you know Lizzie was almost a second victim?"

Jean wiped her reddened hands on her yellow apron. "Heard that too. What are you going to do about it?"

Helen reached for the second cup. "My first stop was here. Anything new I should know?"

"So far, not a lot. Grumblings from a few contractors worried they may not get paid for their work on the restaurant and his house. These are regular folk. They can't afford to have their bills sit on the desk of a fancy Philadelphia attorney."

"I'd feel the same way if Roberto and his company owed me. Any idea if Adrian plans to reopen the restaurant?" She pushed back the sleeve of her sweater and glimpsed at her watch.

"Haven't heard. I'll let you know if I do."

"Thanks for being my eyes on the street. Are you sure you don't want to join my Detection Club? I'm sure they'd approve."

Jean's plastic teapots pinned across her apron danced as she laughed. "I'll stick to selling coffee. Safer."

* * *

Tammi wasn't at her desk when she carried in their coffees. She settled behind her own and pulled up her file on Riding Cross. It sure was a remarkable property. Problem was, who's got three million dollars to spend on it? She printed out her notes and all the legal paperwork, tucking them into her tote. She decided to call Joe.

"Good morning," she said, infusing extra cheeriness in her voice.

"Good morning," He grumbled. "Looking for inside information?" His car radio crackled in the background.

"Actually, I thought I'd invite you to dinner. Are you available tonight? About seven?" She listened to the silence on the other end of the call.

"Do I have to bring dinner, or are we eating frozen pizza?"

"Don't be so sarcastic. I promise it won't be frozen pizza."

"Now that's something to look forward to."

"I'll take that as a yes. In the meantime, is there any news?"

He hesitated. "Analysis of his stomach and blood tests came back. He was poisoned with a liquid extracted from an evergreen called Daphne added to his food. It causes seizures, then death within minutes. Question is, who would know that, and how did they mix it into his ingredients?"

Helen rubbed her eyes. "Someone who knows how to cook?"

"That obviously lets you off the hook," he quipped. "Too bad we have too many candidates."

"Before you go, tell me the latest on the Realtor who got attacked? I know her. She's a good person and a real professional. I'm wondering how I can help her."

"Rick's in charge of that investigation. Ever hear of the Regional Automated Property Information Database? It's RAPID for short."

"Never heard of it."

"We've had the system in place a few years. It means police get real-time data from all the pawnshops and auto-dismantlers. If a seventeen-year-old girl comes into a pawnshop with a power tool, you know it's not hers. Probably lifted. This attacker did us a favor when he stole her jewelry and her car. When he tries to sell any of it, we'll get a tip. RAPID will notify Rick by text and email."

"That's fantastic. Do you mind if I call the agent?"

"Not at all. I'm sure she'd appreciate it. I'll text you her number once she okays the call. See you tonight, about seven."

She went back to returning client calls. First, she set up an appointment for a contract session with the builder of Seasons for Living Friday at ten am. She left a voice mail for Olivia. She hadn't confirmed the tax records for Riding Cross and the plot plan. She decided to open up tax records on the restaurant. Sure enough, both properties' taxes were in arrears. Interesting.

Jean said Dottie from Taylor Lumber supplied all the materials for Roberto's rehabs. That means Riding Cross and Water Street Bistro. She wondered how far behind Barto Enterprises was on her payments. Dottie's family had been in business in Kent County for easily sixty years. She had a reputation for being a good employer. Could Roberto's past due payments cause Dottie to delay paying her subcontractors and suppliers? That could have put her in a real bind.

She opened Joe's text with the agent's number who'd been attacked and took a deep breath. "No better time than right now," she said to the room and dialed.

"Alicia, it's Helen Morrisey from Safe Harbor. We worked together a couple years ago on the Patterson sale in Point Breeze."

The agent sounded warm and familiar. "Hi. I remember. That was a nice transaction."

"I'm calling because I heard of the attack and want to know if I can help you in any way. What a terrible ordeal."

Alicia's voice quivered. "I'm trying to get over the fright. I never expected to have this happen to me."

"I don't think any of us expect it. We're too trusting." Helen paused. "This might be too soon to consider, but I'm wondering if you would be interested in working with me on an awareness campaign. We could approach our Board of Realtors."

"I think that's a great idea. It may help me feel like I'm fighting back. Can we talk about it in a few weeks?"

"Absolutely. I'll check in with you. In the meantime, I'll email the board and copy you. Let's see if an awareness campaign interests them too."

"Thanks for this call. It makes me feel much better."

"I'm glad. Talk with you soon." She set her phone down. She could hear phones ringing. Agents and staff chatted together. This is our world. Looks like we need to work harder at protecting it.

At about eleven-thirty, she packed up her laptop and paperwork and headed to Riding Cross. Unlike the weather on the first visit, today was overcast. The clouds scudded across the sky, spitting rain drips across her windshield as she pulled down the drive. Adrian opened her car door.

"Hi, right on time. I appreciate that. I'm still in the midst of firming up funeral arrangements, but without the coroner's release, I can't pick a memorial service date."

She reached into her back seat and came out with arms full. "I sympathize. I went through it when my husband, Andy, passed away. The waiting was so hard on my family." She stopped and took a breath. Mentioning Andy was still a struggle.

She followed him through the foyer and into a first-floor office. Two huge glass top and chrome desks flanked opposite walls. Public relations photos of Roberto working in his kitchen and demonstrating his recipes with their Flying Pans covered one wall. Awards from international competitions and feature stories in *Chesapeake Bay Magazine*, *Gourmet*, and *Coastal Style* covered another. The room felt like a shrine with him gone. She wasn't sure if it was creepy, but it was definitely sad.

"Must be difficult working here after losing him," she offered.

His partner gave a slight nod and a look of what seemed like surprise. "It is. But you know what they say, 'the show must go on.'"

Helen couldn't help reeling back a tiny bit. That was a cold comment. Where did she hear that same phrase recently? She turned and placed her materials across one desk, hiding her face.

"Let's start with your timeframe. When do you think you'll be ready for showings? We'll need access to the house, starting with my photographer." She glanced around. "I'd expect he has about four to five hours of shots to take inside. He'll do drone shots and videography."

Adrian sat down at one desk and signaled her to join him. He tented his fingers together. "Will you be in the house while they're here? We have a lot of collectibles."

"Yes, of course. Or, I can try to have Lizzie here with me too. Can you remove anything valuable from being displayed during showings? After all these years, I'm still surprised by the occasional thief."

"I understand."

"Let's decide your asking price and review our marketing agreement.

You'll need to complete a seller's disclosure statement for any repairs or problems with the property. Please don't be tempted to skip the smaller ones. Everything should be disclosed. Any questions about that?"

"Not at all. We have nothing to hide. Or should I say we had?" Adrian's shoulders drooped.

She nodded. "I know this process is difficult right now. I'll do everything I can to make this easier. I'll need to work myself through the house, taking notes and photos for my reference. It's helpful if you can walk along with me. I'm sure you know details that would add to my descriptions. We also need to decide if you have any items affixed to the house that you don't want to include in the sale." She pulled out her file. "Are you ready to review all this now?"

Adrian rubbed his short beard with his left hand and offered another weak smile. "Yes. Let's not put this off. Roberto's death only makes this sale even more necessary."

"Is there anything I need to know that could hold up a sale? Liens, overdue taxes?" She waited for him to admit that they were behind in their taxes and owed Taylor Lumber late payments.

He studied Helen's face for a few seconds, then re-tented the tips of his fingers. "No, nothing at all."

"I'm curious. Has anything been decided about the future of Flying Pan marketing without him?"

"Greg Waldron and I will be announcing his replacement by the end of this week. The entire Flying Pan line can't lose its market momentum. Ironically, we were about to announce a new female chef to partner with Roberto. Now, we'll need to move more quickly."

Helen tried to cover her surprise. She weighed her words. "That's fortunate. It's nice to think he had a hand in your choice. Roberto can't be an easy persona to replace in the public's eyes."

The small man examined his nails. "No, he's not. I loved him, and he'll be greatly missed. We worked together for years. But he tended to get involved in dealings that were not always best for him or the company."

Adrian cleared his throat and began signing her paperwork. "Don't believe for a second that his death hasn't shattered me. But I'm pressured to keep Barto Enterprises up and running. There's a lot of employees depending on me."

Helen smiled sympathetically. "I understand. It's a lot on your shoulders. I'll do everything I can to help you through this."

"Thank you. I appreciate that. I have a meeting with our attorney in an hour. Let's walk through the most important areas of the house. Then I'm going to leave you alone."

They headed up the wide circular staircase to the second floor. The upper landing and hallway wrapped around the semicircle at the top of the stairs. Paneled, walnut doors opened to each bedroom. They passed a young woman changing sheets in one of the guest rooms. Adrian led her down a separate hall.

"This was Roberto's private wing. I haven't been in it since he passed. I live on the opposite wing. It's a mirror image." For the first time, he allowed a quake in his voice. "I'm sorry. This is hard to talk about."

Helen nodded in sympathy. She surveyed the room, opening closets and taking notes of built-in cabinets. Heavy pocket doors opened to Roberto's private study. Boxes holding his latest cookbook were piled against one wall. Two lay open on his desk with his signature sprawled in dark black ink across each flyleaf.

"Signed copies?" Helen asked.

"He liked to sign his books for the local bookstores. His fans loved them."

"I'm sure they'll regard them as even more valuable now." Helen noticed more framed photographs and a slew of awards lining one paneled wall. She recognized two local politicians from Maryland. "Is this Senator Goldman?"

Adrian smiled. "It is. Roberto did a charity event for her last year. Great publicity for Flying Pan and our restaurants."

Three photos with a casino in the background showed the star sharing toasts with two men in suits. "Looks like they're celebrating something special."

Adrian shrugged his shoulders. "He enjoyed the casinos as a stress reliever, and since he was so recognizable, everyone pulled him into photos. I doubt he even knew who those people were." He glanced at his wrist. "I've only a few more minutes. Let me show you my wing."

"Sounds good. I'll finish my note-taking and let your staff know when I leave. It's likely I'll be back again tomorrow morning." Helen turned to survey the office again. "One question. Do you have an alarm system?"

Adrian paused. "As a matter of fact, we do. It records visual and sound depending on the doorway. Is that a problem?"

"Not at all. People expect it in this size property." Helen smiled. "I'll need to know the passcode to disengage it for showings. How often are video recordings reviewed?"

He tilted his head in thought. "They operate twenty-four seven. Our security company only reviews them if there's a concern. I'm not sure how long they are retained."

"Thank you. Good to know. Let's run through instructions for the alarm panel. I'd hate to have alarms triggered because I key in the wrong password."

* * *

About three o'clock, she and Adrian shook hands back in the main hall. She watched as his black Mercedes pulled out of the drive.

The house was quiet. Nancy Drew urged, 'Come on. You've never been afraid to poke around where you didn't belong. Let's take a closer look at Roberto's upstairs study.' Helen hesitated. Agatha chimed in. 'Hurry!'

She returned back to the alarm panel and counted the camera angles per room. Good. The study upstairs only had one on the doorway, typical for a bedroom level. Helen raced up the stairs, then turned down a corridor. No sign of the cleaning staff. She snapped a few worthless photos of the doorways to appear official in case a camera picked up her movements.

Inside the study, she started with his antique walnut desk. A couple yellow Post-it notes were tucked along the edges of his embossed leather blotter. A box of ivory engraved notecards with the Barto Enterprises insignia lay open. One note read "Dear Marlo" in thick black ink. He hadn't finished it. There was something about it that felt forlorn, abandoned.

57

She quietly pulled each desk drawer open an inch at a time and rifled through. A passport showed a trip last spring to Italy. Two menus from competing restaurants were tucked away. A brochure of a local casino on the bay detailed their array of services. A few corporate financial statements showed balances. Helen snapped four of the summary pages. She didn't have a clue what they reflected. She tugged on the bottom right-hand drawer. Locked. 'Snakes and Bastards,' Agatha uttered in her ear. Another file marked "Hobbies" held a five by a six-inch lined journal with dates and dollar amounts running down the pages. Big dollar amounts. She quickly snapped more photos with her flash off.

Glancing at the camera angle, she edged her way along one wall and back out the door. Then, she walked back in, knowing this time she was in full view of the camera. She moved over to photos lining the wall. Why did these photos feel different than the ones displayed downstairs? Seemed more personal. She studied the figures, many in suits. Everyone looking prosperous. A few with drinks in their hands. A lot of jewelry on the men. She tried to place the background location, but nothing struck her. Pulling out her cell, she stood back and snapped photos of the room, including some close-ups of all the pictures lining the wall. She wondered whether there were dates on the backs.

As she reached out to take one frame off the wall, the hum of a vacuum cleaner grew louder. 'Time's up, Agatha. You too, Nancy. We'll be back.' Helen stepped into the hall. She gave a friendly wave to the cleaner, headed down the curved staircase and out the front door.

Chapter Ten

Joe was arriving at seven, and Helen was feeling pretty proud of herself. She'd actually planned ahead. Baked Idaho potatoes were rubbed in olive oil and about to go into the oven. She'd seasoned two thick ribeye steaks with some kind of concoction Lizzie had left behind. A large Caesar salad was chilling in the frig.

Watson and Trixie kept winding around her legs. "Stop acting surprised I'm actually in the kitchen," she commanded.

She squeezed in a call to Lizzie. "Guess what! Adrian signed my contract to put Roberto's house on the market."

"I thought he'd at least wait until Roberto was in the ground."

"Me too. I like him, but he's a tough person to read. I can't tell if he's so broken up about losing his partner, he has trouble talking about him, or if he doesn't care. Did you know he and Greg were about to announce a new female partner to go on air and represent Flying Pan? He said it was already in the works before Roberto was killed." Helen splashed around in the sink, her cell crooked between her ear and shoulder.

"That's big news to me." Her daughter went silent while she mulled it over. "I can take a few guesses who it is. Certainly, helps them recover faster from losing Roberto."

"It seems like a gamble, don't you think?"

"Big shoes to fill. I'm predicting they'll expand Dana's on-air hours."

"I don't have enough knowledge to have an opinion. By the way, Adrian agreed to let you help me complete any staging needed. But this time, I really need a George to my Nancy to help snoop around. Nora's not a snooper."

"Gotcha. Let me know which day."

"I'll keep you posted. Let me run." Helen sounded excited. "By the way, I invited Joe for dinner."

"Really? Thought you'd make amends? Are you serving broccoli lasagna TV dinners again?" Lizzie laughed. "You'll never win him over with that concoction."

"Very funny. For the record, I'm not trying to win him over."

"Ah huh."

Her mother ignored her smirk. "Actually, I'm serving steaks. He'll have to grill them. And baked potatoes and a salad. I'm rather proud of myself."

"Very un-Agatha Raisin. Jessica's your best cook in the Detection Club. Are her skills rubbing off on you?"

Helen chopped peppers with a vengeance as she talked. "I admit nothing."

"Does Joe know you're working with Adrian?"

Silence.

"He doesn't know, does he."

"Ah. No. I'm going to tell him tonight." Helen listened to her daughter chuckling. "Glad you think it's so funny. He won't think so."

"Poor guy. You ply him with steak and potatoes and then hit him with that news. Just can't keep your chums out of his business."

"Listen here, daughter. You suggested it. It's our business too. You're lucky to be alive."

"I know, I know. Talk tomorrow."

A little after seven, Helen heard Joe traipsing up the path around the water side of her house and up onto the deck. A Golden Retriever loped behind him.

"Hi, Rocky!" Helen put her hands on both sides of the big dog's soft ears and gave him a little rub on his muzzle, which was slowly turning white. He swished his wide tail from side to side in pleasure. "Looks like you decided to join us for dinner." She stood up and exchanged a kiss on the cheek with Joe.

The detective followed her back into the kitchen, placing a bottle of cabernet on the kitchen island. "I didn't have the heart to leave him home alone."

"You know I don't mind. Besides, Watson and Trixie like him around." She smiled down at the two cats sitting side by side, tails pacing back and forth like metronomes. One set of green eyes and one set of blue glared back at her. "Oh, come on, guys. You know Rocky's just an old softie." They looked him over and seemed to shrug.

"Should I open up the wine? I thought you'd like this one." Joe started sorting through Helen's junk drawer and pulled out a corkscrew.

"Absolutely. It'll go great with that broccoli lasagna you liked so much last time you were here."

He stopped twisting the corkscrew into the wine bottle and raised his head. "Oh. Well, sure."

She pulled over a wooden cutting board with two New York strips covered in black pepper and Kosher salt. "Don't worry. I already got the word from Lizzie that dish was an insult to manhood."

His eyes lit up at the steaks, and he let out a sigh of relief. "These look great. Should I light the grill?"

"Already waiting for you." She handed him a grilling fork. "I know you're probably starving. Bring the wine, and we'll watch them together. These beauties are too good to overcook." He grabbed the board, a fork, and a serving plate. Helen picked up two wine glasses. Rocky trotted behind.

Helen shifted an Adirondack chair near the grill. "Any progress with the investigation?"

He hesitated. "I'll tell you as long as that's not the reason you're serving me steak."

She batted her eyelashes. "Would I do that?"

"Nora Charles would. She's the sweet talker, and the looker." He closed the hood on the grill and reached for his glass. He eyed the khaki and white knit dress that stopped just above her knees. He pulled her close, tucked her hair back, and fingered the ring on her silver chain.

She gave him a soft smile. "How would you even know that?"

He smirked. "I am a detective. I know how to google Nora Charles."

"I'm sure you do. Back to any news?"

He stepped back to the grill. "We found out the Daphne plant in Roberto's soufflé is very common. You can find it along any roadway in Maryland."

"Which means it's even harder to trace who brought it into his studio kitchen."

"Exactly. On the other hand, to hide the plant in the recipe, the killer was adept at chopping it up so finely that Roberto didn't spot it. Or grinding it into a liquid." Joe opened the grill and watched the flames searing his steaks.

"Which points to someone with culinary skills like Dana or Mariah." Helen sipped on her cabernet.

"They're high on my list." Joe pulled the steaks off the grill and placed them onto the platter "What do you say we eat these while they're hot?"

Dinner was on the deck at Helen's family-sized teak table. Three metal lanterns served as light. He grinned at her as he chewed the last bite of steak. "That was fantastic."

"I'm glad you liked it. Was I able to compete with Prime and Claw? I know that's your favorite beef restaurant in town."

"Absolutely. The company tonight is great too." He grinned. "You pushed the image of broccoli lasagna out of my mind. It was keeping me up last night worrying about enduring our next meal together."

"Don't get too excited. Steak and potatoes are pretty basic. Beyond that, it's a real stretch for me. We could be back to oatmeal on your next visit."

"I'd be okay with oatmeal if it was breakfast." His dark eyes twinkled.

"Is that supposed to be a hint?" She reached for her cabernet.

"Quite possibly. I'm trying to set a low bar. No pressure."

Helen blew him a kiss in the lantern light. "Thank you. I appreciate that."

An American Bald Eagle screeched. They spotted him in the moonlight swooping down toward the water. "Looks like we're not the only ones hoping for dinner," she offered.

A second eagle followed the first. "Or companionship," Joe responded. "It's not all bad, you know."

"I know." Helen nodded. "Speaking of companionship, is there any chance Roberto has a love interest we're not aware of? He obviously attracted women."

"No one as yet. Do you think Lizzie heard any rumors? Can you check with her?"

"I'll ask again. We're meeting at his house to plan out staging and photos over the next few days." She slipped in the news.

"Is this your way of telling me you're working for Adrian after all? Just make sure that's *all* you two are doing." Joe glanced at his watch. "I need to head home. Early interview tomorrow. Do you think you and Lizzie could meet us at the studio at three? Rick and I are reviewing security tapes of everyone coming in and out of the building last Sunday for the second time. I'd especially like to get Lizzie's input." He grabbed a platter and headed to the kitchen.

Helen picked up their dinner plates. "I'll text her right now." Minutes later, Lizzie texted back. "Three pm is fine."

"Good." He smiled. He leaned against the island and pulled Helen into his arms. "Thanks for a great dinner. First break since Sunday."

Helen inhaled his musky cologne and gave him a light kiss. "We both needed it."

Joe offered his special upside-down smile. "Need anything else tonight?"

She tucked her arm into his and led him to the door. "A good night's sleep?"

"I was afraid that's what you would say."

Chapter Eleven

ShopTV was buzzing. It was like New York City, the city that never sleeps, and felt almost as big.

Security issued Helen a new badge, her name printed across in bold followed by *Guest*.

Lizzie waved her through the first set of glassed double doors.

"I've been on-air for almost fifteen hours. Hope this meeting isn't long. I'm ready for bed." Her daughter's big blue eyes narrowed. "How was your dinner last night?" Her short bright hair was pushed back with a wide fabric hairband that seemed to be the rage.

Helen ignored her stare. "Great dinner. You would have been proud of me. I cooked and didn't set the house on fire. Nothing more to report."

Lizzie shrugged her shoulders. "Okay, closed subject, I see." She headed down a long hallway, the opposite direction from the live sets. Knocking on an unmarked grey steel door, she waited.

"Good afternoon." Joe opened the door and pointed them toward a couple swivel chairs. A long narrow desk formed a circle running around the darkened room. Twenty-five cameras encircled the room above their heads, monitoring building entrances, and rooms. Rick introduced them to the studio's head of security with a short nod.

"Rick and I have asked you here to review the tapes for last Sunday," Joe started. "In our first go-round with security, we didn't see anything or anyone unusual. Since Lizzie works with the staff involved in the live broadcast, we're particularly interested in getting her reactions. Let's begin the tapes at noon, four hours before our victim died. Remember, there's no sound, but it's pretty obvious what they're discussing."

Everyone was silent. Helen could feel the tension in the room. A technician pulled up a screen showing the network lobby, outside doors to their cafeteria, and the loading docks. They watched as every few minutes, someone involved in the live shows came and went. Network hosts, guest hosts, stylists, studio assistants, and product reps with samples all entered through the main door. They stopped and received custom badges like Helen's, then walked through the first set of interior double doors. Some headed down the hallway and checked in again at the OPS Desk. Most headed for coffee in the green room or sat in the OPS area on couches in eyeshot of the desk. ShopTV hosts came in and out from the sets to meet with guest presenters and review their demonstrations before the live shows. A couple times, Lizzie came out to meet with her guests.

Joe looked at Lizzie. "Busy place. Notice anything odd?"

She shook her head. "Nothing unusual. It's all organized chaos."

"Start your tape with the first time Mariah enters the building that day," Joe requested.

Another security technician scrolled back and forth between camera shots until he pulled up a screen capturing Mariah.

Joe spoke up. "Stop. Where is the time stamp?"

The technician squinted, then replied. "Two fifteen."

Joe turned to the security chief. "Why would Mariah come into the building at two-fifteen when their show is scheduled to start at four?"

The security head pulled a clipboard off a peg on the wall and flipped through computer printouts. "We have a note here that our marketing department scheduled a photo shoot for five products. *Cooking with Roberto's Flying Pans* was one of them."

"Marketing does that to update the still shots they use for publicity. That means that both Mariah and Roberto had to arrive here earlier than the four o'clock actual show," Lizzie explained.

"Who else was scheduled for these photo shoots?" Joe asked.

Frank ran a finger down the list. "Looks like Dana Moore for *Dana's Delights*, along with two clothing lines and one beauty brand."

65

Joe signaled again. "Okay. Roll the tape. Let's see what happens."

Everyone's eyes in the room were transfixed on two flatscreens.

At two fifteen, Mariah, wearing a pink and yellow cotton sweater and pink flowered pants, came through security at the front entrance on the second monitor. She chatted with security, picked up her badge, and walked down to the OPS Desk. She carried a heavy green plastic cooler like Helen would bring to her boat and a tote with a large bouquet of flowers peeking out.

Joe made a move-along motion with his fingers. The tape started to roll again. "Why does Mariah have a cooler?"

Lizzie responded. "I've seen her with it before. She's responsible for bringing any items that help style the dish for the day. The decorative items."

"Who brings the food ingredients?" Rick asked.

"Good question." Lizzie tapped her fingertips against her lips. "That's usually the chef. A good chef wouldn't allow just anyone to pick out their ingredients. Or take a chance an ingredient was missing. Roberto was extremely specific right down to his favorite butter and olive oil." She furrowed her brows. "You might want to check with his head cook at Water Street Bistro."

At two-seventeen, the monitor focused on the kitchen blinked alive, showing a camera operator in jeans and a Ravens baseball cap. He was fiddling with equipment. Mariah entered. They greeted each other and set to their tasks.

"Stop there," Joe said to the technician. "I thought we'd only have a recording of the actual show. Why do we have a tape of Mariah setting up the kitchen?"

"Typically, our security cameras only pick up entrances and hallways. Camera operators film the sets while products are on air," explained the security head. "We've got her activity because the camera operator for the day's airings was testing the video cameras. I see it every so often."

"Lucky for us," commented Rick.

The security room was quiet as everyone watched her empty her cooler. They saw the camera operator adjusting a few box lights around the room. He left the set by walking behind the kitchen cabinet wall and pushing aside a sliding door at the rear. The tape continued to run. At two twenty-five, he returned, shifting two small spotlights on the island. Mariah smiled at him and glanced at her watch. He left again.

"No keys? Anyone can enter the kitchen area?" Rick asked.

"No keys. It's impossible. We have too many people coming in and out.Besides, not everyone comes onto the set from that grey door. Some sets don't even have doors, just drapes. Technicians and camera operators tend to enter from the rear rather than main hallways like I use," Lizzie explained.

"All this expensive kitchen equipment is exposed to anyone?" Joe interjected, running a hand through his hair.

"Pretty much." She hesitated. "Except I've seen Roberto pull out his knives from a locked drawer under the island. Most chefs work with their own custom knives. They cost a small fortune. They're like a violinist's Stradivarius."

Joe squinted at the screen. "Who cleans them and puts them back in the drawer? Roberto?"

Lizzie shook her head. "No way. That's for Mariah to put out just before the show. She's the only other person with a key to his knives, as far as I know. She cleans them along with everything else in the kitchen and locks them away. A food stylist's job isn't all fun. She makes sure the kitchen is spotless, except for the floor. I did hear Roberto chew her out because she put a souffle pan in the wrong cabinet once."

Joe signaled to advance the tape. They watched as Mariah emptied her cooler and arranged fresh red, black, and green grapes with a long loaf of crusty bread on a board.

Opening her cooler again, she pulled out a small glass jar and an artist's brush. With a deft hand, she added a few drops of water into the jar and, after swishing it around with her brush, gently painted the grapes and the top of the bread with the liquid. The display glistened.

"Do you know what she applied?" Rick asked.

"Likely sugar water. It dries on food and creates a natural, edible shine," Lizzie replied.

They watched as Mariah washed her hands. Roberto entered the set through the grey hallway door with a carton in his arms. They gave each other a friendly greeting.

Together, they opened the carton and set out his ingredients. Mariah removed flowers from a vase at the end of the island and set them aside. She put fresh flowers in their place, cleaning them up and tossing clippings along with the old ones into a plastic trash bag. She shifted a wooden sign that read *"Cooking with Roberto"* in red script with a large crab beneath it. From under the cooktop, she brought out a glistening set of dark blue Flying Pans. Snipping a few yellow stems from her display, she intertwined them underneath the pans to add some more drama. The star bobbed his head over the display.

A few minutes later, a photographer arrived with a Nikon camera on a wide strap hanging from his shoulder. The three chatted and pointed. Mariah stood aside, and Roberto posed behind the island. He adjusted his chef's hat over his thick dark hair, picked up one of his pans, and smiled toward the camera. The photographer moved about the set taking photos from different angles. Ten minutes later, he stopped, reviewed the shots on his camera, turned with a satisfied wave, and left. Mariah helped Roberto cover up any perishable food and place it into the refrigerator for the four pm show. She picked up her cooler and left the area. The handsome chef removed his hat and white coat, setting them on the island. Security cameras captured him leaving the set area. The tape went to black.

Joe turned to Lizzie. "How was it that she was still in the building when your mother came to meet you after the show?"

"She went over to Dana's kitchen set and styled it for her photographs."

Rick interjected. "She told us that after she finished with Dana, she walked down to the cafeteria and had something to eat. Café staff confirmed serving her. Lizzie asked her to meet Helen at security and walk her back to the kitchen, which she did."

"How'd she seem to the two of you?" Joe asked.

"Perfectly normal," Helen offered. "It was the first time I'd met her, but she was friendly and calm. Certainly not acting nervous or distracted."

"These notes confirm the photographer did the shoot for Dana after he finished with Roberto," interjected Rick.

Rick and Joe exchanged glances. "Dana and Mariah were both milling around the building that afternoon," said Rick. "We also know Greg and Adrian had meetings that same time."

"And every one of them had access to his set," Joe responded. "Dana checked in with security about one. She turned her badge in to security and left the building at the same time Roberto and Lizzie started their demo. Let's keep going." Everyone studied the tape of Lizzie arriving on set.

"When you began the show, did he act like himself?" Helen asked Lizzie.

"I think so. I walked onto the set about three-fifty. He was tying his chef's jacket and putting on his hat. We laughed because I tilted his hat a bit for him." Her voice choked. Lizzie crossed her arms and rubbed them. "He liked it at a cocky angle."

"Sounds like him," her mother piped up.

Their live presentation began with a warm greeting addressed to the cameras and viewers. Sales were fast and furious. Ten minutes into the airing, Roberto began to act slightly clumsy. Fifteen minutes later, he slurred a few words and began to seem disoriented.

Lizzie stood up from her seat and moved even closer to the screens. "There. Do you see? He began to act weird. I tried to take over more of the conversations with our call-in guests."

They watched as the big man slopped some liquid onto the counter. Lizzie deftly grabbed up the small mixing bowl and joked with him on camera about the spill. He wiped his brow with the sleeve of his white jacket. Perspiration beaded his forehead. He mentioned how the lights seemed hotter than usual. Lizzie quipped about Florida weather in Pennsylvania. As they approached four-thirty and the close of the show, his normally tanned complexion was stark white. She held up his crab cakes and coconut creation, reached for a fork, took a tiny taste, and followed it with an enthusiastic thumbs up. Lizzie thanked everyone for watching and teased about the next product coming on-air.

The security head signaled a technician to key in a few letters. "Let me show what we managed to pick up on camera after Roberto's show ended."

He pointed at a second large wall monitor. "Here's another camera covering the next show. But look again at the first monitor. The camera that recorded Lizzie and Roberto's program caught another thirty seconds."

Everyone watched Lizzie as she turned to Roberto. "You aren't yourself. You look terrible. You need to sit down." She looked up at the camera operator. Roberto gasped and began to lean heavily over the island. They put their arms around him. A moment later, she gripped her own stomach. The big man began to sink to his knees, and she struggled to support him. Seconds later, her mother and Mariah walked through the entrance from the hall and spotted them collapsing to the floor. The tape showed Helen grasping Lizzie, forcing her head between her knees. Then she jumped to her feet, shook Mariah, and pointed to the exit. Mariah bolted from the room for help.

The security room was silent. Everyone's faces paled with initial shock as they saw Roberto's body shudder, then stop.

A few minutes passed. Joe cleared his throat. "We're sorry we had to put you through this again. Is there anything you notice now you didn't notice then?"

Helen squeezed her daughter's hand hard. "I'm sorry, Sweetie. That was painful to see." Lizzie leaned her bright head against her mother's dark one and let out a soft sigh.

"I'm trying to not relive it. Now, it feels like it just happened. I don't have anything to add. I wish I did."

Joe put his hand on her shoulder. "It's okay. Tell us again why you didn't taste his dish until the very end of the demo."

"I usually eat his food because it's great for sales. This time, I warned him. I have a tough time digesting coconut. I told him I'd only taste the dish at the very end of the show for the camera. So, I did."

The detective studied her. "Lucky you. It saved your life. If anything strikes you later, call me. Why don't you head home?"

The younger woman nodded and rose to her feet. With a broken smile, she thanked the security staff. "I know this wasn't easy for anyone here."

Her mother met Joe's eyes. "Keep us in the loop."

Sympathy was written across his face.

Chapter Twelve

Lizzie followed her mother back to Osprey Point. Helen tucked her into bed, changed into shorts and a short-sleeved t-shirt, and brought her laptop to the deck. She texted Tammi and started catching up on emails. One call from a homeowner in her neighborhood asked for a price opinion. Olivia Cantor left a question about possible upgrades for her unit at Seasons for Living. Adrian wanted to know the date of his photography and drone shoot.

Her cell rang. Tammi. "Hi. Did you wonder why I wasn't in the office today? I should have texted you."

Tammi's lilting voice responded. "I wasn't worried until Adrian called, complaining because you didn't respond to his request for his photography date. Something tells me he's going to be a bit of a challenge." The bangles on her wrist clinked in the background.

Helen sighed. "I'll email him right now. I guess he figures a famous owner and a three-million-dollar house warrant an immediate response. Probably can't blame him. He's been pretty accommodating so far." Her cell phone rang with the name Susan Edwards displayed. "Hold on a minute. It's Susan. I'll patch us together on the call."

"Hello there! I've got Tammi added to your call. We were thinking you decided to ditch being my real estate partner," Helen laughed. "When are you back from vacation? We could use you here."

Susan returned the laugh. "I'm tempted to keep testing out every port on the bay. You should try it. Lots of good-looking men with big boats willing to buy me a drink!"

72

"As my childhood friend, you know darn well I head in the other direction when it comes to the bar scene, but I'm glad you're having a good time. With all that's happening, I might need you to handle an out-of-town buyer I'm expecting in."

Tammi spoke up. "You may want to run the other way. She's sticking her nose into police business again."

"That's why I called! That chef's death and Lizzie's close call is national news," Susan exclaimed. "After my nightmare murder charge last spring, I knew she'd get involved. Is Lizzie okay?"

"She's physically fine but shaken up. Joe McAlister is in charge of the investigation," Helen explained.

"We all know he'll leave no stone unturned. He's not suspecting Lizzie, is he?"

Helen sighed. "Not yet. He said she's off the list, but we're still nervous. Lizzie had as much access to poisoning his food as anyone."

"McAlister's no fool. He knows she couldn't be a killer," Susan soothed. "When is his house going on the market?"

"Next week. I'm working with his partner, Adrian Stratton. We've set up the photography session. Technically, it's owned by Barto Enterprises, but he's now the sole owner of the company."

"Seriously, do you want me to shorten my trip and come back?'"

"I have you returning two weeks from now," Tammi noted.

"Let's stick with your plans for now," Helen advised. "If we get desperate for help, I'll give you a shout."

"Then I'm off to the pool. Keep me posted. Anything to help Lizzie. Give her my love."

"Will do," Helen clicked off.

Tammi raised an eyebrow. "Are you sure you don't want her back sooner? You've got a lot on your plate."

"Between the two of us, I'm fine. This was supposed to be Susan's downtime. If I'd sat in jail like she did, I'd need a year's vacation from the real world."

"Where's Lizzie?"

"She's here at my house. We met with Joe and Rick, and the studio's security team this afternoon. She came back with me afterwards and is taking a nap. They replayed all the camera recordings for the day Roberto died. It was so distressing. It was haunting to watch him die." Her voice quivered. "The scene keeps playing over in my mind."

Her assistant was quiet. "Sounds like a nightmare."

"You don't know the half of it. His face was all contorted. The coroner called it Ricket's Grin. To watch such a handsome face become so distorted was shocking."

"I feel terrible for Lizzie. Are they any closer to finding who killed him?"

"Not really. That building is like a revolving door of people. They're working down a long list of suspects. Nothing seemed out of order. Until we figure out a motive, I don't think anyone's actions will stand out."

"Did you say we? I was only kidding with Susan. Does this mean you're working on the investigation?"

Helen tapped in a password as she talked. "I told you. This isn't just horrible, it's personal. Lizzie was nearly their second victim, and the killer didn't care. Someone considered her collateral damage."

"You've been here before. Getting involved with tracking down Al Capelli's killer turned into a nightmare until you figured it out. Be careful. I have no interest in finding a new job because you get knocked off."

Helen sighed. "Thank you. No need to worry. I'm just going to poke around a bit and pass everything off. I'm not interested in disrupting my life again. I just want to be sure there isn't any detail we might be able to help with."

Tammi issued a little laugh. "Uh-huh. Since when have you let someone else take the lead? I'll believe that when I see it."

"After the Capelli episode? Believe me, I'm not getting involved any more than I have to."

"Aren't your Detection Club cronies egging you on?"

"Relax," Helen protested. "I'm putting Roberto and Adrian's house on the market and staying in the background. Very Jane-like. No one will even notice me. Certainly not the killer."

"Now you're kidding yourself. "

"I can keep one step ahead of him," Helen protested.

"How do you know it's a him? And how do you know there's only one culprit? You might need to keep two steps ahead, Jane."

Chapter Thirteen

Adrian rang Helen in her office early the next day. "Change of plans. How soon can you get your photographer in here? The police have released Roberto's body, and I want to have a memorial get-together at the house Sunday. I think it's the kind of event he would have liked."

She tapped into her laptop. "It's Thursday. I'll text my photographer right now and ask him to move it up to tomorrow. It's not much notice."

"Do what you can. Between the press and all the people we know, I'd like to get this over with." He clicked off.

Eight minutes later, her property photographer, Jerome Walker, texted back. **I can switch another client around. See you there 9 am tomorrow. Weather's good. It'll take at least 4 hours.**

Thank you! Thank you! You're the best! Helen grinned at his message. She pulled up Lizzie's number. **Lizzie- meeting Jerome 9 am tomorrow. Can you make that?**

She responded. **Yup. Open until 3.**

Great. FYI, memorial get together at Riding Cross Sunday.

Lizzie texted back. **That was quick.**

Yup.

Someone tapped on her door. Helen looked up to see Joe.

"Got a few minutes?"

"Of course. Any news?" She pulled back her chair and crossed her legs.

"I wondered if you heard anything more about Roberto's money obligations. I stopped by Taylor Lumber to talk to Dottie. She's feeling burned.

Roberto was behind in his payments for building supplies to the tune of a hundred and twenty thousand dollars.

"Wow. That's a lot of money. I'm surprised Dottie let him slide."

"She said she gave him some slack because there was promise of another big job coming up. She wanted to appear more cooperative than the big home centers."

Helen pursed her lips. "I guess that's possible. Jean from the Coffee Pot heard she was being considered for his renovations at the new restaurant in Baltimore. Had to be a stretch for her to give him that much float dollar-wise. You're not considering Dottie a suspect, are you? I can't imagine Dottie would want to kill him. Knowing her as long as I have, I don't think it fits her DNA."

Joe crossed the room and back. "I tend to agree. I don't see how killing him would help her get her money back any faster. Unless she blamed him for her own bad decision. Felt he suckered her in."

"She also doesn't have any physical access to ShopTV." Helen jumped up and started searching across her desktop. "Speaking of money, maybe you'll find this helpful." She opened her cell phone and scrolled through her photo app. "I snapped this the first time I had a chance to poke around Roberto's upstairs office. It looks like a list of dollar figures inside a journal, most of them checked off and dated."

Frowning, Joe got up and stared over her shoulder. "You should have shown this to me sooner. Rick's been trolling through his financials. Tell me you didn't clip the journal?"

"No way. I poked it open with a pencil, snapped this photo, and pushed it back into the drawer."

He sighed. "Good. Email this page to me right now. I'll take it from here."

"I'm sorry I didn't bring it to you sooner. Did you hear Adrian is having a get-together at Riding Cross Sunday as a memorial?"

"Yeah. We didn't have any good reason for not releasing the body."

"I assume you didn't find anything in the coroner's report to help you determine who could have killed him?"

Joe grimaced as he sat back down across from her. "The coroner found enough to incriminate every employee of the studio. I don't think there's anyone who didn't at least brush by the guy."

Helen reached into her desk and pulled out an opened bag of red Twizzlers. She wiggled one at Joe as an invitation. She usually wasn't so open about her addiction. He waved it away. She shrugged and bit off an end. "Breakfast. Probably lunch."

"I've been thinking about the killer's choice of location. Seems like he or she took a big chance poisoning our victim in the midst of all the chaos. Risky."

Helen nodded. "It reminds me of a Jane Marple mystery where there were so many people at a party, anyone could be the killer. Jane has been telling me the studio location was deliberate. The killer wanted chaos. He must have been pretty confident. Think how different your investigation would be if Roberto were killed in his private kitchen back at Riding Cross. Probably a lot fewer candidates for the killer."

Joe protested. "Not only chaos but recorded chaos. How many people plan a murder that's recorded by security cameras?"

"I was thinking the same. It's pretty daring. You do know what Jane would say? Chaos is the great detractor."

"Good point." He pushed himself out of his chair and walked to the door. "But you know I think you're crazy to discuss this with your mystery buddies."

She gave him a playful smile as she reached for her phone. "You have your squad. I have mine. See you Sunday."

"If not before." He closed the door behind him.

* * *

Friday morning, the sun was shining, good lighting for photographs. Jerome Walker was already walking around the perimeter of Roberto's house, shooting distance and close-ups. The bay twinkled in the sunshine.

"Like it?" she shouted across the lawn to him. "Got enough potential shots?"

The big man grinned, his warm smile brilliant. His wiry hair was pulled back in a bushy knot off his face. He gave Helen a bear hug.

"I think I can put together one or two for you." He surveyed the land. "We've worked on a lot of houses together. This place is incredible."

Helen smiled. "Not often you get a horse farm on the Chesapeake. Quite the view."

Jerome picked up a huge camera bag and swung it over his left shoulder. "I think I'd like to cover the inside first. I'll do the stables and drone shots last."

"That would be great. You can finish up the outside shots after I'm gone."

Lizzie walked in as they discussed rooms and priorities. Another warm hug in greeting for Jerome. "How can I help?"

Her mother handed her a stapled printout. "Here's a list of rooms in the order we need them. While Jerome photographs the foyer, why don't you and I rearrange a few things in the great room, the first-floor office, and the kitchen? If we spot anything valuable that needs to be removed, I'll make a note for Adrian."

The two women left Jerome to set up his lighting and headed to the great room. They removed a few side chairs and a display from over the mantel, pulled back draperies, and eliminated pillows. They hauled out split logs in the fireplace and replaced them with candles. Jerome was right behind them, shooting from both doorways and picking up the floor-to-ceiling views of the fields and water.

"This feels weird," Lizzie offered as they entered the spectacular black and white kitchen. She stood between the rear counter and big island, rubbing her palms across the custom-carved edges, much like her last time with Roberto. "It's like I'm back with him, and yet I'm not." Her voice quivered.

"It is definitely eerie," Helen patted her arm. "Can you help me walk through what happened again? Even cameras can lie. Kind of like Jerome. He takes photos of the same room from different angles and ends up with different impressions."

"In this case, I don't think there's much more I can offer."

Helen hesitated. Slowly, her words came out. "You were almost killed with the same poisonous plant. Have you considered it wasn't coincidental? Is it possible you were also intended?" She studied her daughter's face.

Lizzie gulped. Her eyes traveled around the enormous room. "Sure seems like it. The killer thought I would ingest the same food. I always do. Every show."

"It was a miracle the killer didn't know about your coconut aversion. He could have chosen a different show and a different recipe to tamper with if he also wanted you dead. That's a big 'if." Helen grabbed a stool and leaned her elbows on the counter edge, her chin in her hands. "We need to know, was it coincidence? Or was it deliberate?"

"What could be so important to cause someone to hate me that much?"

"Not a pretty thought."

"Mom, now you're really scaring me."

"I'm sorry. Chances are you were just in the wrong place at the wrong time." Helen got up and wrapped her arms around her daughter.

"Is it possible the killer knew I had an allergy to coconut? Maybe they chose a demonstration with coconut so I wouldn't get hurt too."

"That's a possibility. They'd have to know you fairly well." Helen turned and surveyed the room. "We're running out of time. Let's concentrate on styling the office. This kitchen is ready to go."

Lizzie followed her into the office and looked around. "Did you say Roberto had another office upstairs?"

"He did. He and Adrian both used this room. With all these trophies and plaques, it's definitely a shrine. Upstairs, Roberto's study seems much more personal. Lots of photos of friends and shelves of mementos." Helen rifled through paperwork scattered on his desk. "Who do you think will show up on Sunday for the memorial?"

"I guarantee you, all of ShopTV will be here. Whether they loved him or hated them, they wouldn't miss it."

Helen's eyes ran around the ceiling perimeter. She lowered her voice. "If I get a chance Sunday, I may want to take a closer look around his private study. I'll need you to help distract people from noticing my absence. I have to be conscious of any security cameras. My movements will be less likely to be recorded amidst a crowded party. Those cameras will be working overtime that day. Think you can deal with it, George?"

Her daughter pulled her shoulders back and saluted. "You got it, Nancy."

Chapter Fourteen

It may have been a gathering to memorialize Roberto, but most of the Riding Cross guests seemed to have forgotten. Between network crowd and the patrons of his famous restaurants, the chef's absence didn't keep any of them from their share of good wine, strong liquor, and all Roberto's famous food. Helen watched Adrian, now the center of attention as sole owner of their company and the Flying Pan product, enjoying his role a little too much. News stations and newspaper press followed him about.

The only one to put a damper on their imbibing was the arrival of Detective Joe McAlister.

Thirty-five minutes after the front gates opened, Dana Moore of *Dana's Delights* and the assumptive heir to Roberto's show walked in. Mariah Manley, in her usual odd outfit, wore streaky washed denim and a calf-length dismal shawl, followed behind Dana's entourage. Her freckled face was white and drawn.

The queen of ShopTV was doing a poor job of hiding her personal delight that her strongest competitor was gone. Glittery and confident, Dana greeted everyone with little pats and breathless cheek kisses while never marring her lipstick. Her skin glowed. Her reddish-brown shoulder-length hair was styled in a wispy knot at her neck. Her form-fitting black suit with a hint of pink lining was stylish but appropriate for the occasion.

She spotted Lizzie in the foyer. "Lizzie, I hope you received my note. I feel terrible about what you must have experienced, to have poor Roberto collapse into your arms." Dana tsked, tsked, as she stroked Lizzie's arm.

Helen leaned forward, offering her hand. "Hi. I'm Helen Morrisey. I wish we were meeting under happier circumstances. No doubt losing Roberto is sad for everyone. As your colleague, I'm sure you miss him terribly."

Dana's eyes grazed Helen, taking in her Nora Charles gray linen jacket and four-inch heels. Her tone oozed sugar-sweet. "It is an absolute pleasure to finally meet you. You are right. These are sad circumstances." She smiled warmly at Lizzie. "Your daughter is a remarkable host. If she had formal training as a chef, I'd be intimidated. We love working together."

"I'm glad to hear it. She talks about you often. Tell me, how are you planning to help fill in the gaps Roberto has left?" Helen asked, her eyes guileless.

"We'll sort through it. Roberto was an incredible talent, and I was happy to help guide him through the nuances of live television presentations. I helped clear his path to recognition."

"I didn't realize how much you impacted his career. I'm sure he was grateful."

Lizzie glanced from woman to woman, then stepped in. "Dana spent years establishing her fan base. Her success is no accident."

Dana beamed. "Let's just say, without my leading by example, Roberto would likely have struggled to get his foothold with the network's fans."

"Do you think he was appreciative?" Helen tilted her head toward the gathering.

The star pursed her lips. "I'm not sure appreciative is the right description. Let's say he was smart enough to spot a marketing opportunity and made the most of it." She turned her head toward two men across the living room. "Please excuse me."

Helen accepted a glass of white wine from a circulating waiter in a black uniform with Water Street Bistro embroidered in red on the breast pocket. Lizzie interrupted. "Mom, this is Neal Frawley. He's head of wait staff at the restaurant. "Neal, this is my mother, Helen."

"Nice to meet you. I'm Helen Morrisey. Looks like this crowd is keeping you busy."

He scanned the crowd in approval. "I run all Barto Enterprises big events."

"Are you involved in the other restaurant locations?"

"I plan the layouts and staffing for all of them."

"That's impressive. I'm sure Adrian is grateful, especially now."

Neal's eyes glinted. "Be more impressive if I got a title and money instead of just lining their company's pockets year after year." His mouth formed a thin line.

"Did you like that cover article in *Restaurant Magazine* about Roberto and their restaurants?" Helen probed.

"Yea, that should have been about me." He shifted toward a nearby couple and offered out his tray.

"Any ideas as to who's happy Roberto's gone?"

"Other than the obvious," his eyes traveled to Dana. "I don't have an opinion. Besides, opinions are dangerous." He moved away.

Lizzie whispered. "I can't believe you asked that!"

Her mother shrugged. "Why? Jane suggested it. Staff usually know more about our personal lives than best friends. Thought it was worth a stab."

A sharp ring of a glass clinking from the patio drew everyone outside. Adrian stood under the pool canopy. Greg Waldron joined him.

"Thank you for being here to hold this tribute for Roberto. I want to say a few words today about my partner and best friend." Adrian's eyes misted. "Roberto was undoubtedly a remarkable man. I recognized his talents when we first met years ago. He loved creating great food and entertaining people. His pleasure in providing both was obvious. I owe much of our success to him. My skills may have created our unique Flying Pan, but he was the magic that inspired purchasers to bring our organic product line into millions of homes and to dine in our restaurants. I miss him every day." His voice broke.

Another glass clinked. All eyes traveled to Greg Waldron, dressed as the image of a corporate executive, a navy suit cut to show his broad shoulders and trim waistline. He stepped forward. "As some of you within the ShopTV family may have heard, we've been in discussions with Barto Enterprises about introducing a second chef to help cover Roberto's scheduling conflicts as his travel increased. Our decision was supposed to be announced in time to ramp up for the holiday sales season."

Helen spotted Joe at the opposite end of the pool. Their eyes met. 'Where is he going with this?' Nora asked her.

"Given this sad and very unexpected loss of Roberto, both Adrian and I believe we should announce our choice immediately. It's best for the Flying Pan brand, ShopTV, and all the employees affected by its sales. To be very clear, this choice was also approved by Roberto before he died." Greg paused. "We are pleased to present Miss Tara Owen, who many of you may recognize as the number one celebrity chef from a competing station. She will be the new face of Flying Pan and Roberto's cooking show. She will be employed by Barto Enterprises while working closely together with the network." Greg swallowed, small beads of sweat on his brow, then shifted aside. "Tara, could you say a few words?"

The buzz through the crowd of guests took over. Greg and Adrian parted, and Tara joined them.

A diminutive blonde about thirty-five or so, in a short black dress and pale blue heels, she shook the two men's hands, then turned toward the crowd. Tara flashed a bold, confident smile. The press maneuvered for position, their cameras snapping.

"Good afternoon, everyone," she began in a polished, clear tone. "I admit I was a bit surprised this announcement would be made so quickly after Roberto's death. He and I have been quietly working together for the past couple of months to coordinate this fresh marketing strategy. When we lost him last Sunday, the idea of going forward with our plans without him seemed daunting. However, it became clear delaying would benefit no one and could hurt employees in particular." She paused and cast across the crowded room. A diamond bracelet glinted from her wrist. "Like Roberto, I'll be working with ShopTV's talented hosts. I promise you, I'll do all I can to fulfill his very big shoes. Figuratively." She gave a little feminine laugh, glancing at her tiny feet.

"Holy crap," Lizzie exclaimed under her breath. "I didn't see that one coming."

"Apparently, no one else did either," commented Joe behind her.

Complete silence, then polite clapping. Across the room, Mariah seemed glued to the floor. Others stole sly glances at Dana, whose face turned to grey marble. She grabbed a drink from Neal, turned on her heels, and brushed past the others. Adrian winced. Greg leaned over, whispering in Tara's ear while tilting his head at Dana. She set down her drink and began to cut across the patio in Dana's direction.

"Be right back," Helen said softly. She weaved among the little clusters of people, following Tara inside. Through the kitchen, around the main hall, and up the staircase. At the top of the stairs, she followed the staccato of clicking heels. They stopped. Helen halted and tucked herself against the wall outside Roberto's bedroom.

Tara was speaking. "Dana, I'm sorry this was unexpected. We should talk about it."

"Talk about it! There's nothing to talk about! How dare you steal this deal from me!" Dana's voice was climbing octaves with each word. "This is my network! I cannot believe this was strictly a business decision. Were you sleeping with Roberto? Is that how you devised this? Why else would he convince Greg to go around me and hire you?"

"Don't be ridiculous," the younger woman retorted. "They all made this decision based on sales and fan base."

"Sales and fan base. Don't insult me. I had a fan base before you got into the business. Your ranking as an international chef doesn't touch mine. I've sold more bestselling cookbooks than you could even dream of. Have you ever even run a restaurant bigger than a pizza shop?" Dana scoffed.

Tara made a dismissive wave. "Your numbers are dropping, and mine keep climbing. I'm on the way up, and you're on the way down. It's very simple."

"Did Greg fall for you? He's such a pompous ass. He must have assumed you were interested in him."

Tara slowed her words and purred. "Adrian and Greg and I had hoped we could talk this out. Now I realize it's not possible. The press and your groupies are waiting for your reaction. I suggest you pull yourself together and act like an adult."

"Don't tell me who's the adult!" Glass shattered against a wall. Helen snuck a peek around the corner in time to see Tara leaping aside.

"You're crazy," she cried out as she marched back toward the entry. Helen slipped through the next bedroom doorway as Tara passed by. Moments later, Dana stepped out. Helen watched her apply fresh lipstick, her hands trembling, in a hall mirror. She pulled down her jacket and strode back down the staircase.

'Well, chums,' Helen breathed. 'What do you think of those two?' If Dana killed Roberto to take over his product line, she just lost the entire crap shoot. If Tara killed him to seal her new deal, she'll need to work awfully hard to keep the cops from sniffing at her door. They both had a lot to gain with him out of the picture.

She peered down the hall. 'Go for it,' Nancy spoke up. 'Check out Roberto's study again while everyone is distracted. It's right up our alley.'

Helen whisked down and into the study.

She came to a halt, her eyes traveling from wall to wall to wall. Why did she sense something's different in here? She cruised around the room, studying the articles on the desk, the notes and papers appearing pretty much as she remembered a few days before. What was she missing?

She reached to straighten one of the framed photos she'd seen before. 'Wait!' She murmured. They were rearranged. In fact, some were missing! Who removed them? Why?

Helen stood and snapped the wall collection again, then stepped back into the hall and casually walked down the staircase to rejoin the crowd below.

Chapter Fifteen

Her cell rang at eight am Monday morning. Joe.

"Well. What did you think of last night?" he asked.

Helen poured her first cup of coffee and walked out to the deck. "Hello to you too. I'm actually in an Agatha Raisin frame of mind right now. She doesn't think well at this hour."

"Hmmm. I was hoping to talk with Helen."

"Sorry to disappoint. Agatha thinks you have a very long list of people who could gain from Roberto's death. I also discussed your problem with Jessica on the way home last night."

"Does she have anything to say about all this?"

"She is practical. She thinks you need to follow the money."

He grunted. "That won't help much. Tough because so many benefit."

"No, it doesn't. But we could try to consider them in the order of greatest gain. Of course, given I deal with a lot of clients who react emotionally rather than logically, ranking their motives in only money may not help us either."

"Which means both Agatha and Jessica are wrong."

"My squad is never wrong. They're just working through the process."

"Which one would be interested in going to dinner tonight? And please don't tell me it's Miss Marple."

Helen laughed. "No, Jane's not a night owl."

"Nancy?"

"I think she's a little young."

"Agreed. If I remember, you told me Agatha has nice legs," he quipped back.

"She does. Lucky for you, she likes to show them off."

"Pick her up at seven?"

Helen swiped through her phone calendar. "Hmmm. I've got a conflict. I'm meeting a couple in the office tonight."

"Looks like it's me and Rocky."

* * *

By nine-thirty am, she was weaving her way through little Port Anne, determined to pick up a latte for herself and Tammi. Her coffee at home always tasted second-rate. Water Street bustled. She crawled down the one-way street toward Jean's Coffee Pot, searching for a parking spot. Water Street Bistro was still dark, but its sidewalk was replenished with more flowers on its front steps.

The little shop's door chimes tinkled as she entered. The shop was surprisingly empty. "Jean? Hello?"

Jean popped her head out from her backroom. "Oh, hello! I was just getting out more cups. What are you up to? Is Nancy still sniffing around for clues on Roberto?" Her bright eyes twinkled.

"I did want to ask you, have you heard any chatter since Adrian's memorial at the house last night? I figured some of the locals might be buzzing about it while they picked up their brew."

"From everything folks tell me, it was quite the gala for an event that's supposed to be sad. Is that the way they do things if you're a celebrity?"

Helen helped herself to a blueberry scone. "Adrian definitely seemed to enjoy being the sole owner. I imagine it was tough sharing the limelight with Mr. Charm."

Jean reached for Helen's cash. "Did I hear he's been replaced already?"

Helen talked and munched at the same time. "These network people don't seem to waste any time moving on. Their VP of Talent Greg Waldron announced their replacement, Tara Owens. According to him, she was chosen to start sharing Roberto's demos before he died. Awfully convenient if you ask me. Poor Roberto's gone, and now she doesn't need to share the limelight. She has to be thrilled."

"I liked his show because he was our local boy. But I've been following Dana Moore for years. I get the sense she's got a big ego but worked hard to get where she is now. I would have thought she'd be the one to share his airtime rather than someone new." Jean snapped lids onto Helen's coffees.

"You and everyone else, especially Dana. She was ready to tear Tara apart. Probably would have if all the studio staffers and the press weren't watching. I felt bad for her. It was pretty embarrassing." Helen juggled her two coffees. "Keep me posted. You know you're my eyes on the street."

Jean followed her to the door and pulled it open. "Come to think of it, I did hear something new."

Helen leaned on the doorjamb. "Were you planning on keeping it a secret from me?"

Jean pursed her lips. "One of the camera crew heard the liens on Riding Cross are being called. You're the Realtor. Does it make any sense to you?"

Helen paused. "Not really. I didn't get the idea Barto Enterprises was in that deep a financial hole. Unless Adrian and Roberto were in serious arrears on their mortgages, banks can't call loans. But thanks. I'll give it some thought."

The older woman chuckled. "I'm sure you will."

* * *

Helen settled the two coffees on her front seat, turned on the ignition, and stopped to watch all the activity at Tomes and Treasures on the next corner of Water Street. Calli, its long-time owner, and her assistant, Viv, set out their samples of local authors' titles, Love the Bay t-shirts and sweatshirts, and Port Anne local crafts onto the sidewalk. A sign in the window advertised Roberto's latest cookbook. "Autographed copies!" said a sign with a big red crab above it.

She swore she heard Agatha muttering a request for a new cookbook. Helen groaned. If there were two women who didn't use them, it was Agatha

Raisin and herself. She reached for her ignition again, then stopped. Perhaps they did. She needed to stop talking out loud to an empty car. Passers on the street either assumed she was on her cell or she'd lost her mind.

She climbed out of her Mini and strolled into the crowded little shop. It had been a few months since she'd been here. She marveled at how such a small space displayed all this inventory. Buoys hung from the ceiling, fish nets draped the walls, blue crab pottery, Port Anne magnets, stickers, and tea towels were stacked in wooden racks and cabinets of all sizes. No one could enter this store and not smile at its happy aura.

Front and center, Roberto's latest cookbook was on display with its full-color cover photo of him smiling into the camera. A pile of Dana Moore's cookbooks with Dana holding a large wooden spoon sat next to his. Helen flipped open his flyleaf and spotted his autograph signed with a flourish across the title page. Recalling his face frozen in a Ricket's Grin the last time she was with him made her swallow hard.

Calli offered a warm smile as she approached the crowded counter. There was barely three inches of room between handmade soaps and candles. "Helen, I thought it was you. How have you been?" Calli was tall and thin, a woman who had turned this shop into a local favorite with twenty-five years of hard work. Viv, her right-hand, was short, fair, and always welcoming. They made a charming pair.

"I'm fine. Looks like you're bustling as usual." Helen handed her Roberto's cookbook.

Viv took her credit card. "We can't keep this in stock. We wish we ordered more of them."

"I bet you'll sell them out. He was a popular guy."

"People love autographed copies," Calli added.

"It is fun to get them, although my favorite autograph is when one of my clients signs a sales agreement."

They laughed together as Helen stepped back outside with a wave.

* * *

Monday at Safe Harbor was busy with agents and staff catching up with client paperwork from the weekend. Tammi handed her a small stack of invoices as Helen walked past her desk.

"Good morning. I wasn't sure you'd be here bright and early after your big memorial yesterday." Tammi was wearing a scarlet-colored cotton sweater with long gold sunbursts dangling from her ears. "Do you have time to go over monthly expenses? There's not a lot here, but I'd like to get a couple of bills paid for you."

Helen handed her a coffee and a biscotti. "You know I hate accounting. I probably would have ducked past you if I'd known."

"I know. That's why I like to barricade you in your office on the first of the month." Tammi followed her into the room and laid the receipts on Helen's desk with a checkbook. "This is an easy month. A few marketing expenses for Riding Cross and three installations for signs."

Helen flipped through the receipts one by one. Tammi wrote out the checks, handed them to her to sign, and then scooped them all up. "That wasn't so painful, was it?"

"Nice to have a less expensive month. Or is it my fault because the past week has been a little slow?"

Tammi rolled her eyes at her. "You do seem to be distracted with Roberto, not that I blame you. Any news?"

Helen tapped her pen on the paperwork. "Nothing much. Lizzie and I are still trying to wrap our heads around the fact that she almost died along with him. Whoever it was, I hope they realize I'm not likely to forget it or forgive."

"Would it be better if they *didn't* realize you're asking questions?"

"You might be right. Of course, from Joe's standpoint, I need to stay out of it completely."

"Fat chance."

Helen stuck out her tongue.

Tammi tossed back a grin and headed off, her sunbursts swaying.

* * *

Helen decided to give her son and personal district attorney a call. "Shawn, I have a question for you. Call me. Thanks, Hon."

Twenty minutes later, he was on her cell. "Hey, Mom. I'm in between hearings at the courthouse and grabbing a sandwich at a food truck. What's up? Lizzie okay?"

Helen smiled to herself. He always checked on his twin sister first. "She's still shook up. She's having a tough time going in to work. It's nearly impossible to not wonder if she's rubbing elbows with a killer."

"Joe any closer to figuring it out?"

She could hear him chewing in between words. A bus roared behind him. "He's not exactly filling me in hour by hour. Wants me to stay out of it."

"Can't say I blame him. Let him do his job. This'll take time."

"I'm not barging into his investigation," she protested.

Shawn swallowed. "So, you say. How can I help?"

"I want to send you a few photos I spotted in Roberto's private study a few days ago."

"What's special about them?"

"I took photographs, like I usually do the first time I take notes on a house. During the memorial lunch, Lizzie covered for me while I checked the room again. There were at least three photos missing from the walls, and the rest had been rearranged. I thought you could blow up all my shots. You might notice something important. You're used to examining evidence. There has to be a reason they were removed. Someone went to a lot of trouble to do it."

Shawn let out a dramatic sigh. "You just finished telling me you weren't getting involved. Now, you tell me you're snapping photos of Roberto's private study. Why are you doing this?"

"Why? Because your sister almost died along with Roberto. Doesn't it concern you?" Her voice raised two octaves.

"Of course. That doesn't mean you, a private citizen, and my mother, should stick your nose into this investigation."

"Fine. Can you just take a look at these photos for me? I'll scan and email them right now."

"Okay. I will. Call you later tonight. Can you please do us all a favor? Go sell someone a house. It's so much safer." He clicked off.

Helen dug through her bottom desk drawer and unearthed three bent Twizzlers. She bit down in frustration. 'Since when did my son become such a know-it-all?'

Her cell buzzed with a text message. **Love you, Mom.**

Chapter Sixteen

Ms. Olivia Cantor was ready to sign her agreement to purchase with Seasons for Living. She beamed as she signed off on her custom upgrades.

"Can I take you out to lunch to celebrate?" Helen proposed.

"Love to." Olivia's eyes twinkled.

"Follow me. Let's head over to Port Anne Yacht Club."

The little yacht club sat along the bay coastline in between larger marinas, taking every advantage of a bar and dining room facing the water. Views captured spectacular sunsets, the light splaying across the boats. It was already about three o'clock, and Helen led Olivia around the terrace past a group of twelve students from the university sailing team. Helen grinned as she soaked in their high energy and competitive spirit.

Olivia's eyes lit up as she spotted the young sailors launching little Opti racing boats and hoisting sails. The team's sail coach barked orders from across the water.

"This is exciting," Olivia exclaimed as they claimed two wrought-iron chairs. "I'd forgotten the university practices here."

Helen laughed. "Their teams flock back to our docks in late August and the start of fall semester. Still not tired of being with young people? After all your years teaching, I would think you might have lost interest."

The older woman's eyes gleamed. "How can anyone not get pleasure seeing young people take an interest in the water and away from computer screens. If you ask me, that's one of the biggest challenges parents and teachers have today."

"Given Shawn and Lizzie grew up on the water, I completely agree, although I'd have to give Andy most of the credit. He loved boats."

"Do you get out on the water very much?" Olivia set aside her menu after choosing her lunch.

Helen ordered iced tea for them, then shrugged. "For the first two years after Andy died, *Persuasion* was pretty neglected. I wasn't confident about taking her out alone. Lizzie and Shawn would sail with me whenever they could. The last two seasons, I've been mustering up my courage and going out by myself, usually at the end of the day. It's peaceful spending some quiet time by myself on the water."

"I'm glad to hear it, although having too much time alone isn't always good. Take it from a woman who knows."

Helen eyed her neat, diminutive guest. "Now, you sound like my children."

Their lunch arrived, and they both dived into crab salads.

"How is Lizzie handling the terrible scare she had with Roberto?"

"Honestly, she's upset, although she's trying to hide it. These are her co-workers, and the atmosphere, I gather, is pretty tense. I wish I knew more about the people involved with the network. It's hard for me to offer her much solace." Helen paused.

Olivia eyed her. "Given all I've heard about you professionally, you might want to give your abilities more credit. You're known for being good at observing people and places. If I were the killer, I wouldn't want you and your Detection Club sniffing around me."

Helen leaned across their table. "My Detection Club? How did you hear about them?" She said under her breath.

"I've lived in this town a long time. People talk, rumors float around. Your involvement in solving the Capelli case isn't much of a secret, even if law enforcement tried to keep it quiet." Olivia pursed her lips.

"My assistant, Tammi, said the same thing. I truly doubt anyone is concerned about my little observations," Helen protested. "My friends and my family tell me I talk to myself far too often. Strangers probably think I'm simply crazy." She drew a small circle on her cloth napkin with a spoon. "My mental squad is my sounding board. They're just very opinionated."

Olivia laughed.

Helen smiled back. "You realize Jane Marple was the woman described as having a fine sense of evil."

"She was born with it, like having a keen sense of smell," Olivia added. "My sense is you two are much the same. You might as well accept it and put your talent to good use."

Helen stared into the wise teacher's steady blue eyes. "That's a lot to think about. I'm not sure I'm willing to accept the responsibility. You call it a talent. It may be more like a curse." She sat back and gazed at the boats bobbing in the harbor. "You've educated half the people in Port Anne who work at the network. Are you aware of anyone we should consider a suspect?"

Olivia studied her face. "How much time do you have?"

Helen raised her eyebrows. She gave a little wave to the passing server.

Olivia smiled. "Young woman, could I have a martini, dirty, three olives?"

Helen's eyebrows climbed another inch. "I'll have a Sidecar in a coupe glass in deference to Nora Charles. Might as well bring them all in on this conversation. Nancy and Jessica aren't drinkers."

Their eyes met in accord.

With fresh drinks served, Helen started. "You mentioned Greg Waldron, vice president of talent, the first time we met. He was incredibly involved in Roberto's career and brought over a new chef, Tara Moore, to replace him. What do you remember about him?"

Olivia twisted her chilled martini glass between her fingers. "How well does Lizzie know him?"

Helen sat back, surprised. "I have no idea. She deals with him because he's in charge of hiring talent, and Lizzie is what they call 'talent.' They probably cross paths quite a bit. What do you know?"

"Only how he operated as a teenager." She measured her words. "He may be perfectly respectable now, but in high school, he was known as a con artist."

"Con artist! What do you mean?"

"Greg was one of those handsome fellows who was always the instigator, and I'm not talking about the usual immature high jinks. He was the kind who conjured up money-making schemes by passing test answers to friends. He paid more diligent students to write his term papers. He tapped into our grading system. Always crossing the line but getting away with a slap on the wrist."

"How'd he pull it off?"

Olivia gritted her teeth. "His parents' influence. It infuriated me."

"You're wondering if he rose through the ranks at his company by skirting corporate rules. Or, worse yet, had reason for eliminating Roberto."

Slowly, Olivia tilted her head from left to right. "I am giving you background. I worry that he is not the bright, clean company man he portrays." She wiggled her index finger at Helen. "He may have played a part in Roberto's death. I'm suggesting you and your Lizzie should be on high alert."

Helen studied her hands.

"I'm inclined to believe you aren't a person who believes in coincidences." The educator observed. "Someone killed Roberto for a reason and apparently did not care if Lizzie could be considered a suspect."

"Are you sure you aren't Jane Marple incarnate?"

Olivia chuckled. "Only a fan. You didn't answer my question."

"Let's say I'm not usually a believer in coincidences. Least of all when it comes to a poisoning by a rare substance. There must have been a personal benefit. The question is what benefit and for whom." Helen reached for the bill, waving Olivia away.

Olivia rose and gathered her handbag. "I'm simply thinking if you're ranking suspects based on lack of integrity, Greg might be a strong candidate. How he'd benefit from Roberto's death, I've no idea. That's for you to figure out. I'd like to think I've misjudged him. I'm confident I have not misjudged *you.*"

Helen pushed back her chair. "Jane Marple said once a deceiver, always a deceiver."

Her client stared directly into her eyes and offered a tight smile. "She's proof women up in years like me are not quite the daft old ladies people tend to assume we are."

Helen smiled at her. "I think I read that somewhere."

* * *

"Joe? It's me. Do you have a few minutes?"

"Of course. What's up?"

"Have you questioned Greg Waldron yet?" She could hear his car radio squawking in the background.

"As a matter of fact, I'm pulling into the studio parking lot. Rick and I are meeting with him now. Why do you ask?"

"I had an interesting conversation with a client of mine today who knew him as a Port Anne High School student years back. She was principal at the time." She hesitated. "I'll ask that you keep anything she said to yourself, but it might help better prepare you."

"Why would she confide in you?"

"Because she trusts me, and she is concerned Lizzie and I don't know who we're dealing with."

He sighed. "What's she got?"

"According to this educator, his smooth corporate demeanor may not be all it seems. As a student, he had a reputation as a real con artist. Always pulling off ways to cheat the system. Exams, papers, bribes, even hacking into computers to alter grades."

"Did they toss him out of school? How do I know this isn't just hearsay from a frustrated teacher?"

"She said he never got more than a reprimand because his parents had influence. I gather school boards and teachers were more willing to write off bad behavior back then. Schools didn't worry about bullying and hacking and security like they do today."

"True. You trust this source?"

"Implicitly. She's not suggesting Greg is responsible for Roberto's death, but she wants us to be forewarned. The information he gave you might be based on an outcome that benefits him and not the case."

Joe was silent for a moment. "We did run a background check on him. He came up fairly clean. He's a bit over-extended financially, but not unusual for a young hotshot anxious to show off his success. Did this person know anything about his reputation with women?"

She paused. "She never mentioned it. If I take a guess, Lizzie might know more about it. She mentioned he hit on her a while ago. He was pretty annoyed she blew him off."

"Gotcha. I'm just trying to look at him from different angles. Thanks for phoning this into us. I'll catch up with you later." His cell went silent.

Chapter Seventeen

"Hello, my little lovelies, did you miss me?" Helen called out as she walked into her kitchen and greeted her cats. Watson and Trixie blinked, then bolted for their bowls, yowling for dinner. She dropped her tote and her laptop on the counter and pulled out their food. She eyed Watson and his overly round body. "Aren't you lucky you don't depend on my cooking? Not that you couldn't stand for a reduction in calories."

Her cell rang as she headed toward her bedroom to change. Jerome.

"Hello there. Rather late for you to be calling, isn't it?"

Jerome offered a hearty laugh. "I knew your seller of Riding Cross was anxious to get his photos. I just emailed the entire file to you. Once you pick out the photos you like, I'll create your video for you."

"How'd they turn out?" She reached for a wine glass.

"Spectacular. Your biggest problem is reducing your choices. There's only a couple of the lower level. I was running out of time and assumed they were the least important."

"I trust your judgment. Always amazes me how many agents post photos of toilets with the seats up. Ugh."

Jerome chuckled. "If I remember, you found Lizzie her house because the photo of the front was so terrible, no one else was bothering to show it to clients."

Helen smirked. "That listing agent should have been fired. I'll email you with our choices as soon as I can. Thanks again."

She dialed Adrian and left a voice mail. "Hi, it's Helen. My photographer's photos are in. Do you have time to review them tomorrow? Let me know. Thanks!"

A text came in twenty minutes later. **Let's meet 9 am tomorrow my house. Please confirm.**

She tapped her phone. **See you at 9. :)**

* * *

The next morning, Lizzie called as she was leaving her house.

"Dana called me. She wants to meet with me. She's suggesting I leave ShopTV as a network host and join her corporation. She thinks we could combine our fan bases."

"Well, that's an interesting twist. Sounds like she plans to turn up the heat and give Tara and Adrian new competition. What do you think of the idea?"

"I'm not sure I can deal with her on a daily basis. She's a strong personality."

"And you're not?"

"You're right. I'd have to be careful our discussion doesn't get back to Greg."

"You should consider hearing her out. She's obviously a superstar in your business. She may think you can increase her fan base by attracting more younger buyers."

"A possibility. Would you like to sit in on the meeting? Might be useful to have a second set of ears."

Helen paused. "As long as she doesn't think you're not strong enough to act on your own. That you have to bring along your mother."

"I could care less. She might even like it. Gives her the impression I'm seriously considering her proposal. Leaving the network would be a big career decision for me."

"Shouldn't you check with your agent?"

"I'd rather not involve him at this point. Let's consider this a reconnaissance mission. Besides, I think this could be a chance for us to bring up Roberto's death and get her reaction."

"I agree with you there. I'm leaving for a nine am with Adrian now. Text me with a time. We should have Agatha listen in. She's very business savvy."

Lizzie giggled. "Mom, you sound like a crazy person."

"No, I don't," Helen objected. "I'm in the Jessica Fletcher mode today, by the way. She would have made a great real estate agent. Logical and persistent."

"You're crazy."

* * *

Adrian stretched out his hands in a warm double handshake at his front door. "Thank you for getting here early. I'm excited to see the photographs. Let's sit at the kitchen island. Can I offer you coffee?"

Helen was happy to get the warm greeting. "Coffee sounds great, especially if it comes from your gourmet coffee bar."

He nodded agreeably. "It's actually one of the devices I wanted when Roberto designed the kitchen. I am a good coffee addict. Why don't you fix it the way you like it?"

He handed her a large black mug of steaming coffee and pointed toward cream and an entire array of flavorings.

"So, what do we have?" His eyes behind his round spectacles were bright. "Can't wait to see them."

Screen by screen, photo by photo, Helen and Adrian reviewed dozens of numbered shots and eliminated over half, narrowing them down to about thirty-five.

Helen scratched down the number for his last choice and threw down her pen. They both sat back and exchanged pleased grins.

"Whew! Next question," Adrian interjected. "When are all of these released to the public?"

"Should only be a couple days. I have one concern. Your attorney sent me your power of attorney regarding the will and the deed substantiating your right to sell the property." She hesitated, reluctant to disrupt his positive mood. She measured her words. "I heard rumors that you're being pressed to sell quickly. Do you have loans being called on Riding Cross that could halt a sale? Seems an odd rumor, but I have to ask. Both you and Roberto had such urgency to sell. Why?"

"You asked me this before. Why do you feel a need to ask this again?"

"Because in the end, without a clear title, we can't sell this house."

Her seller went silent. His thin, long face started to redden. His voice tightened. "We've always had debt tied into our restaurants. It's perfectly normal protocol in this business. This house is another form of collateral."

Adrian snapped shut his laptop, rose, and walked over to the refrigerator. He pulled out a bottle of Evian mineral water. "I can assure you we have more than enough equity to enable us to close."

Helen offered an enthusiastic smile. "Then we're ready to go on the market tomorrow." Adrian's shoulders relaxed.

"How are you managing without him?"

He cleared his throat. "I miss him very much. As far as Barto Enterprises is concerned, we'll be fine. I expect a few bumps in the road as we transition Tara Owen to take his place. We were fortunate Tara was already prepared to join us. I'm confident business will settle down over the next few months."

"Are you anxious to find his killer?"

"I don't know if anxious is the right word. I certainly hope the police are being diligent. Why? Do you have someone you suspect?"

She cast an eye across the room and back to him. "Some people seem more likely than others, but I don't know much more than you do. Do you think there's any reason Dana or Greg would want him dead?"

He crossed and uncrossed his legs. "I think Greg, like me, had the most to lose with Roberto gone. He's got his reputation on the line by choosing Tara. For me, keeping Barto Enterprises on a growth path without Roberto is my priority, not finding his killer."

"That's certainly understandable." Helen gathered up their paperwork and slipped it into her tote. She hooked her bag over her shoulder and hesitated. "In walking through the house with Jerome, I got the sense you're tucking items away."

Adrian acted puzzled. His shoulders pulled back. His neck muscles tightened. "I'm sorry?"

She gave him an innocent little grin, "It's probably not important, but I want to be sure you've removed anything valuable before we begin showings."

He offered a little chuckle. "I'm beginning to realize you don't miss much. I like that about you. We did lock away a few valuables. I was concerned we kept Roberto's personal mementos private."

Helen could feel his presence shift from friendly to testy. "I'm glad. I'd feel terrible if something private is exposed to the public. Too many curious fans and press."

Adrian showed a rare glimpse of his teeth. "Thank you. I assume you'll concentrate on selling this house and put aside any thoughts on this murder? Remember, it's how you earn your share. You represent me. I don't need ghoulish curiosity-seekers. I need serious buyers."

He clapped her shoulder with a firm hand and accompanied her to the front door.

She climbed into her Mini, turned on the engine, and started to pull up the drive. She slowed as she reached the slight rise and gazed down over the green rolling fields, the horse barns, and the private dock with the bay beyond. The water was dark, and she sensed a late summer storm approaching. 'Why do I feel uncomfortable about marketing this house? Is it the house or the owner? What do you say, chums? Is it instinct, or is it just nerves now that our master chef is no longer in charge?'

Chapter Eighteen

Helen could easily understand why Dana Moore was such a celebrity and queen of all things related to cooking on ShopTV. She was a standout, without question. Confident, not cocky, stunning, yet not perfect, Dana had an aura that inspired a crowd and kept them hanging onto her melodic words. It explained why she moved millions of dollars of her products each year.

Her gold bracelets tinkled as she reached across the white linen tablecloth to shake her hand. Her Chanel perfume wafted gently across the table.

"Such a pleasure to see you again, Helen," she remarked, her lips a perfect bow and her eyes shining in a way that made the recipient feel chosen. "I'm delighted Lizzie suggested you join in on our conversation."

Helen had thrown a wide swath of light cream cape over her too-conservative Jessica jacket and had switched out practical straw wedges for cream-colored high leather heels with silver tips. She watched as the TV chef ran her eyes over her designer handbag. She'd left her bottomless Jessica tote in her car.

"Thank you." Helen returned Dana's warm handshake. "She thought a second set of ears would be helpful to her."

"Let's order our lunch before we talk business, shall we?" Dana offered cheerfully.

She had chosen the Riverside Inn, a few nautical miles across the water from Port Anne Yacht Club. Fresh white tablecloths and polished flatware immediately made diners feel special. The Riverside Inn's history pre-dated the Civil War. Paintings of visiting presidents seeking excellent food and comfortable lodging mid-route between Philadelphia and Baltimore covered the paneled walls. China cabinets brimming with tea sets, one from John F. Kennedy, were lined up beneath them. An American eagle carved in wood from Theodore Roosevelt gazed down at them with a sharp eye. Helen was sure he was listening in on their conversation.

Lizzie and her mother waited for Dana to direct the conversation. Dana questioned the menu's ingredients like the professional chef she was before placing her lunch order with their server. She paired it with a specific white wine and requested three glasses.

Smoothly, the shopping network star began. "Thank you both for meeting. Roberto's passing has been such a shock, and poor Lizzie must have been frightened out of her wits given her close call." She bit her lower lip enough to express sympathy but not enough to mar her shell pink lipstick.

"Greg and Adrian's choice of Tara as his replacement must have been quite the shock for you," Lizzie countered. Helen was pleased her daughter had jumped into the controversy with both feet.

"I'm afraid I didn't handle their announcement very well." Dana looked directly at the two of them. "I admit I was stunned. Frankly, I still don't understand it."

Lizzie leaned in. "I don't either. That's why I was curious about your plans. Why on earth do you think Greg went along with such a choice?"

Dana tapped her pink nails to her perfect front teeth, then sighed. "It certainly was no secret Roberto and I merely put up with each other. I can only assume he felt he had to go along with hiring Tara. Whatever Roberto wanted, Roberto got." She calmly sipped a Perrier and lemon, disdain for the VP in her voice.

"I've dealt with my share of catty competition, but this seemed deliberately vengeful," Helen slipped in.

"Roberto wasn't just competitive. He was jealous of my standing." The chef tilted her head. "Yes, very vengeful." She inhaled, then said, "Which leads me to rethinking how to continue to grow my company in new directions. Lizzie comes to mind. I've decided to launch a new home décor product line and invite you to be my partner." She smiled at her. "I believe you have a bright, fresh aura and personal style. We could complement each other well."

Dana sat back, her shoulders relaxing against the padded dining chair. "Well? Would you like to become the latest Joanna and Chip Gaines, only two women?"

Lizzie shifted her tableware in front of her until the pieces were perfectly aligned. "Whew. That's a bold move, but I admit, I like it. I've often thought of starting my own product lines."

Dana waved her hands. "If you are open to the concept, we could meet again soon to start combining ideas. My attorneys could begin writing a detailed proposal."

"To be very clear, I have no interest in taking a secondary position in a partnership," Lizzie said.

"I understand." Turning to Helen, Dana asked, "What do you think?"

"I've been in business long enough to know the devil is in the details." Helen paused. "I also can see how this could be quite an opportunity for both of you."

Dana smiled.

Helen tapped her glass. "I hope you don't mind, but I'm very curious. Who do you think wanted Roberto dead? I'm assuming the police interviewed you given that poison was inserted into his ingredients?"

For a second, Dana's facial expression shut down. She reset it with a visible effort. "I met with Detective McAllister briefly. He assumed I would know quite a bit about Roberto's cooking habits, and I was happy to provide as much information as I could. Unfortunately, it wasn't a lot. I'm not accustomed to the dangers of using ingredients found in the woods of Maryland. Nor do I need to knock off my competition in order to stay on top."

"How do you think Tara will do as his replacement?" Lizzie asked. "She is a trained chef."

Dana rolled her eyes. "She's a lightweight. She's your age with half your audience appeal."

Helen interjected. "You both used Mariah Manley to arrange your demonstrations. How well do you know her?"

"Mariah is an excellent food stylist, which is hard to find. Typically, former chefs are not good food stylists. The skills seem related but are actually quite different."

Lizzie spoke up. "Where did Mariah train? She never mentioned it."

"I'm surprised she never told you. They both attended the New York Culinary Institute. That's where she and Roberto became acquainted. When they graduated, he was offered the sous chef position in the city's hottest restaurant. I heard Mariah struggled. Worked as a prep cook for a couple years."

"Perhaps she just wasn't comfortable telling you, Lizzie," her mother offered.

"She told me she applied for the new position on his show. It was a foolish idea. She never had the slightest chance. She had no live TV experience and no national reputation whatsoever. And her hippie style worked against her," Dana added dismissively.

"Would you consider Mariah a possible suspect?" asked Helen.

"She had the skills and the opportunity."

"Would she be jealous of Roberto's success?" Helen probed.

"A lot of people were," Dana replied coolly.

"Anyone in particular?"

She studied the two of them. "I heard rumors Neal Frawley resented not being named their general manager."

"Really? Where did you hear that?"

Dana made a coy smile. "A good chef never reveals their secrets." She took a last sip of her wine. "I hope you didn't accept my invitation today to only discuss Roberto's murder. I was forewarned you've collaborated with the police in the past."

"You must admit, it's pretty disturbing to know a killer is in our midst," added Lizzie.

Dana nodded. "Shall we proceed with my concept?"

Their check arrived, and Dana insisted she treat, signing the bill with a flourish. She rose from the table and turned to Lizzie. "I'll send you some brief marketing concepts. If they intrigue you, we can take the next step. If partnering with me doesn't interest you, I'll reconsider a few other personalities."

"I'd be foolish not to consider your idea seriously. This could be very exciting for both of us. Thank you for singling me out." The two women rose, then hugged each other.

Dana regarded her closely. "You are a stand-out among network hosts. It wasn't hard." She threaded her way toward the entrance, giving a little wave and a smile at a star-struck server.

Lizzie exhaled. She flashed her blue eyes toward her mother. "What did you think?"

"Her vision for both of you could be fantastic!" Helen admitted. "She's also calculating and driven. If she were a man, most people would be fine with it. So, I'm fine with it. You need to ask, does it make her a good business partner?"

"She got touchy when you asked her about Roberto's murder."

"She did. I probably would, too, if someone pressed me."

"Could she have killed him?"

"Someone did it. She's got nerve, and there's no doubt she gained from it. You know the expression 'keep your friends close and your enemies closer.' Getting them eliminated is even better."

Her daughter sighed. "I hate this. I'm heading into the studio and don't know who to suspect. It's horrible."

"Try not to dwell on it. I'll call you later."

* * *

Leaving the Riverside Inn, Helen stopped at a crossroads and tapped on her steering wheel. "Do I head to the office or somewhere else?" she asked herself. "Tammi is probably ready to stage a walk-out." She glanced at her Mini's clock, then pulled right, heading toward the opposite side of Port Anne bridge. Time to have a chat with Dottie Taylor, owner of Taylor Lumber, one of her favorite places.

Taylor Lumber was around the back side of Port Anne, cut off from the rest of town by a small bridge washed out in a storm twelve-plus years ago and would likely never be replaced. It was the very opposite of the big box home and garden center a mile down the road and in plain sight. Somehow Taylor Lumber continued to hold its own.

She pulled in, slowing near the rear of a small dark gray building clad in cedar siding in need of redoing. Two yard workers, one with a grey beard and the other with acne and a faded red cap worn backwards, gave her a brief wave. She waved back and pulled open a small door. She stepped gingerly over the threshold and past stacks and stacks of windows, tiles, and roofing samples, careful not to snag her pants. A tiny, brass bell on a metal clasp shook behind her in response.

She pushed her sunglasses onto the top of her head as she peered through the dim lighting past rough wooden shelving to reach the one and only service desk. Its surface was slanted toward the center from a hundred years of handwritten orders scrawled out on green, lined pads with carpenter pencils. A fat gray Tabby was sprawled across the counter, its front paws lying over the register. She never moved, regardless of the conversations or the size of the orders. Helen guessed the cat could write up an order but never saw the need to assist. Her job started after dark as the yard's official mouser.

One of Dottie's daughters was on the phone, jotting down dimensions for a roofing order. A younger daughter, with her baby boy on her hip, spotted Helen as she approached. The baby offered a big toothless grin at their latest customer.

"Hi, Rachel. Good to see you. How's your little guy?" Helen shifted a pine stool to the side, leaned over the counter, and scratched under the cat's chin. He shifted to encourage a little more. The baby followed her fingers as she stroked the cat.

"He's finally sleeping through the night." Rachel straightened his bib. "How can we help you today?"

"I need another quart of high gloss varnish like the one I purchased a few months ago. I ran out of it and can't finish a tabletop I'm working on.

Thought I'd try to get it done. Would you know which it was?"

"Seems to me you were covering barn wood."

Helen shook her head in amazement. "You're right. We decided on a clear coat."

"Give me a minute, and I'll find a can for you."

"I'd be happy to find it myself. Point me in the right direction."

Rachel laughed. "Don't trouble yourself. Sit down and rest your feet. If you can find it, Mom might threaten to replace me." Mama and baby traipsed across wide, uneven wooden floorboards. Helen watched the top of her ponytail weave in between row after row of supplies, most of them with handwritten price tags. She returned with the quart and set it on the counter. "Anything else today?"

She eyed Rachel's mother. Her back to the room, Dottie had her head inside an old metal file cabinet, slowly pulling out invoices. "Actually, I was hoping I could catch your mom for a few minutes. I have a question for her."

Rachel turned and tapped her mother on the shoulder. She tipped her head toward her. "Helen Morrisey needs you."

Dottie shoved the creaky file cabinet drawer back with a vengeance and turned to her.

"Hello. Good to see you. I'm afraid I'm buried in paperwork." The broad, stocky woman in a brown sweater and work boots offered a warm handshake. "How can I help?"

"Actually, we might be able to help each other. Could we step aside?"

Dottie shifted her gaze and signaled Helen to follow her to the rear of the store. "What's on your mind?"

"I'm hearing a few rumors you're waiting for payments from Roberto Barto's company. Any progress?"

The yard owner's eyes traveled across the shelves of stock and back at her. "Why do you ask?"

Helen crossed her arms across her chest. "You may not have heard, but Lizzie was also poisoned on the set with Roberto. She only had a taste at the very end of the show, so she only became nauseous. She was very lucky. I'm not going to be satisfied until the police track down who's responsible.

It's a miracle she didn't die with him."

Dottie studied her worn cotton work gloves. "If she were my kid, I'd feel the same way. I've known you and Andy for a long, long time. When the big garden center opened up, my family thought it might be the death of us. But people like you stuck with us."

Helen's face flushed. "Most of our old house was restored with your materials. And your advice."

Dottie took a deep breath. "I'm embarrassed to admit we got sucked into feeling important by supplying their materials on credit because he was a bigshot mentioned in all the papers. Adrian convinced us this was an opportunity to pick up some really big orders which often go to the bigger companies. They owe us about $120,000 in payments between the restaurant and the house. That's a lot of money to us. Now, the bank is pressing me for repayment. I'm getting nowhere with Adrian and his attorneys."

Helen patted her friend's arm. "If it makes you feel any better, I'm the listing agent for Riding Cross, and it's going on the market any day. I don't know yet what's going on with their money situation. You can count on me to do everything I can to be sure you're first in line as a subcontractor due for payment. Right now, my biggest concern is how much Adrian or Barto Enterprises owes the bank. Bank loans are first in line. Do you have a lien filed with the county on the house or the restaurant?"

Dottie gritted her teeth. "My attorney is working on it."

"You didn't hear it from me," Helen whispered. "But I'd get on the horn and push him."

Dottie nodded, and Helen headed for the back door. The fat gray cat on the counter followed her with calm but curious eyes.

Chapter Nineteen

"Hi." It was Shawn's calm, clear voice in her messages. "I have a meeting in Kent County tomorrow morning. Thought I'd come up and stay with you tonight. I also have some background on those photos you sent me. Let me know if tonight works."

Helen texted him a thumbs up. Seeing Shawn was a treat. Bringing info on those photos made his visit even better.

A few minutes later, Lizzie texted.

Hear Shawn staying overnight. I'll come too. Plan dinner!

Well, sleuths, sounds like we've got the whole clan coming tonight. Pizza?

By seven, Shawn and Lizzie were chomping on their second slice of pizza, content it was fresh and not from her freezer.

She was pouring herself a glass of Sauvignon Blanc when she spotted Watson and Trixie darting across the kitchen toward her bedroom. Across the deck, a swish of light brown tail caught her eye. A grey-muzzled Golden Retriever was loping up the steps and onto the deck with Joe making his way right behind him.

"Hello there, I wasn't expecting you tonight," Helen stroked Rocky's upturned nose.

"Thought I'd stop by and check in with you. Hope you don't mind my crashing your party." Joe smiled over at Lizzie, then tossed his suit jacket over a chaise.

"Not at all. Hungry?"

"Famished." He shook Shawn's hand and grabbed a slice of pie. Lizzie handed him a Corona.

"I thought about calling you," she offered. "I sent a few photos I took of Roberto's study over to Shawn. He told me they might be interesting."

Joe and Shawn's eyes met. "Yes, I heard."

She studied the two men. "Are you telling me you've talked?" She sat back and crossed her arms. Lizzie averted her eyes. "Okay, what gives?"

Her son reached for another beer and flipped off the cap. He took a slug. Helen's eyes narrowed. He was stalling.

He reached into his briefcase he'd set on a canvas chaise, pulled out a sealed yellow envelope, and slid three photographs onto the teak deck table. Everyone leaned forward.

"Here are the three photos you snapped the first time you were in his private office." Shawn lined them up in a neat row. "Here are the three photos you took on your second visit. The same walls." He lined them up in a neat row below the first. Helen felt like her son was in court presenting a case. "Notice anything interesting?"

Everyone studied them. Lizzie pointed at the first photo from the first set. "This shows a wall with seven pictures hanging on it." Her fingers trailed over to the next row and counted. "If I look at the photo Mom took of the same wall, there's only four pictures hanging in the second row. Three in the original photo were removed."

"Exactly," Shawn responded.

Helen rested her chin on her palms. "I knew the photo display wasn't the same! If we were actually in the room, I'll bet the wall may even show faint lines from where the missing frames marked the wall."

Shawn pointed to the second set. "Now, look close at this photo of the other wall. Compare it to the photo taken during your second visit. You'll see fewer pictures on this other wall. Someone removed a couple pictures and spread out the remaining ones to cover their gaps."

Lizzie's blue eyes met the matching blue eyes of her twin. "Why would someone not want these photos seen any longer? Who removed them?"

Joe ran his hands through his thick brown hair. "That's what Shawn and I are wondering."

"You two discussed this already?" Helen's eyes narrowed.

"It's why I wanted Joe here tonight," Shawn said.

"So, this wasn't just a casual stop-by," she eyed the detective and the district attorney. "Spill it."

Shawn inhaled. "These pictures show Roberto with two men with blackjack and poker tables behind them. The third picture is at a racetrack."

"Adrian mentioned Roberto liked to gamble at the Baywood Casinos off Interstate 95," Helen said. "It doesn't surprise me he might be seen at a racetrack. Kent County has quite a few horse farms with some famous horses trained on them. Barbaro was even trained here."

"Agree. But if these photos are innocent, why did someone remove them? I decided to have my technical unit staff create closeups of the faces. Then they ran those closeups against a criminal records database." Shawn hesitated. "These two men are key Mob members. They're involved in gambling and loansharking. The tall one is Gabriel Giano, and the short, heavy one is James Nero.

Lizzie gasped. "Shawn, these are scary people."

"Not people you want to tangle with," Joe grunted. "That's why we're asking you and Nancy here to back away from searching out clues to this murder. Let law enforcement deal with it."

Helen pushed her chair aside and stood up. She turned her back, leaned on the deck rail and stared at the water.

"Mom," Shawn interjected. "All our lives you've been a fixer-upper. Whether it's houses, or client problems, or family. Last year you got involved in Al Capelli's murder. Now, you and your Detection Club think you should solve this murder. You've got to stop it. It's dangerous." His eyebrows narrowed, his blue eyes intense.

She glanced out at the sun sinking over the water and back to the group. "This wasn't just an impromptu pizza party, was it? This was a planned intervention." Helen's face flushed. "I'm pouring myself another glass of wine." She marched inside toward the kitchen.

"That didn't go well," Shawn said. Joe opened another beer.

Lizzie clasped her hands together. "Did you expect it to? This is Mom we're talking to."

Her mother came out with a bucket of ice and wine and plunked them down. She had a legal pad tucked under her left arm. "Anything else you want to say?"

Her daughter cleared her throat. "Actually," she rooted through her purse and pulled out a plain white business-size envelope in a plastic baggie. "Someone stuck this in my tote this afternoon. I don't have any idea who." She looked up at Joe. "Don't worry. I got out gloves to open it and then put it into the baggie. I knew you didn't want it handled."

"Good thinking." Joe pulled a clear plastic glove out of his pants pocket and gingerly reached into the bag for the envelope. They all studied his reaction as he opened the flap and pulled out a folded slip of plain white paper. He read aloud. "Tell your mother to back off!"

"Holy crap!" Shawn exclaimed. His sister bit down on her lip and gave a little shiver.

Helen crossed her arms and glowered at Joe. "Who could have written it? You've been working on this case for a week now. Who's top on your list?"

He glared back. "ShopTV is like Grand Central Station. We're working on it." Rocky dropped his snout down and hid it between his front paws in response to the tension in the air.

"In other words, you haven't got a clue."

"We're interviewing everyone and anyone. Looks like we need to check into Roberto's Mob buddies."

"I sure don't want to be accused of being Miss Fix-It. Nor do my sleuth buddies. Sounds like you need to talk to Adrian again. It also sounds like you ought to give my list of possible suspects more respect."

"Sometimes you really can be stubborn," her son gritted his teeth. Lizzie shot him a warning glare.

"I guess you know where you got it from," his mother retorted. "You're a good prosecutor because you don't give up easily. You know what they say about Jessica Fletcher?"

He sighed. "No, what do they say about Jessica?"

"They say she'd never sit back when there are questions to be answered. I'm in her camp. So's the rest of my Detection Club."

Joe stuck his hands in his pockets and strode back and forth across the deck. "We have two major shifts in this investigation here." He ticked them off with his fingers. "One, we know Roberto was involved in the Mob. Why, we're not sure. He liked to gamble, and these two creeps may have enjoyed rubbing elbows with a celebrity. Or he gambled so much he owed the Mob big money. I think that's more likely."

"With all his success, why do you think he might have been in financial trouble?" Lizzie piped up. "Just because Barto Enterprises are slow-payers doesn't mean they can't cover their bills,"

Helen tapped a pen against her pad. "We know he owes big money to local contractors. Dottie at Taylor Lumber says she gave him $120,000 in credit."

"I still find it hard to believe," her daughter protested. "Why wouldn't he and Adrian go to a local bank?"

"You don't know gamblers," Shawn said. "You'd be shocked at how many athletes and movie stars with multi-million-dollar contracts are operating on their last dime."

"If he's gambling, local banks may not be an option. They'd want to know where he's spending his money and why he'd need more," added Joe. "They'd want to go over the company books."

"Did Adrian know how much he owed in gambling debts?" Helen tossed out.

Joe rubbed his chin. "He may have. Maybe he realized Roberto was putting their business in jeopardy. Having a partner addicted to gambling could be a huge problem. Maybe he was really ticked off about it."

"How else do you think he gambled his money, other than casinos," Lizzie asked.

Shawn turned to her. "Ways you wouldn't even think of, like horses, college football, race cars. My guess, since these pictures show him at Baywood Casino, he started out legally with poker and blackjack. Then he got introduced to a couple backroom players. He gets behind, and they bring in a few sharks. He starts to branch out, placing bets on anything to catch up. After a couple years, he's way over his head. He's lost total control."

"I thought loan sharking was illegal?" Helen said.

"The Mob gets around it by claiming they're investing into a business. Then they collect 100%, even 200% on their money," Joe added.

"They call it hard money loans," Shawn said.

Lizzie stared at her half-eaten slice of pizza. "That's unbelievable. How could a man as smart as Roberto get involved with these people?"

"People get sucked in," Joe shrugged his shoulders. "It's a long way from buying a lottery ticket every Friday night at the local grocery store. My guess, he took advantage of the Mob's offer of hard money, expecting to pay it back quickly."

"One more reason why you have to back off," said Shawn, glowering at his mother.

She ignored him, turning to Joe. "Do you think one of these two Mob guys broke into the bistro last week?"

"Most likely. Good thing he didn't spot you."

Lizzie stared at the two men. "Or maybe he did. Was he the one who delivered this note to me?" She shivered in the dark.

Helen protested. "I think you're all jumping to conclusions. There's lots of options. Dana knows I snoop around. Maybe she left the note. Or Greg may worry I'll find out about Roberto's gambling habits, and it would hurt the company's family-oriented reputation. What about Tara? Is she worried we could disrupt her new deal?"

"Right now, the reasons don't matter. What matters is you and Lizzie have to drop your impersonations of Nancy Drew and Nora Charles." Joe stood up and whistled for Rocky. The lab reluctantly climbed to his feet and followed him to the edge of the deck.

Helen started to clear the table. "I'll think about it."

Shawn glanced at his sister and threw up his hands. "I'm going to bed."

Chapter Twenty

Even with all the speculation swirling around Port Anne about Roberto's murder, Helen couldn't help feeling excited the next morning. Riding Cross was officially on the market as of eight am. She grabbed the heavy oak Victorian door to Safe Harbor Realty and gave their young receptionist a big wave as she passed by.

Tammi flagged her as she came down the hall toward her office.

"Look who showed up this morning," she exclaimed. Bright yellow sunbursts dangled, with a matching necklace at her neck. She wore a highlighter yellow cotton sweater pushed up toward the elbows. "You have a visitor."

Helen stopped short. "Excuse me? Who in the world would be waiting for me?"

"Your favorite police detective." Her assistant fluttered her dark eyelashes. "I told him you were on your way in."

Helen groaned.

"Do I sense there's a little tension between you?"

"You could say that. He and Shawn corralled me last night. They want me to be a good girl and leave any snooping to the law."

"Who broke the news to them it wasn't your style? Jessica? Nancy? Agatha?" Tammi couldn't hold back a little chuckle. "Let me guess. It was Nora, with a martini glass in her hand."

"Not even close. Nora wouldn't be caught dead eating cold pizza. Nor would Jane. When they began harassing me, I broke out another bottle of wine."

"What did Lizzie have to say about it?"

"She was kind of quiet. This whole thing has really shaken her up. She doesn't want anyone else hurt."

"Of course not." Tammi nodded. "But knowing her, she'll keep digging if you ask her."

Helen tugged her hair behind her ears. "That does worry me. I'm not sure what I should do." She reached for the doorknob and opened her office door. "Talk to you later," she whispered to Tammi.

* * *

"Good morning. What brings your officialness here? Haven't you seen enough of me?" Helen tossed her bag onto her desk.

Joe stood up and offered a tenuous smile. "Thought I'd invite you to lunch unless you have plans. We didn't get to talk about my conversation with Greg Waldron. You know I appreciate your insight on people."

"I thought you didn't want me within a hundred yards of anyone involved in your case." She crossed her arms across her chest and offered an unblinking Agatha stare. You and Shawn called it meddling." She scrutinized him up and down. It was annoying that he looked this good so early in the morning.

"I don't. That doesn't mean I wouldn't like your opinion." He rubbed the back of his neck and grinned.

"Don't go pouring on the Mr. Charm. I haven't forgiven you for ganging up on me. Or Shawn for that matter. You've got Lizzie worried. You knew she was on my side. Now she's nervous."

Joe sat back down, crossing his legs. "She should be. My squad's putting out feelers to find out if the Mob is tied into Barto Enterprises' finances. I have an appointment with Adrian today."

"Was he surprised to hear from you?"

"Not particularly. He has to know he's on our radar, along with others."

Helen opened her laptop. "Would you like to see his property? Riding Cross is officially on the market as of this morning." She tapped in her

121

password and pulled up an address search. She spun the screen around. "What do you think?"

He leaned in and whistled. "Spectacular. Too bad it's not in a cop's salary range. By the way, you smell great." He winked.

"You're trying too hard, Detective McAlister. What are you up to?"

Joe held up his hands. "Just trying to set up lunch with a good-looking woman. Most of my interviews are with ugly large men who smell bad."

She laughed. "Lucky you. A lot of my appointments are with anxious moms and kids with sticky fingers."

His cell buzzed. "McAlister." A voice muffled. "Tell them I'm on my way." He stuffed the phone back in his suit pocket. "Well?"

"I'm totally booked until about two. Want to meet at Blue Crab for a burger at four-thirty? Or is that too late?"

"Given this call, it's probably perfect. See you there." He flashed a quick sign of relief and bolted.

Tammi poked her head into her office. "He seems happy. You two make up?"

"Only couples make up." Helen retorted, trying to tamp down a smile.

"He's got it bad," Tammi laughed and shut the door behind her.

Helen dug into her desk drawer, dragged out a stale Twizzler, and chewed. 'You need to improve your breakfast choices,' Jane admonished.

* * *

She spent the morning responding to a flurry of agents wanting more details on Riding Cross. One agent had a client requesting to see it. Two curiosity seekers probed about why it was being sold, usually a waste of time for her. But she couldn't afford to ignore them. Never know where they might lead, she reminded herself. She moved on to double-check the marketing on different luxury homes sites. Most had already picked up the property through her multiple listing info. She left a message with a local bay publication concerning a feature story they were interested in writing, particularly because of the Roberto Barto connection.

Tammi tapped on her doorway. "Planning on getting some lunch? I'm running out for a half hour. I could pick up something."

"That would be great, but I'm packing up in a few minutes. Believe it or not, I had a call on the old Jamison house. I'm showing it to a contractor in about an hour."

"That's quite a contrast from Riding Cross. Didn't you tell me it had a dirt cellar?"

Helen chuckled. "It does. Don't see that very often, thank goodness. Like to not see one again. Let's hope this buyer doesn't need a bank loan. I'd love to get Jamison off the books."

Tammi made a little shrug. "Good luck with the showing. Are you coming back?"

Helen squinted at her watch. "Plan on it. Should be back here about two-thirty, three at the latest."

Tammi gave her a little salute and headed off.

* * *

At ten before one, Helen was creeping down a long gravel driveway toward the Jamison cottage. Tall pine trees and scrubby native rhododendrons grazed the sides of her car. She gently eased over a large pothole near the left shoulder and turned at a wooden arrow nailed onto a stick next to her own directional sign. The two-story cape had real possibilities, in her opinion. She was surprised someone hadn't made an offer since it came on the market sixty days ago. The lot was almost three acres and touched a bit of the Deer River. If this buyer didn't want to fix her up, she'd encourage him to make an offer and consider tearing down the house. The neighborhood, nestled along the water, could easily adapt to a new house three times this size. She was hopeful meeting directly with this buyer could get a conversation going.

A shiny black truck loaded with chrome was parked in front of the house. As she turned off her ignition, a young man with dark sunglasses, jeans, and a Baltimore Ravens cap climbed out.

Helen offered her hand. "Rory? Good to meet you. I hope I didn't keep

123

you waiting."

Rory exposed uneven teeth and looked her over. "Not at all. You're Helen, correct?"

She handed him a card. "Helen Morrisey, Safe Harbor Realty."

He nodded. "I recognized you from your picture. I've been meaning to call you for a couple weeks. I had an appointment with a client in Port Anne and thought it was my chance to see this house." He trailed behind her up the front steps to the door. She opened a lockbox on the handle and swung the door open. She ran her hands down the wall, flipped on the lights, and waved him forward.

Rory removed his sunglasses, tucking them into the collar of his shirt. He stepped in and surveyed the room. "Not a bad layout. Due for rehab, but good-sized rooms." He rubbed his right hand over a scruffy beard.

"Is this intended for yourself, or do you plan to fix it and flip it?" She continued to flip on lights as they made their way upstairs.

The contractor paused. "I'm trying to find my next rehab project. I'll flip it as fast I can."

"I'll tell you, the location brings a lot of value. I'm surprised a builder hasn't already bought it. As much as I like redoing old buildings, this lot could accommodate a much larger house."

Rory walked to a bedroom window and took in the surrounding view of woods and a bit of the river. "Let's see the utilities and the basement."

Helen turned, walked down the stairs, then turned to a small door off the hall. "I have to warn you. This basement is the original, dirt floor and all."

He shrugged. "Not the first time I've been in one. Let's see what we've got."

She pulled out her cell and switched on its light. Her feet felt for the uneven wooden stair treads. Dampness wafted up, filling her nostrils. At the bottom, she groped for a pull chain. The four walls of the small basement smelled moldy, with broken plaster exposing dirt behind it. Two grimy windows on three sides appeared sealed. "Not exactly a man cave, would you say?" She led him to a scratched metal fuse box in the corner. She ran the cell light across the rusted cover. It creaked as she opened it and peered in.

"I'm not an electrician, but I assume we can agree the electrical is obsolete." Helen glanced up to feel Rory's steel gray eyes studying her. A chill ran across her shoulders, and the room's clamminess seeped through her light summer jacket. Glancing around the dark room, a schism of fear streaked through her body. 'Nancy! How could I be so foolish! Showing an empty house alone, especially this one, to a man I don't know. We both know better.'

She eased her right foot, then left, and made a slow step backward, putting him at arm's length. Slowly she wandered around the perimeter of the room, pointing out beam height and floor joists. She inhaled, then launched into a cheery running commentary. "I'm sure you've seen quite enough to get a picture of the condition. Why don't we go outside? I'll walk you along the property line." She turned toward the stairwell, gesturing for Rory to go first. But the contractor's pleasant smile had morphed into a leer. Moving in close, he placed his two hands flat on the wall behind her, pinning her against the uneven, filthy concrete.

She could feel the rough surface pricking at her hair. Helen pressed her hands on his shirt. "I'm not sure what you have in mind, but I suggest you leave now." She returned his stare with a defiant chin.

Rory breathed a mix of chewing gum and Dollar Store cologne. "I am here to deliver a message. Before I do, we should have a little fun, just you and me." He pressed his face into her neck.

Helen eked out a low yelp, turning her face away and trying to push the alarm on her cell. Her assaulter whipped her around, scraping her face against the wall and pinning her tight, shoving his hip into her backside.

"I guess we should stick to business. Here's my message. Stop poking your nose where it doesn't belong. We will not warn you again."

She froze in place, her eyes wide and her hands shaking despite her effort to control them. Nancy whispered in her ear to stand strong. "Who are you, and who sent you?" she said through clenched teeth.

His rough clammy hands reached out and gripped her neck. "Not your business." He took in the room again. "I was told you're smart. You're not so smart. If you were, you wouldn't be down here in this filthy hole with me." He snickered. "All you need to know is I'll be back again when you least expect it if you keep on asking questions. Same goes with your daughter." He yanked her back to face him, and his eyes bore into hers.

"Tell me," she cried. "Who sent you?" Their eyes locked again. He pressed his thumbs into her skin. Helen pulled down on his raised arms, squirming to be freed. Her cell phone dropped from her pocket and skidded across the dirt. He let out a cruel chuckle. Her nails dug a fistful of dirt and concrete bits from the wall, brought a hand around, and shoved the grit into his face. Rory cursed and rubbed at his eyes.

Released from his cage, she darted toward the stairs. He was faster, pulling her down to the ground. She shouted, "Let go of me!"

Rory pressed his forearm down across her neck and used his open hand to cover her face. "Shut up! No one can hear you." Helen continued to struggle, rolling side to side.

"Let me go! People know I'm here. They know you're here!"

The man sneered in her face. "No one knows who I am, but I know who your family is. And your friends. They'll get a visit if you don't follow our orders."

She freed a hand and pulled on his arm. Gasping, she bit his hand as hard as she could as she kicked his groin with her left knee. She rose to her knees.

He let out a yelp, cursing and rearing back, then lunging forward, punched her full in the face with his fist.

Helen fell backwards, smacking her head onto the basement floor. The last she heard was the crash of heavy feet bolting up the stairs before she passed out.

Chapter Twenty-One

Helen's right eyelid peeled back from her eyeball. Her left eye slowly followed. She shifted her eyes painfully across a grey surface. Two long overhead LED lamps came into fuzzy focus. An antiseptic whiff reached her nose.

"Where am I?" She mumbled to herself. A soft ping repeated in the background. Her eyes traveled from her left arm to an IV stand and a monitor next to her bed.

"Mom? Thank God you're awake." Shawn stroked her right arm. Lizzie's tear-stained face came into view. "Mom," she choked.

Her mother reached up and squeezed her hand. "Tell me what happened." But before they began, her moments in a dank basement flooded back. "How did you find me?"

Lizzie smiled, her voice quivering. "Joe found you. You were supposed to meet him for dinner. When you didn't show and you didn't answer your cell, he called Tammi to find out if you were delayed. She told him you were meeting him after a showing. Thank goodness, you mentioned the address. He and Rick raced to the house and found you out cold on the basement floor. EMTs brought you here."

"I was so incredibly stupid. I knew better, but I was anxious to get that ghastly house sold, I fell for his story," Helen's voice quivered, tears in her eyes. "I did everything wrong."

"It was your bad luck he picked you." Shawn leaned in.

She shook her head. "No, it wasn't arbitrary. He was sent there to warn me away from poking into Roberto's murder. He told me if I didn't back off,

127

he'd be back."

Her son's face blanched. "Had you ever seen him before?"

"No. Never. Just an average, everyday kind of guy."

They looked up at a knock on the doorway to her hospital room.

Joe stuck his head around the door and smiled. "Looks like you're awake. Can I come in?" His tie hung loosely around his neck. His face showed a day-old beard.

Helen offered a crooked smile back. "Hi."

Shawn stood up. Lizzie signaled him in. "The nurses say we only have a few more minutes."

He sat down next to the bed and squeezed Helen's arm. He studied her taped arm and bandaged forehead, and swollen cheekbones. "How are you feeling? Are you able to talk about how this happened?"

"We just started," Shawn said. "She didn't recognize her attacker."

"This is the third agent in two weeks."

"I don't think he's your man. He said he was delivering a message. He said I had to stop asking questions about Roberto. If I didn't stop, he'd be back." Helen's lip trembled. Lizzie's eyes watered.

Joe reached for his pad and a pen. "Can you describe him? How tall was he? Was he Caucasian? A minority?"

"Probably about five foot eight. Caucasian. Light brown hair and grey eyes. Kind of skinny."

"What was he wearing?"

She gingerly touched her nose. "A light grey, long-sleeved t-shirt, jeans, and black sneakers. And a Ravens baseball hat."

"Did he have any distinguishing marks?"

She hesitated. "No beard. He had a tattoo on his left arm. It was mostly covered up by his shirt." She closed her eyes for a moment. "It was black with some kind of feathers. Could be a bird with a beak. I did bite his left hand." She made an attempt at a crooked little smile.

Joe chuckled. "I'm not surprised. What was he driving?"

"A black pick-up truck. Recent. Had some chrome trim. I didn't notice the plates."

"Did he steal anything?"

Helen swallowed. "He grabbed my watch, and the bracelet Shawn gave me last Christmas."

Lizzie opened the patient storage locker near her mother's bed. "Looks like your wallet is gone, but your chain with Dad's wedding ring is here."

"Thank goodness for small favors," she muttered.

Shawn rubbed his palms together and began to pace across the room and back. "Any hint who sent him? Was it a man or a woman?"

"No idea. He didn't say. When I tried to push by him, he hit me. I heard him run for the stairs. I must have passed out."

Lizzie patted her mother. "The doctor says you must have fallen and hit your head."

"Is my nose broken?"

Her daughter sighed. "No, nothing was broken. A couple stitches in your left arm."

"Good thing it was a dirt floor and not concrete," Shawn added.

Joe studied her swollen, stark white face. "You had a close call."

"That's what we said about Lizzie the day Roberto was poisoned." Helen breathed in, the smell of hospital disinfectant filling her nostrils. "Jane told me I had a talent for sensing evil. I sure blew it with this guy."

Joe glanced across at Lizzie and Shawn. "Can we agree you need to sit on the sidelines? Let me track down who's responsible?"

She avoided his eyes. "When can I leave here?"

"They're keeping you tonight for observation," replied her daughter. "I can take you home tomorrow morning. No driving for twenty-four hours." They all raised their eyes when a nurse stepped into the room and tapped on her watch.

Joe rose, then stopped. "You didn't answer my question. Do you agree you're off this case?"

"I'd say I'm more important to your case than ever before. Someone is trying to scare me off. Don't forget, you promised I'd be safer if I concentrated on selling houses. Look what that got me."

Joe heaved a huge sigh. "We'll discuss it tomorrow, Nancy."

"Get some sleep." Shawn kissed his mother on her forehead. They all took the nurse's signal and headed out.

Alone, Helen stared at the ceiling, examining the drop panels. 'Snakes and bastards,' exclaimed Agatha. 'What are you going to do?' 'What she needs now is a gin gimlet cocktail,' Nora piped in. 'I suggest a sherry,' said Jane. 'I suggest keeping a clear head,' objected Jessica.

'Quiet ladies,' she thought. 'I need to sleep. Then we'll plan.'

* * *

"What in the world are you doing here?" Tammi practically shouted when she spotted her walking down the hall at Safe Harbor the next day. She trotted alongside Helen into her office.

Helen plunked down her laptop with a swollen hand. She brushed her bangs down and across the large white bandage plastered above her left eye. "I made Lizzie drop me off. One overnight in the hospital and I was stir-crazy. She'll be back in an hour."

"You should be home." Tammi jammed her fists on her waist and glared.

"Doctor says I'm fine. Just have to take it a little slower the next few days." Helen rolled her eyes at her assistant and issued a little laugh. "Fat chance." She sank into her leather desk chair. "Anything new here?"

Tammi's brown eyes breathed fire. "You are the most obstinate person I've ever known." She sat down in the guest chair and crossed her arms.

"If it's true, I owe it all to Nancy Drew. She's the one who helped me fight back." Her face flushed. "You're right. I barely slept last night, trying to decide what my next step should be. Do I retire my Detection Club, or do I ignore everyone, including my kids, and keep digging?"

"Joe must be furious," Tammi uttered.

"Not yet, but he will be if I ignore his advice." Helen pawed around her top desk drawer. "I need some sugar." She pulled out a pen and three Twizzlers. She chomped down on one. "Got any coffee?"

Tammi groaned. "Only the office swill. I'll get us a cup." She headed down the hall, returning a few minutes later.

CHAPTER TWENTY-ONE

Helen took a loud slurp. "It's bad, but I'm feeling grateful."

"Do you know you made the online local news this morning?"

Helen blanched. "What are you talking about?"

Tammi shifted around to Helen's side of the desk and juggled the mouse on the laptop. The screen lit up. "Look at this." Her long, sparkly nails clicked across the keyboard. "Right here on the *Kent Whig* site." A short story framed by a wide black border ran about three inches down the right side of the front page. Tammi read, "Local Realtor attacked in empty Port Anne house."

"Oh, no!" Helen exclaimed. "Why would I hit the news?"

Her assistant's silver bangles clinked together. "It's the local crime beat. Did you think your attack wouldn't be news? It gets worse."

"Worse? How's that possible?" She leaned over the screen and squinted with puffy eyes.

Tammi kept reading. "The second attack on a local real estate agent in two weeks, Helen Morrisey of Safe Harbor Realty was assaulted in the basement of an empty house, allegedly attacked by a buyer who requested a showing. Detective Joseph McAlister of Kent County precinct found Mrs. Morrisey unconscious, and EMTs were dispatched. Morrisey currently represents Adrian Costello, owner of Barto Enterprises and partner of recently murdered chef Roberto Barto, in the sale of their multimillion-dollar property on Riding Cross, Port Anne. Mr. Costello was contacted regarding her attack but had no comment. She is expected to fully recover. "

Helen sat back and glared at Tammi.

"Wait. There's more. Look at this reader's comment under the story." Tammi pointed. "Rumor around town is Morrisey may be privately investigating Mr. Barto's death. She assisted local law enforcement with solving the murder case of developer Al Capelli last May."

Helen mumbled around the Twizzler in her mouth. "Adrian will have a heart attack."

"He might like the extra publicity. More people aware his house is on the market," Tammi offered.

"He made it pretty obvious he wants me to stick to business and focus on getting his house sold. I was trying to keep my sleuthing under his radar."

Tammi scrunched her nose. "I think that ship has sailed, don't you?"

Helen swallowed. "I'm lucky he doesn't pull the property from me. I could lose my chance of selling it, and my opportunities to keep searching for clues."

"Can I help?"

Helen pulled out a Post-It note and scribbled across it. She handed it to Tammi. "Check our list in Google Drive for his upcoming advertising. Run through it and make sure they have their materials and photos. Let's be sure we don't miss any deadlines. Then call Adrian. Let him know we're on track, and I'll call him sometime tomorrow." Her cell buzzed. She snapped her laptop shut and slid it into her case. "Lizzie's here to drop me home. Can I give you my list of credit cards? I'll need to cancel them ASAP. Someone stole my identity years ago, and it was a pain in the rear to get new cards set up."

"Not a problem. Are you going to rest?"

"I need to plan my next steps. My son accused me of being a fanatical fixer-upper, and he wasn't talking houses. Thanks for being a champ."

Tammi jotted down a note.

"Could you check around the office? Ask if another agent can show a client of mine a couple houses tomorrow. I'm just not up for it. Text me if you hear any more news too."

Chapter Twenty-Two

Lizzie and Helen were quiet as they drove through the park woods. It had been an exhausting two weeks, and they both were feeling it. After carrying in Helen's tote, Lizzie gave her mother a kiss and left for work. She had to be on air at six pm.

Helen took a hot shower, tenderly avoiding the large patch across her forehead, then pulled on sweats and a cozy fleece. It may have been late August, but she shivered, and her head pounded. After making a hot cup of Red Rose tea, a toast to her mother, she eased herself down on a deck chaise and turned her head to the sun, soaking it in.

Her cell rang two hours later. Groping for the phone, she pulled herself upright. "Joe, hi."

"Did I wake you?" He sounded regretful.

"I'm glad you did. I must have fallen asleep here on the deck. I'll never sleep tonight if I don't get up and move around."

"I don't want to talk about the case. I'm calling to find out if you need anything."

"I'm fine. I'm just beat." She stopped. "Sorry, poor use of words. Is there anything new?"

"I suppose you saw the article in the *Kent Whig*."

"Tammi showed me. Not good, especially when it comes to selling Adrian's house. I really didn't want him to know I was sleuthing." There was silence on the other end of the call. "Joe?"

"He's not the only one," he grumbled. "Adrian called me early this morning and complained you were asking him questions he didn't appreciate."

"What did you say?"

"I blew off his concerns. Said you were just another nosy, middle-aged Realtor hoping for a bit of gossip. I started describing you as an elderly knitter like Jane but stopped. I thought it might be overkill."

Helen laughed, then stopped short. It hurt the bruises on her cheekbones. She loosened her grip on the phone. "I hope I'll be as sharp as Jane when I'm in my eighties. Right now, I'm more concerned someone deliberately planted that rumor about me. I'm not sure why. There are some buyers and sellers who might not hire me if they think I'm a gossip. People have secrets they don't want the outside world to know."

"You and I need to talk about all this. You know how I feel, but you're not listening."

"I realize you're upset with me. I'd probably feel the same in your position. Can't you accept me as another Jessica Fletcher?"

"If I had to choose, I'd pick Nora Charles. A lot sexier."

"True. But Jessica is very logical. Or Agatha? Neither of them is afraid to speak their mind."

"That's the problem. They're too bossy."

She paused. "I'm not supposed to drive for another day. I also haven't been out on my boat in two weeks. Would you want to come with me tomorrow? I know I shouldn't sail *Persuasion* on my own, and I'd love to get out on the water. We could talk then."

"That's a great idea. We could both use the break. I'll pick up sandwiches."

"Good." Her voice sounded pensive. "I can't just back off. You must know that."

He sighed. "I know. It's in your DNA. Let's stop tugging at each other and figure out how we can work this out."

Helen breathed a sigh of relief. "I'm so glad you feel that way. We're a force to reckon with if we work together."

"Is your sleuthing squad coming along tomorrow?"

She chuckled. "You know they can't be kept silent. Besides, they need a day off too."

"You know you're delusional, right?"

She laughed again. "For good or for bad, you're stuck working with all of us."

"Hmmm. I'll be there about noon. Get some more sleep."

"Night." She leaned back and watched the beginnings of a sunset. 'We're back, ladies.'

* * *

At noon on the button, Joe's unmarked black four-by-four pulled in the drive. He strode up to the deck side, whistling with Rocky waving his plumy tail right behind him.

"Oh, ho! I see Trixie and Watson have a visitor too."

"Thought you wouldn't mind. He can sit on the porch and get some fresh air, watch the eagles." Joe handed her a cooler with Corona Lights on ice and hoagies wrapped in white deli paper from Little Creek Market.

Helen gave his gentle lab a head-scratching and led him into the porch. Joe put out a dish of water.

"You ready? We've got a beautiful day." She tucked a white t-shirt into navy shorts and picked up a faded sailing cap with PAYC lettered across the brim. They both traipsed down the stairway to the lower dock. *Persuasion* bobbed up and down in greeting. Helen was sure she was smiling.

"Poor girl hasn't gotten much attention lately." Helen loosened the dock lines and pulled the boat closer to the finger pier. She hopped on. Joe tossed on the cooler. Opening the companionway, she reached in for the chart plotter and keys to the diesel engine. In minutes, the motor was warmed up. Joe tossed off the lines, gave the boat a little shove, and hopped on the stern.

"Let's motor out a bit and try to pick up some wind." She adjusted her cap to deflect the full sun. "Looks pretty quiet."

"Doesn't matter," Joe eyed her. "Great to be out on the water. He reached over and tucked a strand of her hair behind her ear. "That bruise looks sore."

"I guess my attempt at covering it with makeup didn't work." She shrugged. "Looks worse than it feels, thank goodness. It's the back of my head that's tender. As creepy as that basement was, thank God the floor wasn't concrete."

He scanned her face. "You're lucky he didn't do worse."

Helen frowned. "No need to get heavy. I can't forgive myself for being so stupid. Do you know how many Realtor safety training classes I've taken over the years?" She ticked off her fingers. "Leave any property address you're showing with your office. Ask for a driver's license ID. Don't show a house by yourself to a stranger. Have a code word to call into your office if you need help. Keep pocket mace on your handbag. I could go on and on." She lifted her hands in disgust.

"That's because we never think assault can happen to us."

"Okay, mister tough guy. Are you any better?"

"I'm paid to be in tough spots. You're not."

"I did decide, after this case is wrapped up, I'm going to give a testimonial story during agent training as a real-life example. I'm hoping someone else will listen more carefully before it's too late for them." She breathed in the air. "Let's eat. I'm starving."

Joe chuckled. "Even bruised and beaten, you don't lose your appetite." He started to unwrap the hoagies and handed her a light beer. Helen leaned back against the wheel and took a big sip. She sighed, her shoulders relaxing. She regarded the large man as he chomped on his sandwich, oil and vinegar dripping down around his fingers.

"I've also made a decision." He swallowed a big bite and took a slug of his beer. "Trying to get you to back off on a murder case when your daughter was nearly a second victim is probably a waste of my time."

"And we certainly don't want Detective McAlister to waste his time," she mocked in between bites. "What's your solution?"

"It seems we'd make more progress if we agreed to work together rather than at odds."

She made a face, then winced, patting her bandage. "Isn't that what I suggested in the beginning?"

"Yes," he chewed, "but I didn't want you or Lizzie to get in any danger." He pointed at her forehead. "Case in point. I wasn't wrong."

"To him who lies in fear, everything rustles. Sophocles."

"Sophocles wasn't a detective."

"I know." She dropped her eyes. "My sleuths have had their share of danger. They've all survived."

"Humph. Yes, they have. On paper. Unless they go out of print."

Helen frowned. She put her left hand on her hip. "Don't be ridiculous. They'll never go out of print."

He raised his hands in acceptance. "Let's not go round and round."

"Got a solution?"

"I agree, we can work well together. Notice I said *can*. You are exceptionally good at reading between the lines when it comes to people. You also know this county and its people far more than I do. I'll bet you can tell me the history of almost every property in the area. Who bought it, who sold it, who lived there, who died there. You're a walking encyclopedia."

She grinned. "Nowadays, I think I'd be described as a Google search site. What's the catch?"

"We need to make a pact. Going forward, you're going to fill me in on anything you're doing before you leap ahead. No surprises."

Helen gazed across the water toward a distant peninsula. She spotted a crab boat chugging past Buoy Two. "I'm not good at reporting in. That's why I'm a real estate agent. Neither is Nora. She's terrible at it. Same with Agatha and Nancy. They're stubborn and independent. Jessica becomes obsessed if she's solving a case. You know Jane Marple will work on her own. She'll just not tell you until she's ready."

"You're killing me." He leaned over and dug out another beer. "Ball is in your court. I have to report to my higher-ups. I can't work with you if I can't trust you to report in, before and after. You'll need to keep your snoops in line, especially with a hired thug watching you. We have to keep this under the radar."

"That's the second time I've heard that expression in the past twenty-four hours," she mused, stroking her bruised chin. "We need to rethink who could be the culprit."

"Makes total sense. We're missing something. Are you suggesting we work up a better list?"

"I am, but not today. Takes too much concentration." She rubbed her forehead. "Do you mind if I reach out to Mariah tomorrow? I'd like to chat with her."

"Mariah. What makes you interested?"

She shrugged. "I can't picture her sending a goon to threaten me. Yet, there's something about her that seems kind of funky. It could be her Woodstock persona. I keep wondering if she knows more about Roberto than she admits. Dana told us she and Roberto met in cooking school."

"You and Lizzie might get her to open up. Don't you think it's odd she never mentioned it?"

"Yes, I do."

"Does this mean we have a deal?"

She took off her cap and shook out her dark crop of hair, then resettled the cap. Leaning over the wheel, she landed a light kiss on his lips with a swollen lip. "We have a deal."

Joe's dimple on his chin deepened. His eyes traveled up the mast and along the boom. "Good. That's settled. I'm hoping I don't have to remind you again. Shall we raise the sails and try to catch some wind?"

"Hoist the mainsail, Mister Christian! Full speed ahead!"

Chapter Twenty-Three

W hen Tammi walked back into Safe Harbor after lunch the following day, she found Joe and Helen in a conference room, hunched over a scratched-up legal pad with the shades pulled down over the glass door.

"Do I ask what you two are doing?"

Helen held her index finger to her lips. "Shush. Ignore us." Tammi gave a little wave.

"Why can't we use your laptop for this?" Joe frowned.

"Not for my pros and cons list. It's always handwritten. It's like the Ben Franklin pros and cons list I create for clients when they're deciding which house to buy." She raised her chin. "It worked for the Capelli case, remember?"

"Got it."

Across the top of the pad, she wrote in big black letters, *Motive plus Opportunity Equals Crime.*

"First is Adrian, the friend and business partner. We need to dig deeper into Roberto's financial situation. *Pro, Adrian gets the business and the properties.* He cuts his ties with his partner who's gambling away their profits, especially if Roberto had debts tied to the Mafia. *Con, now he's stuck dealing with the Mob directly. Second Con, without Roberto's charisma, their business is in serious jeopardy.* Adrian's got a lot more to worry about than creating their next crab bite. Everything they built could tank. Their patented Flying Pan collection is on a huge international TV network. Their cookbooks, their restaurants. Everything was centered around a fanbase crazy about

Roberto. He wasn't just about great food. He was theatre. Lizzie would tell you that."

She took a sip from a Safe Harbor coffee mug and made a face. "Any progress with those Mob photos Shawn identified?"

"I sent them to the State's Attorney's office. They've put out feelers, trying to pick up on any rumors tying those two henchmen to Barto Enterprises." He stopped.

Helen tapped her pad. "I get the idea you were going to say something else."

He groaned. "Getting the State's Attorney's office involved is tricky. I'm buddies with a retired state trooper who now drives part-time for S.A. Scott Harris. Law enforcement can't stand him. The guy's got an ego bigger than the state of Maryland."

"How'd he get elected?"

"In Maryland, it's an appointed position. He's good at working the political system."

"Is he a ladies' man? I could introduce him to Nora. She could handle him." She made a suggestive wiggle in her chair.

"I'd feel sorry for Nora. Who's next?"

"Dana Moore. Competing celebrity chef and queen of the shopping networks until Roberto arrived. *Pro, her sales ranking, which kept dropping, will turn around with him gone.* She's extremely competitive with an ego as big as his. According to Lizzie, the rumors were flying. She was getting more and more difficult while he poured on the charm. Sounds like he smelled blood."

"Let's hope it wasn't his own. Cons?"

"I keep asking myself, why wouldn't Dana wait it out? That's the Con. *She's a fighter, and he wasn't the first golden boy she's dealt with.* He could have been a flash in the pan." She grinned. "Did I say that? You get it. Flash in the pan. Roberto was part owner of the Flying Pan invention."

"That's a terrible joke." He examined the list. "She'd know how to hide a poison inside a recipe."

"Agreed. But every one of these people had opportunity."

"Who's next?"

"VP of ShopTV's Talent Management Greg Waldron." She drew a big star next to his name. *Pro, he hitched his wagon to Roberto.* He discovered him and signed Barto Enterprises to a long-term contract. The network moved him from midlevel management to being a top dog overnight. He had and still has a lot riding on them."

Joe reached for a bottled water and chugged. "That sounds like con to me. Why would he want to kill his golden goose?"

"The last thing he needed was his celebrity chef being indebted to the Mob and the studio blaming him for not knowing. They've spent a lot of money promoting Barto Enterprises and their product line. Maybe he talked to Adrian, and together, they decided they had to clean house and introduce Tara Owen. She appears to be the next rising star chef and ready to replace Roberto."

"What do we think of her?"

"*Pro, with Roberto gone, she takes an even bigger leap into a larger network to scoop up his fanbase.* If sales for Barto products start to sink, the network would likely slide her into other product lines. She's young, beautiful, and ambitious. *Con, she'd have to work even harder to convert his fans to hers.*"

"I'd put her low on our list of suspects unless Roberto changed his mind and withdrew his offer to put her on his show. They were days away from an announcement. If she'd already burned her bridges with her previous network, she might have been furious."

Helen nodded. "Furious. Lizzie tells me there aren't a lot of networks searching for on-air talent."

Joe tapped his pen on her pad. "I have a new suspect to add to this list. Neal Frawley."

"Why's that?"

"Rick interviewed him. He's the one who supplies Roberto's food for his shows. Roberto ordered what he needed, and Neal put together a box of supplies. Ingredients, spices, oil, everything. Our chef stopped by that Sunday to pick up his food."

"Makes perfect sense." She jotted down Neal's name. "*Pro, access to food.*

Any motive?"

"My squad's been asking around. Neal's had a couple drag-out arguments with Roberto about making him general manager. Neal thought he put in too many years running all the restaurants without the title or the money. He told Roberto and Adrian he was quitting if it didn't happen soon."

"Did anyone confirm this with Adrian?"

"Rick did. Adrian confirmed Neal's been difficult lately. Some of the staff described him as a hot head."

"Con?"

"Was Neal that resentful?" Joe stared at the list. "How about Mariah Manley?"

Helen jotted down her name. "Last but not least. *Pro, opportunity* since she prepared the set before the show. *Con, She seemed genuinely shocked and upset when Roberto died.* She's very competent, but kind of ditsy. Smokes too much pot, is my guess. She ushered me down the hall and onto the set. If she arranged the poison, she's got nerves of steel. Or is an incredibly good actor."

"I also haven't found her motive," Joe added. "Our medical examiner tested the inside of her cooler she used. Clean as a whistle unless you count a pinch of oregano stuck to the inside edge."

"Was it cleaner than expected?"

"I don't think so. She does touch food. I'd expect her to keep it clean."

"Didn't she bring in flowers?"

"Checked them out too. Clean."

She sat back. "Anyone else?"

"One more person I can think of. Lizzie." He offered a poker face.

"Very funny." She sighed. "I guess from where you sit, she has to go on the list. *Pro, she leaps past Roberto, Dana, and any new candidate Greg, Adrian, and Roberto were considering.* She's smart and ambitious and the viewers' favorite associated with the product line. The network needs her more than ever."

Joe interrupted. "*Con, she'd have to orchestrate an assault on her mother* after her mother refuses to back down on her sleuthing. Given all my years in law enforcement, I can confidently say she's the one person we can eliminate."

CHAPTER TWENTY-THREE

His dark brown eyes twinkled.

Helen smiled back. "When I study this list, I see three major problems." Her index finger slid back to the heading at the top of the pad. *Motive plus Opportunity Equals Crime.* "I'd add this." In black ink, she wrote *Motive plus Opportunity plus Chaos Equals Perfect Crime,* then read aloud.

Her eyes met his. "First problem, everyone on this list had motive and opportunity which could equal the crime. Second, each one of them, except Greg, had the talent to hide a poisonous plant inside the ingredients."

"Greg could have gotten the help of one of the others," he interjected.

"True. Third problem, the killer deliberately chose a location with chaos and cameras. The exact opposite of most crimes. Most crimes like this are done privately. That couldn't have been by accident."

"Until we reviewed those security tapes, I didn't realize Mariah styled the set twice on Sunday. Once, for the special promo shoot. Again, at four o'clock as he was about to go on air."

"Me either." Joe ran his hands through his hair. "As did Dana, Greg, and Adrian. They all had reason to be in early."

"Don't forget. Neal didn't even need to come into the building. He arranges for the victim to carry in his own poisoned food."

"All this incriminates everyone and no one. Our murderer was extremely clever."

"Chaos. Let's split up some tasks. I'll invite Mariah for a drink along with Lizzie. Let's see if she knows more about him than she admitted. I also want to stop by Adrian's. He's my client, and I need to deal with him on a business level aside from this murder. I'm hoping I can get another peek around."

Joe stood and reached for his jacket. He tucked his pad inside a pocket and adjusted his Glock on a black leather belt. "He's already asking questions about your involvement. Be careful. It wouldn't be hard for anyone, including Adrian, to find a creep like Rory to deliver a message as long as he's well paid."

Helen blinked. "Jane would say everyone is capable of anything if there's motive. I'll let you know what Mariah has to say."

Joe squeezed her arm and headed down the hall and out. He was whistling.

* * *

A few hours later, she walked under the huge ShopTV sign and up to the security front desk. "Good afternoon. I'm Helen Morrisey, and Lizzie Morrisey is expecting me."

The guard at the desk inputted her name in his computer log and printed out her name badge. A few minutes later, Lizzie pushed open the double metal door leading from reception and smiled. She wore pearl drop earrings, a light pink top, and a full, dark pink skirt.

"Hi! I'm running about thirty minutes late. Tara and I are just about to go on air. The OPS Desk rearranged our schedule after your text."

Helen followed her daughter at a trot. "How are you getting along with Tara as the new Roberto? We haven't had a chance to talk about it."

Lizzie gave a little indifferent shrug and pinched her bright pink lips together. "This'll be our first official show, which means everyone from the top down will be tuning in. Greg was on the set, pacing back and forth. He's been told to watch from the green room. Which means you'll get a chance to watch him sweat during our show."

"Oh boy. Does that mean Adrian will be there too? We're meeting tomorrow at Riding Cross. This'll be awkward." Helen rolled her eyes. "I'm sure he'll wonder why I'm here."

"You'll manage it. Believe me, prepping for this show in Roberto's kitchen has been weird on so many levels. Feels like I'm walking across his grave."

"You'll do great. It will only remind Greg and Adrian how much they need you as the familiar face for all the Flying Pan and Roberto followers," her mother responded.

"Thanks for the pep talk. I'll catch up with you later." Lizzie headed toward the OPS Desk.

* * *

Helen pulled open the green room door. The heat of the day may have been climbing to ninety degrees outside, but inside she could sense Greg and

144

Adrian's chilly reception when she greeted them. Greg offered a brusque hello, then turned to a studio staffer. Adrian's clenched jaw told her he wasn't pleased to see her either.

"Well now, why are you here today?" He accepted her hand with a lukewarm shake.

"Hello. Nice to see you here." Her deliberate Jessica tone of confidence tried to inject a bit of warmth into the room. It wasn't working. "Lizzie asked me to sit in and watch her first cooking show with Tara. She's still grappling with the idea she's back in Roberto's studio kitchen. This must be even more difficult for you too." She tilted her head to the side in sympathy.

With a blank face, he studied her for a moment as his voice morphed from annoyance into a sad low pitch. "It's very hard for me. We're fortunate Tara barely knew him. It's easier for her to move ahead without him." He turned and followed Greg to claim two large gray chairs facing the wall of multiple screens.

The show started exactly at five o'clock, with fresh new graphics. Lizzie broke open the intro with a calm yet upbeat aura, welcoming Tara to ShopTV and its viewers. The new face of Barto Enterprises products expressed her pleasure in joining the family with a warm, slightly mournful story of her initial plans to partner with Roberto. Lizzie added her own stories, reminiscing about his cooking shows, then transitioned into their presentation of Flying Pan's latest products to the listeners. Tara introduced a crab with steak recipe from Water Street Bistro's menu, and they were launched.

Greg had begun pacing with the show's onset. Adrian sat stone-faced, his eyes shifting from one screen to another. Helen watched the men's shoulders begin to relax when the initial sales inactivity began to shift as listeners' attention focused from their favorite chef's absence to Tara's step-by-step demonstration. Fourteen minutes into the show calls for their Flying Plan collection took off, and the numbers flashing on their computer monitors climbed. The two men exchanged glances. She watched as they refrained from a high-five and kept it to a sigh.

Chapter Twenty-Four

"Mariah! How are you?" Helen was three steps behind her as she dropped off her badge at security after the show.

Mariah's long pigtails swung from front to back as she turned and spotted her. "Hi. Here to see Lizzie?" She shifted her green cooler from one arm to the other. They followed each other to the lot.

"She needed a little moral support. She and Tara had their first cooking show together. She dreaded using Roberto's kitchen again."

"I don't blame her. I styled the food. It was weird knowing he wasn't about to walk in the door. How'd it go?"

"Pretty well. I don't think their sales were what the studio would expect if Roberto was here. Greg and Adrian watched from the green room. They seemed pleased."

"The execs are on Greg's back to prove Tara was the right choice."

"That's a lot of pressure." Helen reached for her keys. "I was thinking. Lizzie and I are catching dinner tonight at Water Street Bistro. Want to join us?"

Mariah glanced down at her beaded sandals, then up. "I'm not crashing your party?"

"Not at all. We'd love to have you. Meet us there at six."

* * *

The restaurant was in full swing for the middle of the week. Staff bustled, and chatter spilled out from the bar. Neal Frawley approached Lizzie.

Helen gave a little wave to Mariah when she stepped through the door. "Hi, I'm glad you could make it. Let's grab a drink and wait for our table."

"Mom, do you remember Neal? You met during the luncheon at Riding Cross last week. Adrian just promoted him to General Manager."

"Of course, nice to see you. Congratulations. Sounds like a big job." Helen gave him a warm smile.

"Not really. Been doing it for a long time now. Happy to finally get the recognition."

"I'll bet you're glad to see this restaurant reopened."

Neal smiled back and gestured to a table in the far corner. "We all are. Everyone's been holding their breath. A lot of people were depending on it." He handed them menus. "Hi, Mariah, good to see you." He headed off to a nearby table.

"I didn't realize you knew Neal," Lizzie commented to Mariah.

Mariah gave a little shrug. "I come here quite a bit with other studio staffers after work."

Helen chimed in. "I guess it was one way for them to get to know Roberto away from the studio."

Mariah took a long sip of her red wine and regarded Helen's purple and green bruises. "I read about your attack. Terrible. Any idea why it happened?"

"Not a clue. I should never have met that guy alone. It was so stupid of me. If he wanted to, he could have killed me."

"Let's not talk about it," Lizzie shook her head.

"Is it true you have a group of detectives working with you?" Mariah asked, disbelief on her face.

Helen shifted in her seat and made a little laugh. "I wouldn't call it a group of detectives. It's more like some close friends giving me a few ideas. I'm upset Lizzie was nearly a second victim. Whoever the killer was, they didn't care if she was hurt or even died."

Mariah frowned. "I hadn't considered it that way. I doubt hurting her was intentional. I'm wondering if his death was accidental. Maybe someone wanted to make Roberto sick. Or look drunk? Maybe they never thought he'd die from that plant he ingested?"

Helen blinked. "That's a good point." She decided to change course. "I heard you met Roberto years ago while you were both in culinary school in New York. Did you become friends?"

"We did." The young woman made a rueful sigh. "It was about seven years ago. We were in a lot of classes together."

"Roberto was here in Kent County, and his parents didn't have a lot of money. I'm surprised he managed the expense of starting in New York City," Lizzie said.

Mariah gave a little shrug. "He won a national chef competition. The prize paid off his student loans, and landed his first job in a prestigious steak house. That was a huge breakthrough for him. He ended up being offered their Executive Chef position a few months later."

"Why did you decide to go into food styling?" Lizzie said.

The young woman sat back. Her pencil-thin hands, tipped with bright yellow and blue nail polish, folded and unfolded her cocktail napkin in front of her. "It was a hard decision. The economy was slow, good chef positions were hard to come by, and cooking shows were getting more popular. I had a friend in New York in the television business. He suggested I consider food styling. It's a related career, but the hours are a lot less stressful. The downside is you're far less likely to be paid well. Not like the big time. My parents were disappointed. They didn't think food styling was very prestigious, especially after all my training."

"Like Roberto?" added Lizzie.

Mariah shrugged. "Every time they saw him on air or rubbing elbows with the Hollywood set, they'd whine to me."

"How did you come to the network," Helen asked.

"I followed his career a bit. Watched it take off. Then we lost track of each other. About eighteen months ago, I spotted him on his show. I called him and asked if he could put in a good word for me when they had an opening. A couple months later, I came on board. I like working here."

"Do you ever regret giving up on becoming a chef?" Helen watched as Mariah picked at her cuticles.

"Sometimes. I have the talent, but I think I found a better niche. All food stylists are chefs, but not all chefs are food stylists. Roberto would never have the patience. I'm expanding my resume to include food photography. The people we have at ShopTV are strictly mediocre."

"That sounds amazing," Lizzie enthused.

Mariah smiled and reached for her wine. "I figure I can benefit by being on both sides of the camera."

"I'm happy to hear Neal got a promotion," Lizzie interjected.

"We both know what it's like to be passed over."

"What did you think of our photos of Riding Cross?" Helen asked.

"They're excellent. I've been to the house a few times. It's amazing how a photograph can lie."

"Excuse me?" She protested. "Our photos don't lie. We're making the best of each room. Do you consider making food appear delicious for television lying?"

Mariah shrugged, reaching for her glass. "You're right. Poor choice of words. I guess I'm a little jaded. What you see isn't what you always get. It took me a while to realize that, especially when it comes to people."

Helen considered her woeful words. "It sounds like you've had some disappointments."

"I have. But I've moved on. I'm in a good place. I like my job, and I've made some good friends." She lifted her chin. "Tell me about your investigation. Are you really trying to find Roberto's killer?"

"That's just gossip. Wish I knew who started it. Nothing like a small town," she responded. "I'm just nosing around, hoping to help put the pieces together. Can't say I've gotten very far."

Lizzie grinned. "My mother has a problem with minding her own business." They all laughed. "She's a mystery story fanatic. Anytime she can't figure out what to do about a problem, she consults her favorite sleuths."

"My kids accused me of talking to myself, so I decided I needed some smart women who would listen to me and offer great advice. Unlike my kids." Helen laughed.

"Shawn and I offer great advice. You just don't like it," protested Lizzie.

The redhead pulled on her braids, winding them around her fingers. "What does your club have to say about this murder?"

"Not a lot. ShopTV has a lot of people coming and going. It's pretty tough to eliminate anyone. You have any ideas?"

"Dana was obsessed with how popular he was. She was quick with the snarky comments." She stopped, then lowered her voice. "If I tell you something, do you promise to keep me out of it? Her eyes traveled back and forth between the two, seeking confirmation. They both nodded.

"I found this note stuck inside a kitchen drawer a few days before the murder."

Helen leaned over, and Lizzie followed. "Why didn't you show this to the police?"

"I was afraid they might think I planted it." She dug into her fringed suede pouch and pulled out a square white envelope. She slid it across the table between the glasses.

Helen pulled the cuff of her white linen jacket over her hand, covering the tips of her fingers. She reached for the envelope, touching only the edge, and opened the flap, pulling out a matching sheet of thick textured paper. "Pay up or be sorry," she read. The letters were large and printed in all caps with what appeared to be a black Sharpie marker.

She sat back, frowning. "When did you find this? And where?"

Mariah gulped. "I was straightening up the studio kitchen the Wednesday before he died. It was jammed between two spice containers."

"Did you ask Roberto about it?" Lizzie asked.

"Never had the chance. The next time we spoke, it was before his Sunday show with you."

"Any idea who might have written it or what it's about?" Helen surveyed the restaurant from their corner. A high-pitched laugh burst out from the bar.

"There's been rumors he liked to gamble at Baywood Casino. And on horses at Far Hill. About three weeks ago, as I was walking across the ShopTV parking lot, I overheard him talking to a couple guys. It was pretty heated. They had him backed up against his car."

CHAPTER TWENTY-FOUR

"Did they see you?"

"I don't think so. We were about five cars apart. They were in his face. One of them gave him a little shove."

Helen sat back and sipped her wine. "We'll need to get this to Detective McAlister."

Mariah grimaced. "I was afraid you'd say that. I'm trying not to get involved in this mess."

"He was your friend. Don't you want to know who killed him?" Lizzie broached.

"He wasn't a friend. He was a work colleague. We crossed paths over the years. He's gone. I care we get back to normal. Wouldn't you?"

"I guess it's a question of what's normal. Normal isn't having a killer wandering the halls of ShopTV."

"How do we know it wasn't someone completely unrelated to the network?"

Helen and Lizzie glanced at each other. Helen returned the note to the envelope and slid it into her pocket. "We'll keep this quiet, but don't be surprised if Joe McAlister contacts you with more questions." She reached over and grasped Mariah's hand. "Thank you for trusting me."

The redhead gave her braid a nervous twitch with a flowered tattooed wrist. "I didn't think I had much choice. Someone was threatening Roberto, and it certainly wasn't me."

The three pulled back as Neal approached their table.

"How is everyone? Do you need another drink?"

Helen smiled at him. "That would be great. Can we order dinner?"

"Absolutely. I'll get your server."

Tilting back her head, Mariah finished her wine and set down the glass. "Thanks for the drink, but I need to get home. As I said, keep me out of this. As far as I'm concerned, no news might be good news." She scooped up her satchel, gave them a quick wave, and scooted around the tables towards the door.

Lizzie shifted toward her mother. "That was rather abrupt, don't you think?"

"Really odd. She didn't seem very happy about Neal. Do you know what Jane would say about it? She'd say, 'whenever there is a question of gain, one has to be very suspicious.'"

"It doesn't sound like Neal gained from Roberto dying. He was already counting on this promotion."

Helen rested her face in her two hands and watched as a diner clapped him on the shoulder. 'Was he? I wonder.'

Chapter Twenty-Five

At eleven o'clock the next morning, Helen cut through the Kent County Sheriff's Office parking lot. Nearing the entrance, she passed a tinted-out black Chevy Tahoe with *Office of the State's Attorney* inscribed on the license plate with two uniformed officers in the front seat.

She asked the young deputy at their visitor's desk. "Is Detective McAlister in?"

"He is. Is he expecting you?"

"I'm Helen Morrisey. He is not." She gave him a bright smile. "I hoped to catch him in person rather than on the phone."

"He's in a meeting right now. I expect him out shortly."

"Not a problem. I'll wait." She took a seat near the entry and texted him an FYI. **Stopped in to see you. In lobby. Will wait or I can come back.**

Ten minutes later, Joe strode out from the direction of his office, a second man beside him. "Helen, good morning. I want to introduce you to State's Attorney Scott Harris. He's here to discuss the Barto case."

Harris's eyes roved over her pale blue sheaf dress and high-heeled open-toed sandals. He held out his hand and offered a wide, overly bleached smile against a fake tan. "Helen, I've heard so much about you, I thought I'd say hello."

Helen turned on her Nora charm and showed him a wide-eyed, you're so important blink. "A pleasure to meet you. I hope what you heard is good. I didn't mean to interrupt your meeting." She returned his examination. About six foot two inches, he wore black cowboy boots with two-inch heels

153

and a custom-looking, oversized badge on his belt.

"Could we step inside a private room and talk?" He opened his palm, pointing back down the hall. She nodded. He placed his hand on her back and escorted her into a room and to a seat.

"I'm sure you realize the Barto murder is creating public interest not just in Kent County but around the country," he began. The State's Attorney tugged on the cuffs of his white dress shirt, matching each of them an inch below his custom dark suit. He took a seat across from her. "Joe contacted my office about the photos you provided. Very helpful." He paused. "Given the questionable people in those photos, my office has taken a particular interest in collaborating more directly with Joe on this case. The press is watching, and they'll get more persistent if the word 'mob' leaks out."

She tilted her chin at his comment. "Understandable, Roberto is a hometown boy success story. His death could have immediate impact upon our local workforce."

His eyes glided from her face to her neckline and back. "I've been discussing with Joe the need for us to oversee this investigation more carefully. I'm not sure trying to solve this murder at the Sheriff's Office level, as experienced as Joe is, will be the right route. I've also cautioned him about your involvement. I gather you have a penchant for your own investigating which I strongly advise against. We certainly don't want to involve you in a case that could lead to your own personal harm." He tapped his cheek. "You've had one close call. A beautiful woman at risk will only impede our efforts."

Jessica rang little warning bells. She recognized a letch when she saw one. So did Helen. She calmly folded her hands on the table and smiled up at the State's Attorney through her lashes. "Are you aware my daughter, Lizzie, was almost a victim at the same time? Her near death has caused me to have a strong interest in this murder being solved. Can you understand that?"

Harris pulled back and studied her for a moment. "My office will vigorously pursue this case. You can be assured we will do all we can to bring the right person to justice. At the same time, we have a responsibility to keep the public, including you, safe."

Raising her chin, she said, "I appreciate it. Be assured, I have no interest in impeding your case. Should I come across anything that might be material to the investigation, Joe will be contacted. I have *complete* confidence in Detective McAlister and his people." She turned toward Joe. His expression was controlled while his fingertips tapped the tabletop.

Harris twisted his Rolex. "I haven't had any breakfast this morning. Could I interest you in an early lunch? Joe is tied up, but you and I could discuss this further." He stood up, exposing a chrome semi-automatic pistol at his waist. "I assure you, you'll be well protected."

Helen strained to bite back groans. She held out her hand. "Thank you, Scott. This meeting has been extremely useful, and I appreciate your valuable time. Unfortunately, I have a prior commitment. Perhaps another time you're in the area? Let me know if I can be of any help to *you*." Turning to Joe, she held out her hand again. "Detective, a pleasure." She tucked her handbag under her arm and strode out, her heels clicking on the tiled floor along the way.

* * *

Joe called twenty minutes later as she was in line at Jean's Coffee Shop.

"Hi. Where are you?"

"I'm picking up coffee at Jean's. Oh my God. That guy is insufferable! I really don't know how you can deal with him." She edged up in line.

He gave a little chuckle. "Practice. I tried to warn you. He's got his boxers in a knot because he saw the news article about you. Now that he's seen those casino photos, he thinks he can create press opportunities with the Barto case and make some big political points."

"Ugh," Helen muttered. She glanced around the shop. "Do you want to meet for lunch? I'm starving. I also have something to show you."

"Sure. Meet you at Prime and Claw."

* * *

155

She spotted him out on the little patio. "Phew. Glad you suggested this. You would think meeting Harris would make me lose my appetite."

"You've never lost your appetite. He thinks a custom-made, oversized badge is going to woo all the women. His eyes lit up when he saw you." Joe signaled a wait staff. She took their orders and headed off toward the bar.

"Let me guess. You told him I looked like Jane Marple."

"Pretty close." He snickered. "After you left, he said he understood why I let you get involved in the case. Said you were eye candy, for your age."

She groaned. "Such a jerk. Who even says that nowadays? Like I'd give him two seconds of my personal time." She added lemon to an iced tea and stirred. "Is he going to give you grief?"

"He'll come and go. He did tell me I can't let you affect my evaluation of Lizzie as a suspect, given her access to Roberto's food."

"Seriously? Did he have an opinion on her likelihood of arranging an attack on her mother?"

Joe rolled his eyes. "As long as I let him take the podium in front of the press, I can ignore him."

She glimpsed over her shoulder and back. "Let me see those photos again?"

He pulled them out of his vest jacket pocket.

She studied each one, then lifted her head and pointed. "I recognize this man. He's the guy who broke into Water Street Bistro. The man in the black Lincoln town car."

"Hmmm. Two reasons for me to track him down. Wonder what he was searching for. His plates were fake, by the way."

"I want to show you a note Mariah Manley gave me last night over drinks." She reached into her bag and pulled out the folded note.

"Pay up or be sorry." Joe rubbed his chin. "Sounds like the Mob."

"I agree. Unless someone else wanted to lead us to that assumption."

"How'd she get it?"

"She said she found it in a spice drawer in Roberto's kitchen the Wednesday before he died. She was going to talk to him about it after the Sunday show, but, of course, he died. What do you think?"

"Not sure. The problem with considering this a Mob hit is the way he died. It's not their style. Too complicated. They believe in dark alleys. If they want to kill someone in public, it's usually at a restaurant. They walk in, shoot, and leave."

"What do you plan to do with this?" Helen chewed on her soft-shell crab sandwich. "This is delicious, by the way."

Joe smiled. "I'd like to sit down with Adrian. Watch his reaction. I'm definitely not showing this note to Harris. Thanks for not telling him about it, by the way."

"Of course. Why would I help him? But you owe me a favor."

"Really? Why's that?"

She tapped her index finger against her sore cheek. "You need to stop by to see Adrian while I happen to be there."

"Oh, ho. You sure know how to work the angles."

"It's an Agatha Raisin trait. What do you say? I'm there tomorrow at eleven."

Joe scooped up the check and dug for his wallet. "Let's hope this favor doesn't cost me more than lunch."

Chapter Twenty-Six

Helen weaved through the state park to home, her cell service dropping off a few miles from town. The water on her GPS widened as both sides of the narrowing peninsula leading to the lighthouse came onto her screen. A few minutes later, she could see the actual green-blue peek through the trees. Pulling into her drive, she let out a little sigh of relief. Good to be home.

Watson and Trixie greeted her at the door, singing a duet for their dinner. She silenced their clamor, changed into shorts and a light t-shirt, and made herself a vodka tonic. Nora and Jessica approved. It was after six, but her central air kept blowing on and off to combat the late-day sun and sticky humidity. Pulling her kitchen sliders open, she stuck her face outside, groaned, and turned back inside. She threw herself onto her living room couch facing the water and studied the wall of books jammed with mostly mysteries.

"Ladies," she uttered aloud. "There must be advice here." She fingered the yellowing bruise on her forehead. The swelling was down.

Watson hopped up next to her and started to knead his paws into a cushion. She stroked his head and watched Trixie march back and forth across the upper shelf of books, her tail flicking against the likes of Dick Francis, Robert B. Parker, and Dorothy L. Sayers. 'Trying to tell me something, Trixie? I wish you would be more specific."

She poured herself an iced tea and stood in the living room, staring at a table lamp beside the window. She set down her glass, picked up the lamp, and carried it to a small table near the front door. With a grunt, she slid a navy leather chair from one corner near the fireplace to the opposite. Then, picking up a small stack of books on a side table, inserted them into the bookcase. A bookend was moved onto the mantel with her clock shifted to the left. She removed a large brass bell from the mantel and placed it on her glass coffee table with a tall cluster of lemon-scented candles.

Her phone rang. Lizzie.

"I'm checking on you. How's your head?"

Helen perched on an arm of her couch. "Much better. I no longer look like I was hit by a golf ball."

"Good. I'm so relieved. Joe have any leads on the thug who hit you?"

"He's working on it. They've got a partial print on the sunglasses he dropped. As of now, no one has recognized him."

"That's not good. Can I help?"

"Your brother will kill us both if you offer to do more."

"I'll deal with my brother if I have to," Lizzie replied. "He'll get over it."

"I've been wondering if you've spoken to Dana lately."

"Actually, we're meeting for lunch again tomorrow at two. We'll be at the Old League Hotel. We both have airings scheduled up until one. Want to join us?"

"I'd love to. I have a meeting with Adrian to finalize his marketing at eleven. I'm dreading it. Our relationship has been a little strained ever since the news story about me and my sleuths came out."

"The odd thing is, I would think he'd be your new best friend if he's interested in discovering the killer," Lizzie said.

"I feel the same way. On the other hand, if he has dirty laundry he doesn't want aired, he might be more interested in getting us focused on another direction. Roberto is dead, and Adrian's priority is keeping their business going. It doesn't mean he killed him."

"Do you think the Mob could be pressuring him now that Roberto is gone? Are they holding him responsible for paying off Roberto's debts?"

"Could be. They're people used to twisting arms to collect their money, or worse. Joe's showing up at Riding Cross tomorrow while I'm there. I'm sure he'll ask him."

"You sounded as if you were exercising when you picked up the phone. What were you doing at this hour? You're supposed to be taking it easy."

Helen groaned. "I was rearranging my living room furniture. I just finished shoving my couch from one side of the room to the other. And a chair. Rearranging furniture helps me think, and I've got a lot to think about."

Lizzie laughed. "Shawn and I hated helping you move furniture when we were kids. I'll tell him he missed out. Night Mom."

"Night, sweetie. See you tomorrow at two." She surveyed her rearrangement as she turned off the lights. "What do you guys think? Nice?" The two cats, weary from all the redecorating, issued baleful comments and traipsed behind her to bed.

The next morning at Safe Harbor, Helen was glued to her laptop, scrolling through Jerome's photographs for Riding Cross. Adrian had requested a specific shot of the docks showing the house in its background.

Tammi tapped on her door.

"You're here bright and early." Today, she had red crabs swinging from her ears with a matching necklace.

Helen groaned. "I had a terrible night's sleep. I kept dreaming my entire Detection Club was sitting at the bottom of my bed, pointing fingers at me. I couldn't figure out what they were telling me, other than the fact I was blowing this case. It was quite a group. Jane was in her cotton nightie, Nora was dressed as if she'd just gotten in after an all-night party, Jessica was dressed to bike into town, Nancy was swinging her car keys at me, and Agatha was demanding coffee."

Tammi tilted her head at her boss. "Wow. I thought I had it bad when my five-year-old climbed into my bed in her PJs and begged for pancakes before school."

"Don't complain. You'll miss those days when Kayla gets older. I know I do."

The pager went off in the hallway. Tammi turned her ear toward the muffled words. "I think they're paging you. I'll check." She scooted out. Five minutes later, she was back.

"This should improve your day." Her round dark eyes sparkled as she carried in a huge bouquet of late summer flowers in a tall, square silver vase and placed it in front of Helen. "Who's the admirer? Joe?"

"What a nice surprise! It's been a long time since I've gotten flowers. Andy used to bring in bouquets every so often. Remember?" Helen buried her face in lilacs, lavender, honeysuckle, and white roses and inhaled. "Heaven." Smiling, she twirled the display around.

"I remember. Andy was very thoughtful."

"They're from Flower Basket Florists down the street. They're gorgeous." She poked her fingers into the stunning arrangement for the card. "Saw the news," she read. "Hope you're on the mend. Let's do dinner. Love, Pete."

"Who's Pete?" Tammi sat down as Helen cleared a place of honor on the corner of her desk.

"I don't think you've ever met him. Pete Askins's a long-time friend. We dated back in high school. Even college. He's an attorney with a law firm in Philadelphia. He's stayed in touch. Nice guy."

"What's the nice guy look like? Handsome?"

Helen sat down and admired the bouquet. "Very. Tall, thin, athletic."

"So, why aren't you dating? He married?" Her assistant's eyes twinkled.

"No, divorced. His kids are about Lizzie and Shawn's age. He was a huge help when Andy died. Got me through all the horrible will stuff. Keeps his boat at Harborside, so he's in and out of town."

"What's the problem?"

Helen wrinkled her nose. "Don't get started. He's hinted a few times, but I pretend not to notice. You know I'm not interested in dating."

"So, you say. I'm surprised Joe isn't discouraged. He's not going to survive forever on a midnight kiss."

"Hurry me, lose me, is my attitude." She moved the flowers a little to the side.

Tammi let out a huge, long sigh. "Does he know about Pete?"

"He met him last spring. We were having lunch at Prime and Claw. Pete spotted us from the bar. Besides, there's nothing to know."

"Sounds to me as if handsome and available Pete Askins expects a call. Besides, Joe could use a little healthy competition."

"There is no need for competition." She put her hands on her hips. "We may not agree on my sleuthing methods, but we have a friendly, working relationship."

"Does Joe know that's what it is? A working relationship?" Tammi crinkled her forehead. "For someone good at reading people, you're kidding yourself."

"No, I'm not. Besides, he hates rearranging furniture. He told me that once."

"How does rearranging furniture have anything to do with your relationship?"

"I'll explain another time." Helen gave her a shooing motion. "Go away."

Sitting back down, she fingered Pete's card, then reached for her phone.

"Pete? It's Helen. How are you?" She began to laugh at his response. "I had to call right away and thank you for the gorgeous flowers. How did you know Lily of the Valley is a favorite of mine? It always reminds me of my grandmother. That was thoughtful of you."

"You told me years ago." Pete sounded pleased. "When I saw the news clip, I had to send them. Are you okay?"

"It's a long story, but I'm fine. I was incredibly stupid and very lucky."

"Why don't you tell me all about it over dinner. Does tonight work for you?"

She held her breath for a second or two. "I'd love it. I'd love to catch up."

"Excellent. I'll pick you up at seven. Do you like the Beacon House?"

"Sounds perfect. See you tonight." She clicked off and sat back, gazing at a photo of Andy, Lizzie, and Shawn with her on *Persuasion* four years before. She sighed. She swore she felt Jessica, the widow, give her a little pat on the back.

Chapter Twenty-Seven

Halfway down the long drive at Riding Cross, Helen brought her Mini to a gradual stop. Climbing out, she leaned against the side of the car. Heat radiated off the dark blue paint. She gazed across the acreage flowing down to the bay, with the stately mansion and pristine stables nestled in the middle. A power boat streaked across the water, its engine whining. 'This place is so peaceful, so beautiful. Why did its owner die? How does his murder tie into the network?' she mused. The mid-day sun baked her arms. She slid back into her car, shifted it into gear, and approached the front entrance. The housekeeper answered her ring and led her down the long main hall into the commercial-grade kitchen. Adrian sat at the nine-foot-long island, concentrating on paperwork spread in front of him.

"Adrian?"

He raised his head.

Her summer dress felt damp at the collar, yet little goose bumps ran up her arms as she entered. Ever since Roberto was killed, the yards of marble countertops and stainless steel chilled her. The room's mirror image of the ShopTV kitchen was unsettling. How could Adrian sit here, detached from the sad aura surrounding him? His partner's missing ebullient personality created a palpable void, the silence unnatural. Thank goodness buyers were unlikely to sense the same vibe. She knew too much, she thought. Or far too little. She took a deep breath and plastered on an energetic smile.

Adrian got to his feet and welcomed her with a small hug. "Good morning. I'm glad we could schedule time alone. I had a few ideas."

She joined him at the island, relieved her client was in a positive mood. "Of course. I'd like to get your feedback now that you can see all the materials online. It helps inspire some tweaking."

The slight man moved to the espresso bar. "Can I offer you coffee?"

"Thank you. You haven't experienced bad coffee if you haven't had a morning cup at Safe Harbor."

Adrian chuckled. He handed her a large white mug with Riding Cross in blue and gold script. She filled it, then pulled a stool closer to the island.

Flipping open her iPad, she scrolled to his website displaying Jerome's full-screen photo of the overall property with dramatic classical music playing in the background. A second photo slid into focus showing iron gates with a blue and gold *Riding Cross* entrance sign. It overlapped the first. "What do you have in mind?" Together, they began shifting elements around the site until he was satisfied.

About an hour later, the doorbell rang. Joe strolled in. He reached out to shake Adrian's hand. "Hope this is still a good time for us to talk," he started.

"We're just finishing up," smiled Helen. "I do need to ask Adrian about the floor plans he leant me." She leaned over the sheets and guided his eyes with her index finger across the drawing of the basement, now a finished lower level. "You converted most of this space into your movie theatre, pool room, and workout area. It starts under the front door, runs underneath two-thirds of the first floor, and ends directly under the expanded kitchen. Here are the new steps and walk-out sliders installed to reach the patio from the workout room. I'm wondering, what's directly under the kitchen? Do you know?"

Her client's sharp eyes studied the plan. He rubbed his chin in thought. "I've never gone beyond the finished basement. Roberto said there was an old root cellar near our new wine cellar. He was very particular about where his wines were stored." He scratched his head. "Is it important?"

"Only to a curious building inspector. Is the pitched area next to Roberto's bedroom storage?"

"I doubt it. The roofline is steep, and the architect designed enormous closets."

Helen marked the plan in pencil. "I'm not concerned either way. I only want to be sure your seller's disclosure statement is accurate. Rather correct it now than after an offer comes in." She gave him a reassuring nod. "Buyers get suspicious if we leave information out and they discover it later."

Joe cleared his throat. "Speaking of disclosures, we need to review information our forensic accountants found in Roberto's personal bank account." The detective pulled out a sheaf of papers. "Given Helen is bound by client confidentiality, can I assume we can talk with her here?"

Adrian's shoulders tightened, and his thin lips drew a line over clenched teeth. He nodded. "What information?"

Joe ran his hand down a list and stopped. "Barto Enterprises's business account is with Kent Bank. Is that correct?"

"Yes, all our company accounts are with them. I told you before. Why?"

"We have a journal from Roberto's desk listing what appears to be debts due. We also discovered Roberto was writing checks between ten and twenty thousand dollars on a regular basis to a couple small LLCs. They match his figures in that journal. Were they his share of your partnership agreement, or was he stealing from you?"

Silence. Helen sat back and studied the two men. Adrian swallowed, his Adam's apple jumping. Clearly, this was a time for her to emulate Jane. She examined her hands, then lifted her eyes to the two men. She said not a word.

Adrian sank onto a kitchen chair and buried his face in his hands. "No. I tried to get him to at least keep his income inside the account so our bank would see we had strong company float. He wanted the cash right away. Money this past year got tighter even though business was great. We were in the expansion stage, and it was expensive. I believed him when he said it was a shortage of cash flow."

Joe pulled out Helen's photos of Roberto with the Mob. "We saw these photos hanging in his second-floor study. I understand they've been removed." He stole a glance at her. They already knew the answer.

Adrian stared at the photos, then put them down. "I took down a few after Helen suggested I remove more personal items." His eyes were cold, his expression blank. "Why is that a problem?"

The detective sat down across from him. "We know you had reason to remove them. I believe you discovered your partner was skimming money from the business. You also did not want anyone to know about Roberto's gambling habits and his debts to the Mob? Isn't that right?"

The small thin man stood up and started to pace. "Absolutely not! I knew his gambling was out of control, but I didn't know he was taking from the company. I thought he was funding his gambling out of his share of our earnings. I even leant him some of my share of the profits as a short-term loan to buy him time." His hands trembled, and his voice quaked.

Joe didn't flinch. "Given your reputation as a businessperson and his large withdrawals, it's hard to believe. They could cancel your contract if they learned about his gambling. His skimming funds was a motive for you to eliminate your partner when he wouldn't stop."

"That is ridiculous!" Adrian became furious, his face red-hot, his voice elevated. "I agree, I did not want his problem to become public. But he was my friend, and I was trying to help him."

Joe's voice softened. "Let's talk calmly. Are you aware of him receiving any threats?"

Adrian ran his hands through his hair. "Roberto told me he'd been followed. A couple guys accosted him in the studio parking lot one night."

"And because you didn't want to damage your company's reputation, you decided not to tell me. You also removed the photos of him drinking with the Mob because Helen and the public might see them." The detective's statement hung in the air.

Adrian threw up his hands. "Yes. Can you blame me? Bad enough we'd lost Roberto, the face of our company. The last thing we needed was for his name to be tainted. We were equal partners, but he was the personality everyone was buying. Now I'm stuck trying to keep it all afloat."

"I thought the plan was to have Tara share in the limelight," Helen said softly.

"It was, but that could take months. Whoever killed him short-circuited our entire plan. Don't you see that?"

Joe slid an envelope across the island. "Mariah Manley gave this to Helen last night."

"She found it in the studio kitchen," she added. "Does it look familiar?"

Adrian studied the note. "No. I've never seen it." He flashed a glint of distrust toward Helen as he shoved it back toward the detective, scattering a stack of her paperwork with it.

The detective stood up, shoving the note back into his file. "I need you to come down to the Port Anne Station this afternoon. I'll have a handwriting expert collect writing samples. If you wish to have an attorney present, you can."

Her client regained some of his cool, tossing an indignant smirk at both of them. "I don't need an attorney. I'll be there about four. And you better get this house sold fast," he said, pointing at Helen.

* * *

Joe called Helen as she was finishing up a call with a client.

"How'd Adrian do?" she asked.

His car radio squawked behind him. He sounded disgusted. "He held his own. His handwriting could match the note. Unfortunately, our expert said the wide black marker works against us. It blurs distinctive characteristics like angles on the letters and spacing. Using it was smart thinking by whoever wrote the note. Or they were just lucky."

"Dammit. According to Lizzie, anyone could have wandered onto his set and placed the note in a drawer that week. Cameras aren't on if there's no show."

"Back to your chaos theory again. With all those people streaming in and out, no one would consider it odd to see Adrian, or remember. Until Roberto died, it was just another day."

"They wouldn't notice anyone else either. Could have been Greg, Dana, or Mariah. Even a camera operator or a maintenance person. Lizzie says even Neal has admittance to the kitchen for deliveries."

"A possibility. If someone asked you to drop off an envelope in Roberto's kitchen, would you think anything about it?"

"Not in the least. Just another day at ShopTV," she groaned. "I am beginning to wonder how long it will take for Adrian to cancel my listing agreement. Whether he's guilty or not of murder, he has to see me as a nosy nuisance, at the least. At the worst, a threat. He knows very well I'm the one who tipped you off about the missing Mob photos."

"You have to admit, his explanation sounds plausible. When are you meeting Dana Moore again?"

"We're meeting tomorrow at two. I'll let you know what we learn." She stopped. "That's a buyer of mine calling in. I have to take this. Catch you later." She clicked off.

* * *

On Helen's way home, Tammi called her.

She picked up. "Haven't you left the office yet?"

Tammi gave a little laugh. "Kayla's having dinner at my mother's tonight. I'm shutting down my computer now. Guess who stopped in?"

"I don't know. Someone interested in buying a multi-million-dollar property?"

"Ah, no. Your favorite detective. And not the fictional kind."

"Really? We talked not thirty minutes ago. What did he want?"

"He said he was passing by. I'm afraid you'll have some explaining to do."

"Me? Why?" Helen frowned.

"He dropped something off on your desk. Guess what he spotted?"

"Uh, oh. Pete's flowers?" Helen winced.

"Yup. He asked me who sent them, and I said it was an old boyfriend."

"Thanks a lot! You were supposed to cover for me!"

"Thought it might help spur him along," Tammi defended.

"What did he say?"

"Nothing. He got quiet, then flipped over the card and read it. Stuck his hands in his pockets and headed out the door. Let's say it did not make him happy."

Helen sighed. "I seem to be doing that a lot lately. Okay, thanks for the heads-up. Talk to you in the morning. Get home to your munchkin."

Chapter Twenty-Eight

With its peninsulas and bridges separating towns from villages like a sea creature with long tentacles, dinner on the Chesapeake Bay often required weaving from point to point. A trip by power boat to the Beacon House from Helen's spot on Osprey Point took twenty minutes. By land, it took forty. Pete's Porsche Boxster lapped up the road around two bay points to enter the tiny town of Port Breeze. He downshifted smoothly over a bridge and the car purred as he settled it into a parking spot less than ten yards from the restaurant.

The Beacon House was set at the water's edge of a busy shipping channel linking the upper bay to the Delaware River and north. Barges and carriers traveled across the world to pull through this little canal, conveying goods between Baltimore and Philadelphia. Helen thought it remarkable the same narrow passage was just as important to commerce today as it was centuries ago.

Built in the 1780s, Beacon House evolved into an inn and tavern. With formal white tablecloths on the upper story and a tiny tavern below grade, it stood its ground against the more flamboyant competition of oyster bars, beer pubs, and all-you-could-eat, Jimmy Buffett-styled crab shacks. Helen loved its charm, its history, and its views. To enjoy it with a handsome old friend was special, and Helen was looking forward to enjoying the evening and getting away from thoughts of murder.

The host wound them between small tables of two and reached one nestled in a corner against the glass with a reserved sign. Running lights from boats traveling through the canal in the pitch dark cautioned others approaching from the opposite direction. Only a sliver of moonlight helped the travelers by water tonight.

Pete pulled out her chair and then sat down, his grin wide with pleasure.

"I'm so glad we're together. How long has it been?" He eyed her in the white simple dress, its soft neckline creating a wide oval that showed her shoulders. Her heavy silver chain hung from her neck below a small diamond pendant. Her dark hair glistened against silver earring drops. Helen silently thanked Nora for her fashion advice.

"Easily three or four years. You helped me deal with Andy's will."

Pete's expression darkened for a second. "That was a terrible time for you. I wish I could have been more helpful."

Their server introduced himself, then handed them leather-clad menus and took their drinks order.

"How are you now? The last time we bumped into each other was in Port Anne in May. You were having dinner with a local detective, if I remember."

"You do have a good memory. Joe McAlister. He's a good man. We worked together on the Capelli case."

"I got the impression he may have been interested in more than your real estate expertise." He raised light eyebrows.

"You're right, although he might be rethinking it now. I'm not exactly a fast mover. I also seem to be developing a habit of intruding in his cases."

Pete's laugh was low and sexy. "Has he figured out you're not likely to be contained?"

"Oh yes." She reached for her vodka tonic. Ever the man-hunter, Agatha whispered in her ear. 'He's very charming.' Helen tried to wave her away.

"Tell me about the assault in the basement. How did you end up there?

She glanced away and then back to him.

"I got a call from a guy who said he was a contractor and wanted to see a house I have on the market. I met him. We ended up in the basement, where he grabbed me and delivered a message. I'm lucky it's all he did. We struggled, and he knocked me out. I woke up in Kent Hospital with a concussion. I was stupid to go into an empty house alone with a complete stranger." She grimaced.

"What was his message?"

"Stop nosing around in Roberto Barto's murder case, or he'd be back."

Pete rubbed his chin. "You have no idea who sent him?"

"We're trying to figure it out."

"What was the newspaper referring to when they said you have a Detection Club?

Helen laughed. "I was trying to keep it quiet. As you can see, I failed. You might say I formed a small group of famous sleuths, and I consult with them."

"Who are these sleuths?"

She hesitated, wondering about his reaction. "You may know them. Nancy Drew, Agatha Raisin, Jane Marple, Nora Charles, and Jessica Fletcher."

Pete pursed his lips. "Now I understand why your detective friend isn't excited about your input."

"Let's say you and Joe aren't the only ones who think I've lost my marbles. But it's okay. I have to go about this case in my own way."

"Except when it threatens your life." Pete sat back and studied his drink glass. "What does Shawn say about this?"

"My son says I'm obsessed with fixing things. If I listen to Jane, she says I have a talent for thwarting evil. Nancy says I want justice served. Is there something wrong with that?"

Their server stopped back, setting a white wine in an ice bucket on their table and pouring them each a glass. Pete nodded his approval.

"I'm afraid I side with Shawn and Joe."

"I'm not surprised." Helen read over the menu and picked out fresh fish. "Since you're an attorney, do you know much about the Maryland State's Attorney, Scott Harris?"

Pete's eyes widened. "Since I'm in corporate law in Philadelphia, I haven't dealt with his office often. He has a reputation for being very tough and very egotistical. Rumor has it he's considering a run for governor. Why?"

"I met him. He decided to encroach on Joe's investigation. We think he smells opportunity for publicity. He also wants me off the case."

"He's definitely a press hound. I wonder who can be more persistent and annoying. Harris or you. Puts Joe in a tough spot. I don't envy him," Pete chuckled.

"Thanks a lot," Helen laughed. "Do you know anything about gambling in the area?" she tossed out.

"Gambling!" He leaned in and uttered under his breath. "Don't tell me you think the Mob is tied into this murder."

"We think it's possible. It could be the most likely reason."

"I'd steer clear of anything Mob related. You should too."

"You sound like Joe, and Shawn."

"Why don't you tell me about Roberto's house?"

She perked up. "It's gorgeous. On the market for three million. Want to buy it," she teased.

"Be nice to live close to you." His tone was low and even as he reached across and touched her hand. "Can I interest you in an evening sail this weekend? Be a lot healthier than chasing down clues and dodging threats."

Helen gently reclaimed her hand. "Pete, getting back into the dating pool for me is like jumping into freezing cold water. I've never liked it. I still miss Andy. It's taken almost four years to even consider joining this Polar Bear Club."

"Is that a no? After all, it's August. How cold can the water be?"

She studied the handsome man in the well-cut sports jacket and open-necked dress shirt, his nails immaculate, his trimmed beard cut close. "Actually, it's a yes. You know I love water sports." She offered up a contented grin. "By the way, this dinner is divine."

"Good. They say the shortest way to a man's heart is through his stomach. Does it work for women?"

Helen took another bite. "It works for me."

Pete poured them both another glass of wine.

Chapter Twenty-Nine

The following morning, Helen pulled into Olivia's neat little neighborhood. She was looking forward to this meeting, and now, she was even more excited. She'd brought along Lizzie as a surprise. They rang the front bell of the moss green and white trimmed cape cod and waited. Olivia's footsteps grew louder as she approached the front door.

"Hi, Helen. Come on in." She gave a wide smile to Helen and then stopped in her tracks. "Is this Lizzie?" Olivia's face lit up. "Oh, my goodness! If this isn't the best surprise!" She opened her arms to the tall young woman, and they hugged on the doorstep.

"I'm so excited to be here!" Lizzie beamed. "I hope you don't mind me infringing on your business meeting?"

"Mind? I'm absolutely thrilled. Come in, come in." She led the two into her living room and out to a screened porch filled with spider plants and hanging baskets of flowering red petunias. "Let me get you some iced tea." She bustled about in the kitchen and came out with a large round tray with glasses.

"You look absolutely marvelous," Olivia exclaimed.

"I was thinking the same of you," Lizzie responded. "You appear just as I remembered."

Olivia sat down and continued to eye Lizzie up and down. "You always were pretty as paint. Tell me everything you've been up to. I see you on ShopTV almost every day. It's so much fun watching."

Her former student blushed. "Not every day, but enough to keep me busy. Tell me about your plans. Mom says you're moving to Seasons for Living.

174

I've been there. It's a beautiful spot."

Her former principal's eyes gleamed. "I admit, I am excited to move somewhere new. I've been here thirty years, ever since I built this house."

"From all I can see, this is going to be a great house to sell. Exactly as I predicted." Helen gazed around, taking in the small, well-groomed yard and the freshly painted porch. "I'd like to arrange for my photographer, Jerome, to stop by in the next few days."

"He can come early next week. I'll be out of town this weekend."

"I'll ask him to call you directly to confirm a time. I know you'll love working with him. Let's walk through the house."

The owner gave a tour, opening cabinets and closets, with Helen taking notes. As they returned to the sparkling clean and organized kitchen, Helen spotted a row of cookbooks.

"Is this Roberto's latest cookbook?"

"Actually, no. It's his first one. I've been meaning to pick up the newest one."

Helen flipped open the cover and its first few pages. "That gives me an excuse to pick up the new one for you as my gift."

"Thank you! That would be lovely," Olivia responded.

"I see this one's autographed. I don't think I can promise you the next one will be, but I'll try." Helen snapped the book closed and slid it back onto the kitchen shelf. "We need to head off. We're on our way to meet with Dana Moore. Do you watch her show?"

"Who doesn't know *Dana's Delights*? Although I must admit, I didn't watch her as religiously once Roberto started his cooking show. I tended to bounce back and forth."

"We'll promise not to tell Dana," Lizzie quipped. She clasped the educator's two warm hands in her own. "Seeing you has been wonderful. I hope we can see each other again soon. Shawn will not believe I've been here."

"That devil! You tell your brother I still keep my eye on him. He may be a district attorney, but it won't prevent me from hauling him in for detention if he gets too big for his britches."

Lizzie laughed. "I'll be sure to warn him. I'm sure he's more afraid of detention from you than any felon he interviews."

* * *

Helen and Lizzie headed out of Port Anne to meet Dana at the Old League Hotel in the tiny town of Upper Ferry, fifteen minutes away.

"Dana sure is intent on keeping our meetings confidential," remarked Lizzie

"It's not a bad idea. If you decide to leave the network and partner with her, she'll want to time it to your advantage. I'd want to do the same. It's smart business."

Dana waved them to a table as they walked in. A woman in charming, early Revolutionary dress, apron, and cap welcomed them with menus. After a bit of chit-chat, Dana steered the conversation to business.

"I need to know if you've considered my offer to join me. I've already outlined a marketing effort, but it's based on our working as a team." Her eyes regarded Lizzie closely. "I'm giving you the opportunity to make not just a major leap in your sales career. You could be seen as a home décor influencer."

Lizzie glanced at her mother and back to Dana. "I'm giving this offer a great deal of thought. The idea of launching a new brand is very exciting. But I'm not ready to move forward, as much as I'm honored by your interest in me."

"What's your reason for hesitating?"

"I need to see Roberto's murder case resolved first."

Dana gazed across the room, then back. "Any other reason?"

"I'm not sure we're the best match style-wise."

Dana sat back, her mouth slightly open. "Style-wise? That's an interesting way to put it. Reminds me of what Roberto said to Mariah when she applied to be the alternative chef on his show. That one I could understand. He wasn't about to align himself with a carrot-top vegan nut cruncher."

Helen tented her fingers. "I didn't realize they ever had in-depth discussions."

"She may have thought so. I doubt he ever did. Although, he never had a problem paying her peanuts to create recipes for his cookbooks."

"You can't be serious."

Dana's eyes gleamed, her heavily mascaraed lashes fluttering. "I'm very serious. In fact, she said he had a history of stealing her ideas. She told me he promised her co-author status on his new book just released, but he didn't. Stupid woman. They never signed a contract. She couldn't say or do anything without fear he'd sue her for slander."

Lizzie frowned. "They seemed to get along well. And she never mentioned anything to me."

"She knew better. Being head food stylist for our network is a pretty good job. She'd have to search long and hard to find a steadier one if Roberto told Greg to get rid of her." The network celebrity raised two fingers to signal their server. "Could you bring me another Manhattan?"

Helen tried not to blink. It was a strong drink for a lunch meeting.

"Why in the world would he do that?" Lizzie didn't do as well tamping down the disbelief in her reaction. "I worked with him. He was a very creative chef. I can't picture him needing anyone's help." Lizzie rattled the ice in her glass.

"Smoke and mirrors." Dana let out a satisfied sigh. "If I hadn't been generous enough to train him, he'd have been lost. He was a copycat."

"Did Greg or Adrian know about this?" Helen studied Dana's face.

"I don't know about Adrian. Greg certainly did. But then, he's a smoke and mirrors kind of guy too. They got along fine. Greg saw his opportunity to find a famous personality to bring into the network and get himself noticed. He transformed himself into the young network hotshot. Now he has his sights on becoming the next Senior VP."

"Who do you think would kill Roberto? Certainly not Greg." Helen decided to use Jessica's no beating around the bush approach.

Dana tapped her polished nails on her rock glass. "I'm not sure he'd be cocky enough to kill him all on his own, but he did benefit. Greg's got Tara Owens drooling over him. She's at his beck and call. He loves playing big man on campus. Adrian is swamped with the details Roberto used to oversee. He doesn't have time to keep track of Greg's program changes."

Helen studied the cool businessperson across from her. "Do you think it took the skills of a chef to prepare the poison?"

"I don't think it took a master chef and a carving knife to poison his food. As a chef myself, I wondered why Roberto wouldn't notice a change in the flavor of his food during the show. Then I rethought it. To be fair, when I'm cooking on air in front of millions of shoppers, I'm focused on cooking shortcuts and chatting with my viewers, not accuracy. Do you agree, Lizzie?"

"I do. It's the last thing we worry about."

"Did you ever hear people talking about his gambling?" Helen interjected.

Dana's voice grew deeper. "I hear he was way over his head. He joined Gamblers Anonymous. I guess he was trying to get it under control."

"It's very sad," Helen commented.

Dana considered the younger woman in silence. " 'I'm very disappointed you aren't ready to join me," she mused. "Do you have an opinion, Helen?"

"I see two sides of this offer. You are a pro at generating sales by building rapport with customers on air. You've proven your expertise in creating great products. That is very obvious. On the other hand, Lizzie has done well building her own brand in a fairly short amount of time. I also know from experience partnerships can be challenging."

Dana pulled out a compact mirror and applied fresh lipstick. Reaching into her handbag, she pulled out a blank square of stationery with her initials at the top in fancy script along with a pen. She scrawled across the card in large letters, and signed and dated it with a flourish.

"I am going to go ahead and consider my options. However, I hope you'll reconsider. We'd be a powerhouse if we joined forces." She turned the piece of paper upside down and slid it across the white tablecloth. "Get back to me soon." She stood up, offered her hand to them both, and sashayed out of the dining room.

Lizzie picked up the note and flipped it over. Her eyes opened wide.

Chapter Thirty

"You're awfully quiet. Thinking about Dana's offer?" Lizzie clipped her seat belt while her mother touched the ignition. "Do you think I should consider it?"

"As tempting as the money is, I wonder if you'd regret it." Helen shook her head. "Hand me the note she gave you."

Lizzie dug into her bag and pulled it out.

Helen studied the note. "Does this paper look familiar? I'd swear it's the same note card Mariah gave us. The one she found in the studio kitchen drawer."

Her daughter turned it over and over. "It seems like the same thickness and quality." She ran her fingers over Dana's initials in dark blue script. "Except Mariah's note didn't have any initials on the top. It was plain."

Helen tapped her steering wheel and gazed across the parking lot. "Could the paper used for the threat come from Dana? Could she have written the note and tucked it into a drawer for Roberto to find?"

"You think it's possible this plain card is from Dana's stationery? We'd have to find out if she orders plain cards along with initialed ones."

"She may order them online. On the other hand, she's all about liking custom service. Is there anywhere in the area where she might order hers?"

Lizzie pulled up her phone and opened a search bar. "There's the office supply store on Route 50."

"Not Dana's style. Where would she order custom invitations?"

Lizzie continued to scroll. She looked up at her mother and pointed to an online ad. "It reminds me. Did you know Calli's Tomes and Treasures sells custom stationery? I had a girlfriend who ordered her wedding invitations there. They were very pretty, I asked her where she got them."

"Looks like you and I have to make a stop." Helen put her Mini into drive.

With free curbside parking, Port Anne was a throwback to catering to shoppers. Its citizens would storm town hall if the mayor suggested installing fancy credit card meters. Helen and Lizzie grabbed a spot in front of the store.

"What's our storyline? I don't want us to barge in and ask if Dana shops here," Helen said.

"Why don't I tell her I'm planning a party and need to see samples? Shall I turn on Nora's charm?"

"Perfect. Nora loves planning cocktail parties. Let's go."

* * *

Calli offered them a delighted smile.

"Hello! This must be my lucky day. Both of you!"

"Hi, Calli," Lizzie grinned. "I was just telling my mother about the beautiful wedding invitations you printed for a friend of mine. I thought we could see your suggestions for cards I can use for invitations and thank you notes."

"Sounds like congratulations are in order," she beamed. Viv raised her eyes with interest.

"No, no. Maybe someday," Lizzie winked back.

"Promises, promises." Helen mocked. "I'll be using a walker to get down the aisle by the time she and her brother get around to it."

Her daughter reached for a book of samples on the counter. "I'd like a note card on really nice paper I can use for business and personal. Something with my name or initials on it."

The older woman's face scrunched in thought as she flipped through another book. "Is this the type of thing you might like?"

Lizzie peered at the page of aqua and white crabs scattered across a card. "These are fun, but I need something more serious."

"Hmmm. I'm guessing you may know Dana Moore from ShopTV."

"Of course, we're friends and co-workers."

"Let me show you what we've done for her. We keep samples of all our orders for frequent customers."

Viv brought out a folder marked Dana Moore. "Is this closer to what you have in mind? It's pricey."

Mother and daughter put their elbows on the counter and studied the sample. "That's exactly what I need." Lizzie approved. "Let's find a different font for my initials. May even print my address at the bottom in small letters. Does she order these with blanks, so she has a second page if she needs it?" Her voice purred.

"She does," Callie nodded.

Helen spoke up. "Sounds like a handy idea."

Her daughter closed the sample books and handed the shop owner her business card. "Thanks very much for the suggestion. Can you email pricing and some font choices to me?"

"Happy to. Viv'll work on it today."

"Take your time. I'm glad we stopped in." She held up her hand. "Could I have one of Dana's initialed cards? It would help me decide the size of my own initials."

"Absolutely," Viv said, handing her one.

Helen turned toward their stack of books from local authors. "I promised a friend I'd buy Roberto's newest cookbook for her." She took one off the pile and opened it. "Oh! You haven't run out of the autographed copies. That's great." She handed them her credit card, and they bagged the book and receipt.

"We got lucky. Viv called Adrian Stanton's assistant, and she offered to drop more off to me," Calli explained.

"That was clever of you."

Lizzie and Helen bowed out of the store as a couple walked in.

"Thank you!" Lizzie called back.

* * *

Helen dropped Lizzie off at her car parked at Safe Harbor, taking Dana's note from lunch and the sample from Calli. She dialed Joe's cell as she walked inside.

"Do you have time to stop in at Safe Harbor? I have something to show you."

She could hear his cell switch from phone to Bluetooth as he opened his car. "I'm on my way to meet with Harris. Could probably be there in about an hour or so."

"I'm here for the rest of the day. Stop in when you can. Could you bring along the threatening note Mariah gave us?"

"No problem." He clicked off.

Helen studied her phone. 'Snakes and bastards,' Agatha commented. 'He doesn't sound warm and fuzzy.' 'No, he does not,' Helen responded.

* * *

It was almost five when he walked into Helen's office. Papers were scattered on her desk and in piles on her guest chair. She raised her head from a stack at his tap on the door jam.

"Looks like you're swamped."

"You and my Shawn keep telling me to go sell houses. Thought I should take your advice." Helen swept up the files to give him a place to sit. "Besides, I have a mortgage to pay and an assistant I can't afford to lose. The good news is I'm meeting another agent and their buyer at Riding Cross later this week. How was your meeting with Harris?"

Joe took off his suit jacket and sank into one of her chairs. He rubbed his temples. "Didn't get much sleep last night. Off the record, he's a pain in the rear. He wants to hold a press conference and give a public update on Roberto's murder. He's pretty pissed we haven't nailed anyone."

"Heaven forbid he assigns more investigators to help you on the case."

He folded his hands. "He asked about you."

"Me? Now what? Did you tell him I'm behaving myself?" She rolled her eyes.

"I'm not sure you know how. Why did you want me to stop by? I brought the note card from Mariah." He reached over and pulled a plastic bag with the note from his jacket.

"Lizzie and I had a meeting with Dana Moore this afternoon. She gave us this." Helen handed him a note. "Anything familiar?"

He fingered the card. "I'll be damned." He set the card he'd brought next to it. "Identical." Their eyes met, and he smiled. "Think Dana is our killer?"

"Definitely pushed her to the top of the list."

"Could be coincidental."

Helen contemplated. "Do you know Jane's opinion of coincidences?"

Joe sat back, crossing his right leg over his left knee. "No. But I'm sure you're going to tell me."

"She says coincidences do happen, but they mustn't happen too often."

"I'll try to keep it in mind."

"Lizzie and I stopped over at Calli's Tomes and Treasures Shop after we met Dana. She prints custom stationery. She gave us a sample of her stationary orders, some of it initialed and some blank. Same paper stock as the one Mariah found."

He fingered the two cards. "As much as we want a breakthrough, we have to remember. Dana's probably not the only one in town who likes this style card. I'll ask Calli to provide me with a list of all her customers who've ordered this. See if we can match them up with anyone else who knew Roberto."

"Great idea. I'll ask Lizzie to go ahead and place her card order right away. We don't want Callie to think she was wasting her time with us. I'm in sales. I know how that feels."

"Sounds like I need to reexamine finances beyond Roberto and Adrian. I'll start with Greg. Find out how much Roberto's popularity cut into Dana's income."

"Exactly."

Joe cocked his head toward the corner of her desk. "Nice flowers. Who's the guy?"

"Why do you assume they're from a guy?"

"No woman sends those flowers to another woman."

She bit her lip. "You met him. Pete Askins. Old friend. He heard about the attack and checked up on me."

He clenched his teeth. "I remember. Not that old. The Philadelphia lawyer." Standing up, he grabbed his jacket. "Are you seeing him?" His dark eyes seemed darker.

Helen smoothed her short hair behind her ears and pulled on an earring. "We had dinner together last night. We're going out for a sail on his boat over the weekend. Joe, I've known him forever."

He fingered his black leather holster on his belt and studied her as she came around the desk. Joe pulled her close and kissed her hard and long. "Talk to you tomorrow." He whistled on the way out of Safe Harbor.

'What do you think, ladies? I may like trying to fix everyone else's life, but I sure don't know if I'm able to fix my own. Besides, who says my life has to be fixed?'

Chapter Thirty-One

Her cell rang as she unlocked her car. Lizzie.

"Mom, can you do me a favor?"

"Of course, What do you need?" Helen responded.

"Mariah needed a ride home after we finished a show. I came in for a cup of coffee. I tried to bring up the investigation, but she didn't want to talk about it. Said it was too upsetting. After I left, I realized I forgot my new sunglasses on her kitchen table. I'm already late to meet Jason. Could you stop by there tomorrow and pick them up for me? I hate driving without them."

"That's easy enough. I'll run by about nine on the way to the office. I'll leave them with Tammi if I go out."

"That would be great," Lizzie sighed. "I'll text you her address in Port Anne Isles and tell her you'll come by."

"Text me her cell number in case I need it." Helen clicked off and headed for home.

* * *

Two miles from the center of town, Port Anne Isles was an easy stop for Helen. She'd sold a number of homes in this small townhome community nicely placed on the water. Many of the units came with boat slips. If a client wanted a reasonable price range along with water access, it was a smart choice.

Mariah's unit was a one-floor, lower level. Helen rang her doorbell and waited. A neighbor nearby came and went. She tried again.

"Mariah, it's Helen," she called out. She glanced at her watch and texted Lizzie. **Are you sure of the address? She's not answering.**

She responded **Yes, has a little garden flag at the doorway?**

Helen glanced down at a flag stuck into the flowerpot. She rapped on the door and then walked around to the rear deck. Hiking her skirt up above her thighs, she managed to climb over the locked deck gate and knock on the sliding glass doors. Nothing. "What do you think, Nancy?" she asked under her breath. "This is your kind of problem. Did she forget us?"

Helen tried to peek in the windows. The drapes were closed except for a tiny crack of light. She cupped her hands around her face and peered. Mariah lay motionless, face down on her living room couch. Helen shouted out loud. "Mariah!" She banged on the glass. No reaction. She banged again.

Turning, she yanked up her skirt again and hopped back over the gate, tripping on the grass below in her sandals. Running to the front door, she jiggled the doorknob. This doesn't look good. She ran back to her car to grab her phone.

"Nine-one-one," An emergency operator answered.

"Operator, I am at 7347 Port Anne Isles in Port Anne. I can see a woman inside her house who may need help. I can't open the door to check on her. We might need an ambulance."

"Please hold on while we confirm your location."

Seconds later, the voice returned. "We have medical assistance on its way. I need your name and contact information. Please remain on the line until police and emergency services arrive."

Helen spit out her information. Then she put the operator on hold and called Joe.

"I'm in front of Mariah's townhouse in Port Anne Isles! I can see her lying on her couch. She might be unconscious. I keep banging, and she hasn't moved. When I call her cell, I hear it ringing in the house."

"Did you call an ambulance?"

"Yes, they're on the way. I'm going to try to break the lock to get in."

"Help is probably a minute away. The station is around the corner. I'll leave right now. Don't touch anything!" He hung up.

She rummaged through her glove compartment and pulled out a tiny, flat-edged screwdriver. Running back to the door, with the emergency operator still on speaker in her pocket, she jammed the screwdriver into the keyhole. 'Not the first time I've forced open a lock,' she said to herself. Two years before, she'd smelled gas coming from a house on the market. She pulled out the elderly owner while she waited for the fire department.

"Come on, come on, come on," she cried. The lock refused to give. She heaved her shoulder against the door and gave the lock another upward thrust. It popped, and she tumbled into the front hall.

Mariah was face down. Helen kneeled down, turned her over, and placed her ear on her chest. Nothing. No pulse, either. Helen probed inside her mouth, feeling for any obstruction. She pushed up her sleeves, tilted back Mariah's head, and started mouth-to-mouth and chest compressions. Four minutes later, two EMTs barged through the door.

"Thank God!"

"Step aside, ma'am. How long has she been out?" The smaller of the two tugged open her blouse and attached a heart monitor.

Helen sat back on her knees. "I don't know. I just got here."

"Does she have any medical conditions?" He opened her mouth and examined her glazed eyes with a penlight. "Does she do drugs?"

"Drugs! I don't know. I barely know her!"

"I'm sorry." He shook his head at his partner. "Judging by her skin color and cold temperature, this didn't just happen. She's been gone a few hours. There's nothing we can do for her." He frowned at Helen just as Joe strode in the door.

He flipped open his badge. "Detective McAlister, Sheriff's Office." He stared down at the lifeless young woman. "Is she gone?"

"Yes, Sir. Probably five, six hours. Could have overdosed unless it was a heart attack. I don't see any needle marks. We'll need to call the coroner." They began to pack up their equipment.

He nodded, placing his hand on Helen's shoulder and drawing her to her feet. "Did you touch anything?" He handed her paper shoe covers and rubber gloves.

She shook her head. "No, I went straight to Mariah. She's young. Any chance this was suicide?"

"Let's search for a pill container." His fingers probed around her body and in between the creases of the couch.

Helen kneeled down. "Is this important?" She extracted an empty wine glass, handing it to Joe.

He began canvassing the other rooms one by one. "Helen," he called. "Come in here."

Helen followed his voice into a bedroom. He pointed at Mariah's dresser. An empty prescription bottle sat next to a slip of paper.

She watched as he reached for his phone. "Rick, Mariah Manley is dead. Looks like an overdose of Loroxide. She'd been drinking too, which accelerates its effect. There was a suicide note in the bedroom." He lifted his eyes towards Helen. "She confessed to Roberto Barto's murder." He hung up, shaking his head.

She listened, her arms wrapped across her chest, her feet as if glued to the floor. She stared at the empty container and the letter as he dropped them into clear baggies.

Her eyes traveled back to the dresser. "What's this?" she asked, pointing. A small plastic vial had been lined up next to the note. He picked it up, holding it to the light. He placed it into another clean baggie. "Looks like an empty test tube."

Helen frowned as she held the baggie toward the window light with two fingers. "You're close. It's not a test tube. It's a flower tube. Florists fill them with water and preservative. They stick them on the ends of flowers, so they arrive at their destination still fresh. I saw a few on those flowers I had in my office."

Joe twisted his mouth.

"Sorry, sore subject." She slowly turned the tube around. "Your forensics team never figured out how the poison was brought into the building and mixed into his dish. Mariah's telling us how she did it. She'd bring in fresh flowers and remove old ones before each of his demonstrations. We saw her do it on the security tapes. I think she liquified the Daphne and carried it into the building in this flower tube." She pointed to a small round plug at the top of the tube. "The flower is stuck into the rubber plug and into the tube. The rubber plug keeps the liquid from leaking out and mixing with the rest of the flower water."

"I'll be damned. I need to review those security tapes again."

"Very, very clever," she added. "She takes a fresh flower with the tube of Daphne, twists open the tube, and dumps the poison into Roberto's ingredients. Then she sticks the empty tube onto the end of one of the old flowers and carries them all out to dump them in the trash down the hall. She's completely safe from any police discovering the tube on her or her styling equipment she used that day."

"Right in front of everyone's eyes."

"The next question is, why would she kill him? There's no way she killed him because he stole her recipes. Was she that jealous of his success? Or was she furious because he wouldn't hire her for his show?"

The detective rubbed a hand over the back of his neck. "Is there anything else we don't know about Mariah Manley?"

* * *

Helen followed Joe back to his station and called Lizzie from a private room. Her daughter's stunned silence on the other end of the phone turned into quiet tears.

"Why on earth would she kill Roberto? And then herself?"

"I don't know, hon. There had to be something between them we didn't know."

Lizzie's voice calmed. "Was she furious because he refused to hire her as his on-air partner?"

"Could be. How did she act yesterday afternoon when you gave her a ride?"

"She seemed tired. Like we all are. Roberto's death and this investigation are wearing everyone down."

"Are you okay at home?"

"I'll be fine. Jason's with me."

"I'll call you if I learn anything more. Love you."

"Love you, too." They hung up.

Joe stuck his head in the door. "It's after two. Can I get you anything?"

Helen eked out a sad smile. "No. I thought I'd head home if it's okay with you."

He checked his watch. "Almost two o'clock. There's nothing more for you to do."

"Before I go, could I see Mariah's suicide note again?"

Joe handed her the file tucked under his arm.

"Roberto cheated me too many times. I'm not sorry," Helen read. "What do you think?"

"She was a very bitter woman." She sighed, handing back his file.

* * *

The sizzling summer air engulfed her as she opened the sliders onto her deck at home. Helen inhaled, then exhaled. As relieved as she was that Roberto's killer had confessed, it saddened her that it was Mariah. She turned back inside.

Damp from a long shower, she bundled into sweats and a t-shirt and logged onto her laptop with Watson and Trixie flanking her. She punched in a slew of keywords connected to NY Culinary Institute. Jessica, the best at research, kept nudging her to drill down further, and Helen agreed. Why did Mariah kill him? What drove her to it?

She'd done this web search after Roberto was killed. Could she come from a different angle? She inputted 'Mariah Manley Chef Food Stylist.'

Up popped photos of a tall woman with short curly hair and a very round face. Helen leaned over her laptop, enlarging the shots over and over. Could this be Mariah? This woman was easily forty pounds heavier, but her nose and hairline were similar. She got up and began to pace.

A fourth photo seemed familiar. Who was it that said cameras lie? Mariah.

She commented on the photos of Riding Cross. She was training to become a food photographer, Helen told her feline chums.

Trixie reached out and pawed at her hand on the keyboard as if to say, "You're getting close."

Chapter Thirty-Two

T he sun on the bay sparkled, and the fields rolling to the water were green and freshly mowed. It was a beautiful day to show a house, especially Riding Cross. Helen resigned herself to drinking her own coffee on the short drive. She'd texted Tammi with her schedule. Ever since the basement scare, Tammi stalked her like only she could. With Adrian out for the day, she was determined to do some discreet searches in his office for any background on Mariah.

Hustling from room to room, she opened doors and turned-on recessed lights and music. She'd gotten jaded over the years with homeowners expecting to sell houses with wet toothbrushes sitting on sinks and kids' laundry on the floor. Here, everything was impeccable. Helps to have daily housekeeping, she thought. It was a treat not to straighten beds or tuck away dirty dishes.

This was the third set of buyers seeing the house since it came on the market eleven days ago. Given the three-million-dollar price, she was pleased. Adrian appeared unimpressed. Like most sellers in a luxury range, he assumed the world had been waiting for his house to become available, cash check in hand. When she'd reminded him Kent County wasn't Manhattan, he shrugged.

"Good morning." She stretched out her hand to the Realtor and a couple in their early fifties, leading them into the center hall. "Louis, great to see you again. You've a lot to consider today. Let me help you get started." She gave them brochures and data sheets. "Feel free to take your time. I'm here when you're ready with questions." She gave them a warm smile and headed toward Adrian's first-floor office. This was her chance to hunt for more personal background on Mariah while the buyers walked through the property.

Carefully, she poked under paperwork and flipped open business reports. Nothing but colored restaurant brochures, fan requests, and stacks of cookbooks. Adrian had notes and photos of vacation destinations. Italy, Spain, and the Fiji Islands. Nice taste. Wouldn't mind going there myself. Looks like business wasn't so bad, debt or no debt. She walked from corner to corner, studying his awards and group photos. Still nothing.

Conversation floated out from the kitchen as she skirted upstairs to tackle Roberto's private office. Conscious of the hallway camera, she pulled out her iPad and stood in the hallway, deliberately making notations of lighting details. She entered Roberto's bedroom suite and turned on another light on a side table. Casually, she re-entered the hall and turned the bronze knob on his office door. It was closed, not locked. Phew. She didn't want to try her lock-picking skills for a second time in twenty-four hours. She'd be pushing her luck.

The drapes were drawn. She wandered around the darkened room, eventually approaching his desk. She sat down, pulled out her iPad, and appeared as if she was taking more notes. She lifted up a sticky note and made an elaborate effort to find a pen, lifting up his calendar and the "Dear Marlo" notecard still sitting there since her last visit. Was it the same paper? No. Similar. Nothing gave a hint about Mariah.

She glanced at the time on her phone. She needed to check on those buyers downstairs. She stood up, scanning the photos and awards on the walls. Nothing had been moved again since the last time she'd looked.

Reaching the door, she came to a brief halt. 'Snakes and bastards,' Agatha grumbled. Why did this photo feel familiar? Wait. It reminded her of the group shot at the Culinary Institute she pulled up online last night. Roberto was shaking hands with another man as he received an award. Helen twisted and untwisted the silver chain around her neck, studying the photo. Beneath it was a headline, *Restaurant Competition Winner Named*. She scanned the other photos and awards for descriptions.

Her cell ringing made her jump. "Hi, Louis. Do you need me?"

"We have questions about the lower level."

"No problem. Let me finish up a call. Give me five minutes." She snapped a photo of the awards ceremony and turned off the lights.

She decided to slip down the hall into Adrian's bedroom suite. So different from his partner's, his decorating was contemporary and clean. Each grooming item on the bathroom sinks was neatly aligned. A folder of more vacation spots was tucked inside a nightstand. She can certainly tell the contrast between a creative artist and a businessperson.

She glanced at her phone for the time. Shaking her head, she straightened up. Another waste of time, she thought. She turned and headed back downstairs.

Louis' buyers had a gleam in their eyes Helen liked. Their questions were far more detailed than either of those during her previous two showings. She walked them through the specifics of the house's mechanicals along with the movie projection room devices.

"I understand you are serious wine collectors. I have a treat for you." Helen unbolted a heavy door and led them into a room at least fifteen by fifteen. She flicked on recessed lights to display dozens of wine bottles. Hues of glass from clear to deep reds glimmered under the lights.

The husband's eyes lit up, and he peppered her with questions about its temperature controls.

"One last question," their agent interjected. "Do you know where this other door leads?"

Helen tried not to sigh. "I did check the floor plans. We think it provides access to a crawl space and an old root cellar. Remember, this section of the lower level is directly under the kitchen. When this wine cellar was renovated, Roberto replaced the old door with a new one for better insulation. I think of it as part of an old house's charm." She guided them back upstairs and out through the front door.

"There's a small, old icehouse at the water's edge," she pointed. "From the early 1800s until the early 1900s, the bay was a major source of ice farming, with crops of ice loaded on wooden barges and shipped by water. Remind me to show it to you. The inside is lined with tick cork which insulated the building. It could make an amazing bar near the docks."

Louis's buyers gave fascinated nods.

"Are you ready to walk over to the stables?" asked Helen.

Another hour later, she said goodbye to the couple, with their agent promising to get back to her quickly.

Once they were out of sight, Helen texted a message to Joe. **Finished my showing at Riding Cross. Any news on Mariah's death?**

Still waiting for medical examiner finals. Suicide likely.

Okay.

Hungry?

Always. Helen punched in a smiley face. Need to stop by office first. Wooden Mast 1:30?

Done

* * *

Tammi cornered her as she walked into Safe Harbor.

"How was your showing? Any luck?" Today, she wore blue sea glass around her neck and dangling from her ears. Her hair tumbled over her eyes.

"It actually went well." Helen loved her assistant's shared enthusiasm. "Their agent just texted me. They may make an offer. Besides, it gave me an excuse to be in the house while Adrian was gone." She opened her laptop. "I wanted to pull up a photo online. I'm meeting Joe at the Wooden Mast at one-thirty to grab a burger." Helen paused and regarded her assistant's sunny expression. "I have sad news. Close the door."

Tammi sat with a plunk in front of her. "Kids okay?"

"They're fine. It's Mariah Manley, Roberto's food stylist. She overdosed on Loroxide. I stopped at her house yesterday and found her." She hesitated. "There's more, but if Joe knows I told you, he'll have my head."

Tammi made a sign of the cross.

"She left a suicide note. She said she killed Roberto."

Her assistant sat back, her dark eyes wide. "Oh, my, Lord. You did say she had the easiest access to his food. Why did she do it?"

"That's what we're working on now." She glanced at the time. "Can you do me a quick favor? I'll send this to the office color printer along with the scan from my phone. Can you pick them up before anyone else sees them? I need to show them to Joe." She pressed print, and Tammi headed down the hall. She was back in minutes with two printouts.

"Thanks. Remember, you can't say anything about Mariah." Helen stopped and picked up Pete's flowers. "Why don't you put these out on the front desk? They've caused me enough trouble."

* * *

The Wooden Mast at the start of Water Street felt more like a quirky diner than a restaurant, with its artificial Tiffany hanging lamps and Formica countertops, but locals loved it. For vacationers, it was the perfect all-day stop for hot pancakes, waffles, and home fries ordered off red and white plastic-coated menus. It also made great burgers and steak fries.

Tom, their chef, loved to come out from the kitchen as the lunch crowd slowed. He greeted them both with a broad, crooked-toothed smile. His body shape was an advertisement for oversized portions.

"You're a sight for sore eyes!" He patted Helen's shoulder as she sat down. "I've been worried about you ever since I read about your attack in the papers."

She gave him a little groan. "You know me, always where I don't belong."

"It's a character trait we can't seem to correct," Joe grunted.

Tom gave out a hearty laugh diners four tables away couldn't miss. "She and I go back a long way. Believe me, she's not about to change," he told the detective, then headed back to his kitchen.

Helen glanced around the room and then lowered her voice. "I have more on Mariah."

"Show me."

She pawed around in her tote and pulled out the two-color copies, placing them before him. "Last night, I did some googling for Mariah and came up with this photo."

He studied it. "Other than Roberto, do you recognize any of these people?"

Helen pointed at the heavy, curly-haired woman on the screen. "Who does this remind you of from the studio?"

He held the photo under the light. "I can't believe it. That's Mariah."

"Exactly. She's one of the students standing near Roberto as he's congratulated for a big New York City restaurant competition seven years ago. They were both in school together, do you remember?"

He nodded. "Didn't she say they graduated together?"

"Yup. She told me and Lizzie the same story. According to her, Roberto won a big competition. It got him his big break. He was hired as a chef at a Michelin-starred restaurant. His career took off. Good chef positions were rare, and she decided to turn to food styling. Her parents are disappointed in her."

"What's your point?" Joe bit down on a handful of fries.

"Jealousy? Envy?" She chewed on her burger. "To mention this contest to Dana and Lizzie and me, she obviously resented it."

"So jealous that he won and she lost, she decided to kill him?" His brown eyes narrowed in disbelief. "There has to be more to it."

"I'm getting there." She shifted photos, handing him the second. "This is my shot of a similar photo hanging in his private office. It used to hang next to the photo taken at the casino, which Adrian removed. Take another look."

"Roberto cropped her out. It only shows him accepting the prize."

"Exactly. Why would he be proud of this award but not want Mariah in the photo?"

Joe shrugged. "He had a big ego. Didn't like sharing the limelight."

"Could you ask Adrian? He knew them both back then. Could he know why?"

"If they didn't get along, why would Roberto help her get a job at ShopTV?" Helen sat back. "Good question."

He tapped open his phone. "I left him a message to call me this morning. I need to tell him Mariah killed his partner. I can ask him then." He studied

Helen's face. "I can see your brain churning. You want to come with me?"

She gave him an innocent roll of the eyes.

Joe stood up and pulled out his wallet. "I'll let you know what time. Remember, you're quiet as a church mouse. You've got nothing to say unless I ask you a direct question."

"I'll bring Jane Marple to slap my wrist."

"Uh-huh. Don't you dare bring that smart-mouthed Agatha. I'll toss her out."

"Why don't I pay for lunch this time?" She made a pout.

Chapter Thirty-Three

J oe called her an hour later. "Adrian and Greg are meeting with me at the studio at four. Harris is holding a press conference at seven during the evening news. We don't have much time. Meet me there."

Helen signed in at security at three forty-four. Joe was right behind her. Security directed them to a meeting room. Spreadsheets covered the conference table. Neither Adrian nor Greg appeared happy to see them.

Adrian stood up. "We already know about Mariah's suicide. It's all over the building." He glowered at the detective. "Frankly, I deserved better. I should have been told first, not through studio gossip."

Joe crossed his arms across his chest. "My apologies. My department's been busy trying to nail down the details."

"So why are we here?" Greg asked, shoving aside a stack of papers. "In fact, why is she here?" He glared at Helen.

"I thought we could go over the events more completely if you were here together. Helen is the one who found Mariah." The two of them sat down across from Adrian and Greg. Joe opened a file folder and showed them Mariah's suicide note.

Greg read it, then pushed it toward Adrian in distaste. "We should have known. We all knew she was wacko."

Joe gritted his teeth. "Wacko or not, she had to have a motive for killing him, which we're missing. A source tells me she was upset with Roberto because he plagiarized her recipes for his newest cookbook. We also knew she was angry he didn't offer her the position of co-chef for his show. You all chose Tara Owens." He stared at the two men. "How angry was she?"

Adrian rolled a black pen back and forth through his fingers. "Very. She was furious. She refused to admit she didn't have the on-air experience. I tried to let her down easy. We told her we'd increase Dana's airtime and have her cover his shows if he couldn't be in town."

"Did she threaten Roberto at the time?"

"She said he owed her," Greg responded.

"She was jealous of his success," Adrian added. "They started in the business at the same time. He took off like a rocket, and she petered out."

"What about her claim he stole her recipes?"

Adam rapped on the tabletop. "That was nonsense. Roberto asked her if she was interested in testing a few. He paid her for her time. They were always his recipes."

"Was there anyone who could have encouraged her anger? Dana, perhaps?"

"Dana!" Greg stood up. "Let's not disrupt my talent lineup any more than it has!"

Joe pursed his lips. "Did you pull those sales numbers comparing Dana and Roberto? I'd like to see them."

Greg shuffled through a stack of printouts while Adrian glared. "Dana's numbers dropped by easily twenty percent the first year Roberto came on-air. This second year, they dropped again by fourteen."

Helen's face blanched. Wow. No wonder Dana was jealous of him. He was cleaning her clock.

The VP stood up and began to pace. "Dana wanted him out of here. He cost her at least two hundred thousand last year."

Adrian spoke in a low tone. "If you told me Dana killed him rather than Mariah, I'd have believed you."

Joe scowled. "Why didn't you say this before?"

Adrian buried his face in his hands. "Because until Mariah killed herself, I thought the Mob was responsible. They were squeezing him to pay off his debts."

"Have they approached you recently?"

He sighed. "Yes. Phone calls. I told them I needed time to sell Riding Cross. I agreed to pay them an additional fifty thousand if they'd give me

200

sixty days to sell it. If it's not sold, I sign over the property and lose it all." His eyes drilled Helen.

She couldn't hold back. "Do you think the note could have come from the Mob or Dana?"

"I don't know. She could have used the note to cast suspicion away from herself," Adrian said.

"One last question." Joe drew out the awards photos. "These two photos are the same with one exception. Mariah was cropped out of the photo hanging in Roberto's office. The one online showed her at the award ceremony. Why would he crop her out?"

"Why would he frame a picture with another chef who competed?" Adrian glared at Helen. "I warned you the first day we met that he was a prima donna."

"Are we done here?" asked Greg.

"Yes, gentleman, we're done." Joe stood up. "Our press conference will be held here at seven."

* * *

Helen watched from home as State's Attorney Scott Harris, in a dark suit, blue-striped tie, and French cuffed white shirt, preened on the wide steps of the studio entrance.

"We are announcing today ShopTV employee. Mariah Manley died by suicide yesterday morning. In a letter to police, she confessed to killing Roberto Barto. It was apparent our Kent County Sheriff's Department was close to her arrest when she did so. We will continue to wrap up this investigation and her motives over the next few days and will provide you with more information when appropriate. Special thanks to our state level office for their close supervision over local law enforcement's efforts to bring the facts of this case to light. Thanks also to ShopTV and their willingness to help with this investigation. Again, we want to extend our sympathies to Mr. Barto's family for their loss."

He looked directly into the news cameras from the temporary podium and offered his big, ingenuous smile. "Any questions?" The press started to call out.

Helen clicked off her television. "Supervision over local law enforcement. What a jerk!" She poured herself a large glass of Sauvignon Blanc and sprawled across a deck chaise to brood.

* * *

About three in the morning, Helen was stumbling around her kitchen in the dark. Mariah's dead eyes, mixed with the State's Attorney's cool ones, kept circulating around her brain. Watson and Trixie traipsed around with her, clearly unhappy she'd disturbed their night. "Sorry, guys. At least you can catch up in the middle of the afternoon." She made herself a cup of her mother's Red Rose tea and defrosted a scone she'd buried in the freezer, taking them out to the deck. Sitting in the dark night, she listened to an old hoot owl perched in a forty-foot-tall oak tree a few yards from her. "You here again? You're supposed to be smart. How about helping me out?" She covered herself with a cotton blanket and fell asleep on the chaise.

Sun fought its way through the morning mist. An osprey screeched down at the water's edge, and Helen jumped a mile. She gave up on any more sleep, washed her face, pulled on shorts and sneakers, and started off down a path through the woods leading to the point. Sometimes she did her best thinking at the lighthouse.

Anyone who'd visited the park knew the lighthouse had sketchy cell service. Helen walked closer to the edge of the cliff and studied the bay. Miles and miles of green-blue water stretched along both sides of the peninsula. White foam from the waves washed over the rocks. It was barely seven am. Helen opened her text messages and pulled up Dana Moore's number.

Dana, it's Helen Morrisey. Any chance we could meet for a quick coffee about ten? Jean's Coffee Pot?Back room. Surprisingly, she texted right back. **Why?** Helen responded, **About Mariah.** There was a long pause. **Ok. Jean's. 10 am.** Helen texted back, **Thank you.** Good job, Helen. Let's hope she tells you the truth. She trotted back down the gravel path to home.

* * *

She called Joe as she drove into town.

"What's up?" He sounded half asleep.

"Could we search around Mariah's house this morning? I've got an idea."

He grunted. "Is it your idea or your club's idea?"

She laughed. "Since you asked, it was Nancy's idea. The rest of them agreed with her."

He grunted again. "I could be there by eight-thirty. Much later, and I'm booked."

"Great. I'll meet you there." She texted Tammi to tell her where she was heading.

Port Anne Isle was quiet with a few parents waiting for a school bus, and a teenager walking his dog. Yesterday's excitement had passed. Sad how quickly people around you move on, she thought. Maybe, it was actually healthy. She glanced down at Andy's ring.

Joe was perched on a railing next to the door talking to Rick on his cell. "Helen's here. See you later."

"You seem perky. Sleep last night?" he asked.

"Actually, I had a terrible night. Finally fell asleep out on the deck and woke up with a stiff neck." She rubbed her neck.

"Would you like a massage?"

"I'm more interested in seeing her house."

He handed her gloves and swung open the door.

She flipped on the lights. "I'm hunting for anything that tells us more about her time at school with Roberto and the contest he won."

They worked through the living room. In the bedroom, he tackled the closets while she rustled through every dresser drawer.

She stood up, pushing her hair off her forehead. "Anything?" Joe shook his head.

They entered the second bedroom. A desk was positioned against a far wall. Above it hung a large bulletin board with photographs forming a border. "Looks like the different sets she created for Dana and Roberto." Newspapers, magazines, and online stories filled the center. *"Roberto Barto Named Best Chef MidAtlantic,"* Helen read aloud. *"Baltimore Welcomes Barto's Latest Restaurant,"* *"Barto Cookbooks Hit 1 Million Copies."* She stared at Joe. "Do you get the idea she was a bit obsessed?"

She dragged her fingers across the board. Barto Winner NYC Best New Chef! Young Chef Wins National Prize! Prize Winner Breaks onto International Scene! Helen sat down at the desk chair. "In every one of these articles, Barto's name was crossed out and Manley written above it. What's that about?"

Joe studied the postings. "Looks to me like winning this contest was important in the restaurant world, and Mariah resented it big time."

"More than that. Something tells me she thought she should have won." Her lips drew tight. "Was she right?"

"I don't know," he said in a low, even voice. "I need to get on the phone to anyone who participated in this contest and find out if they'd heard anything odd about Roberto's win." He pulled out a pen knife from his pocket and began to unhook the bulletin board from the bedroom wall.

"I'm meeting Dana for coffee in half an hour. I wonder if she knows more about this."

* * *

Jean handed Helen a large latte brimming with foam and tilted her head toward the back of the store. Helen could see Dana talking on her phone. She hung up as she approached.

"Dana, thank you very much for meeting me. I know your days are packed." She settled herself into one of Jean's metal bistro chairs.

Dana gave her a tight smile. "It sounded important. Did you hear more about Mariah? I still can't believe she killed herself."

Helen stirred Stevia into her coffee, taking her time. "It is incredibly sad. That's why I asked you here." She raised her eyes at the attractive woman across from her. "I think you know why she might have hated Roberto so much."

Dana kept her eyes on her coffee. "She was furious because he wouldn't consider her as his co-chef. She told me he owed her big time."

"Why? Why did he owe her?"

"He took her recipes?"

Helen sat back, and her tone turned colder. "Dana, get real. She didn't kill him because he plagiarized her recipes. It had to be bigger than that." Dana said nothing. "Can I tell you what I think?"

The woman gave a slight shrug.

"Whether he did or not, Mariah was sure Roberto cheated her in that New York contest years ago. Winning it set him on a course for stardom as a chef and left her to struggle. It opened all kinds of doors for him. Am I right?"

Dana set her spoon on the table. "She mentioned the contest when I first interviewed her as my stylist. I got curious. I dug around, made some phone calls. Then I pressed her on their history. She told me she was leading the contest until the last day. When the judges tasted her final dish, it was sour. Roberto won. She was sure he tainted her food to beat her."

"Did she complain to the judges?"

"They didn't believe her. She couldn't prove it."

Helen studied her. "Why would she kill him now, after all this time?"

"Maybe she couldn't forgive him. Setting up his shows and cleaning up afterwards sent her over the edge. She decided to press him for money, but he refused to pay."

"Here's my theory." Helen's green eyes traveled from left to right and back to focus on Dana. The shop was noisy with chatter. "You heard rumors Roberto owed the Mob. You stoked her fury to add to his worries. Did you write out the note for her and suggest she plant it in his kitchen drawer? Did you tell her she'd enjoy making him sweat?"

"Don't be ridiculous."

"The police are assessing your handwriting on the notecard you gave to Lizzie and the card from Mariah. They'll match, won't they?"

Dana's voice faltered. "She wanted to scare him into paying her. I suggested the threat. I never dreamed she'd go crazy and decide to kill him. It was supposed to be a prank."

Helen sipped up her coffee, then licked her lips. "I'd like to believe you. But in the end, you regained your number one status with the network and got rid of Roberto as your competition. You're not really worried about Tara outranking you. She's a pebble in your shoe. Reminds me of a case where a girlfriend bullied her boyfriend into killing himself. All in all, not a bad outcome." She pushed back her chair.

The star glared up at her. "I thought her threat would help her get restitution. I'm not responsible for her going over the edge. Killing Roberto and herself was on her and her alone."

Helen studied her stony face. "Thank you for your time. I really appreciate it." Picking up her bag, she left Dana staring at the tabletop.

Chapter Thirty-Four

"Joe, were you trying to reach me?"

"I thought you should know. Another real estate agent was attacked this morning. She's in Kent Hospital."

"My God. Will she be okay?"

"She was beat up pretty badly, and her jewelry and car were stolen. She might have a broken arm."

She swallowed. "You need to find this creep before someone's killed."

"I know. This is the exact same MO. Took her car, jewelry, credit cards. Looks like we've got a serial thief on our hands."

"I'm feeling guilty. I haven't called our local board and offered to help with publicity for safety awareness."

"I'd say you've had a lot on your plate," he defended.

"Do you think I could visit this agent? I understand how frightening it is."

His police radio crackled behind him. "Not a bad idea. I'd have to check with her family first. I'll let you know."

"Thank you." She changed gears. "I had an informative conversation with Dana. Mariah was convinced Roberto had cheated her in the New York contest. She believed he tainted her recipe in the finals to win first place. This contest was no small deal. It skyrocketed him onto the national chef scene. She blamed him for her financial struggles. Kind of fitting she poisoned his recipe to kill him. Tit for tat." She stopped. "Are you ready for this? Dana admitted she wrote the threatening note Mariah said she found in the kitchen. Dana said it was a prank. She never expected Mariah to turn violent."

"That's quite a statement. I could haul her in for obstructing an investigation. I won't because it isn't worth my time. It explains why Mariah killed him."

"I can't help but wonder if Mariah didn't really mean to kill him. That it was a prank."

"Any progress on checking with past students at Culinary Institute?"

"Rick's working on it now. If we confirm the contest story, we'll have proof of her motive."

"I agree. I need to run. Have a showing with new clients this afternoon. I do work on commission, you know?"

"I'm not stopping you. It's those snoops you listen to that are slowing you down."

"You're jealous. You wish you had all their talent working for you. Not my fault you're stuck with an egomaniac State's Attorney." She laughed and hung up.

* * *

A week of heavy air and temperatures in the nineties broke. Helen practically skipped along the docks at Port Anne Yacht Club and out to the finger pier. Pete had tied his boat up to the transient dock and was waiting.

"Hi," he called, jumping down from the stern, and taking her sail bag from her arm. "We timed this perfectly. Look at the wind picking up!" His light hair tousled in the wind, and his grey eyes matched his blue-grey polo shirt.

Helen laughed as he gave her a hand up onto the boat's deck. "I can't believe it, after all this heat and humidity."

"What's all this?" He peeked into the tote.

"Sandwiches for lunch. My favorite Manchego cheese and Di Bruno flatbread for a little later. I'm assuming you brought drinks?"

"Fully stocked. Give me a hand, and we'll shove off." He unwound his stern lines, and Helen jockeyed the sloop's bow around a piling. They turned south toward the open bay.

Pete grinned. "I'm not used to having a woman on board who knows their way around a sailboat."

"You'd have to thank Andy. We started sailing on our honeymoon with a Sunfish. I'd forgotten how beautiful your boat is," Helen admired the long sleek hull and bleach-white sails. She tugged her navy sailing cap over her dark hair and flashed a broad smile.

With long arms, Pete reached over to crank in a winch and tighten the jib. He glanced at Helen with her bright green eyes, her face pink. "I'd forgotten how beautiful you are."

"Your eyesight has degraded over the years." She waved him away and turned to watch their progress as they cut across the wake of a nearby powerboat.

With the main and jib raised, they chose their tack and sat back, relaxed in the warm sun.

"Any activity on your big property?"

"Riding Cross? It's had three good showings during the first ten days, so I'm happy. Let's hope Adrian doesn't fire me before an offer comes in. I'm showing it myself tomorrow at noon. Buyer responded to a luxury website."

"Really?" Pete reached for his drink. "Where are they from?"

"Switzerland. The wife is an executive with a pharmaceutical there. I haven't dealt with an international investor in a long while."

"Now you're talking my business. I'm on the legal end of multi-currency investors. It's a fancy word for moving funds country to country to purchase property."

"Any kind of property?"

Pete tugged on the main. "Depends upon the country. Could be residential. Could be commercial. It's not that complicated in most cases. Given Barto Enterprises's expansion, I wonder if they would have opened up in Europe if Roberto was alive."

"If I wanted to buy a house in Spain or Italy, what would I need to do it legally?"

"In most countries, you need to apply for a residence permit as a foreign national. Money-wise, cash is the easiest, of course. Often, the buyer takes monies from self-directed IRAs. Perfectly legal. If they need more, they can borrow on lines of credit here to use there. Not much different than buying a property in the states."

"Got it."

"Any more on your chef? I saw the press conference about Mariah Manley. Why'd she kill him?"

"They met in New York at the Culinary Institute. She was convinced he cheated her in a national restaurant competition and ruined her professional life. There's a lot of people at the network in shock. No one but Joe's squad knows about the contest issue. Keep it under your hat."

He shook his head. "Amazing what people do. Are they any closer to catching your attacker?"

Helen shrugged. "Still tracking him down."

"Probably not hard for anyone to hire a low life who wants to make extra money. Finding them can't be easy unless someone turns him in." He paused. "Let's throw anchor in a cove. We can have lunch and swim."

"Thought you'd never suggest it!" She jumped up and climbed below into the galley. "Want another drink?"

* * *

The sun was low as they pulled back into the little club harbor, sunburnt and still damp.

They tied up and sat on the rail's edge to watch a glorious sunset. Pete reached over and slipped his arm around her shoulders. "How likely is it Riding Cross goes for the asking price?"

Helen studied his face. "Adrian needs to sell it badly. He'd listen to a decent offer. Why?"

He inhaled. "I've been thinking about buying here. I love the water and the house's location. And it's only an hour into Philly and my office. It has another big plus. We'd be able to see each other, a lot. What would you say about that?"

Her eyes widened, and she let out a nervous chuckle. "That's a huge investment." She reached down and examined the silver chain and ring on her neck. "As your Realtor, I'd say buy Riding Cross because it's a beautiful property and a sound investment. As your long-time friend, I'd say don't buy it because of me. I'm barely putting my toe in this whole dating pool thing. I don't even know if I'm ready to swim."

"Is the cop part of the pool?"

"His name is Joe." She gave a little smile. "He's definitely part of it."

"That's okay," he smiled. "I'm not afraid of competition." He leaned in to kiss her. She pulled back and squeezed his arm.

"It's been a great day. Thank you. Time for me to head for home."

Chapter Thirty-Five

Adrian called her early the following morning.

"Helen, we need to talk." Tension reverberated over the phone. "I had a visitor last night. About two am. Bottom line, I'm out of time. You're out of time. I either have a buyer in the next three days, or I sign over Riding Cross to an investor."

"An investor?" She wasn't getting it.

"*The* investor." His frustration jumped an octave. "I sign it over for a million four hundred and move out, or they take me out and dump me into the bay. They'll put it back on the market for easily three and pocket the difference."

She sat at the desk in her home office and stared at the water. She gulped. "I'll get on the phone with our best shot, the couple I met earlier this week. I'm sorry, Adrian. I feel terrible you've been forced into this situation."

"You and me both. Roberto was burying us, but I thought we could dig ourselves out in time."

"How about the business? The restaurants?"

"No, thank God. They're not in immediate danger. The house will cover all his gambling debts."

She put in three calls to buyer agents, then dialed Joe.

"Made some progress," he said. "We've confirmed Mariah made a complaint with the institute's judges about their contest results. Of course, it's been almost ten years, and memories are a little fuzzy. They chose not to believe her. She had no proof, and he was already being wooed by half the restaurants in the city. The school had no interest in perpetuating a

212

scandal."

"Sounds like they had a lot in common with Adrian. He had a visitor late last night. He has three days to sign over the house or pay up. He's desperate to keep this out of the public eye and protect his company's reputation. I don't know if I can help him. There's so little time."

"Not the first time the Mob takes over a property by offering hard money loans gamblers can't cover. They claim the property for peanuts, then sell it and recoup the debt plus a big profit on top. I'm curious. Is Barto Enterprises doing well with Tara Moore as the chef's replacement?"

"According to Lizzie, they're holding their own. Dana definitely benefited. Her numbers have turned around. Greg's good with the higher-ups at the studio."

Helen's cell buzzed. "Hang on, Pete's calling me." Ten seconds later, she was back. It's a long shot, but I might have a buyer for Adrian from Switzerland. I asked Pete about residence permits for people wanting to buy in the U.S. and Americans who want to buy internationally." Helen could swear she could hear Joe grinding his teeth. "His law firm deals with international banking."

"Cut to the chase. What did he say?"

She inhaled. "On a whim, he did an unofficial search on the Swiss buyers interested in Riding Cross and anyone else connected to ShopTV or the restaurant operation. Greg, Dana, Neal, everyone. Guess whose name popped up?"

"Tell me."

"Adrian Costello. Nine months ago, he purchased a property on the Fiji Islands for two million."

The detective let out a low whistle.

"Mariah may be Roberto's killer, but I keep thinking there's something more to this story."

"There's nothing wrong with his partner investing in his own property. Partners do it all the time all over the world. Adrian could be building a cushion in case Barto Enterprises imploded."

She drummed her hands on her desk. "I might have done the same thing.

Protect myself by moving my investments where Roberto couldn't borrow against them."

"Can Pete provide us with this list?"

"He asked me to come up to Philly. He doesn't want to provide anything in writing. We can run over the reports. They can help you fast-track your own squad's searches."

Joe grunted. "I don't like it."

"Would you rather have to go to Scott Harris and ask him for the staff power?"

"I'll have to eventually get him involved."

She waited. "This is your chance to lay the groundwork."

"It's likely Adrian's investments were completely legal."

Helen could practically hear the wheels turning round in his head.

"Arrange a meeting with Pete, and we'll drive up together. Get back to me."

"Call you back." Helen stood up and walked out to the edge of her deck. If Adrian learned she dug up his investment, she'd be fired, guaranteed. Helen leaned on the rail, her cheeks in her palms. Given she had three days to get a buyer to sign on the dotted line, it wouldn't matter. Her reputation would drop like a rock, and, with client confidentiality, there'd be nothing she could do to defend it publicly.

* * *

By eleven the next morning, they were speeding north on Interstate 95 along the Delaware Bay and into the city. Views of billboards and sports stadiums converted to restaurants tucked along cobbled streets. Their pace slowed to a crawl down the narrow, historic streets of Philadelphia's exclusive Rittenhouse Square section. Revolutionary War era horse-drawn carriages stopped and started in front of them. Cabs halted and honked to pick up riders, and businesspeople scurried across crosswalks as police officers directed traffic. Clumps of tourists with enraptured expressions and clicking cameras listened to guides describe the birth of a nation. They spotted signs for a private garage and Pete's brick and corniced building. A uniformed door greeter opened double glass doors, and they signed in with the condominium's security.

Pete greeted them on the ninth floor. He kissed Helen on the cheek.

"Thanks for driving up. Hope the traffic wasn't too bad," he said, offering a hand to the detective. The two men exchanged handshakes. Helen wondered who squeezed the hardest. She could sense the testosterone exchanging.

"Pete, I'd never been in this condo. When did you move here?" admired Helen, taking in the high ceilings, glossy floors, and charming, leaf-filled view of the square below.

"Do you like it?" He beamed.

"What's not to like? You're front and center in the heart of the city." Helen surveyed the tall bookshelves flanking one wall and the contemporary kitchen on the opposite.

"I bought it after my divorce about six years ago." He rocked on his heels, pleased with her reaction.

"It's gorgeous. Are you sure you'd really want to give up city life to live in quiet little Port Anne?" As soon as the words slipped out, Helen bit her lip hard. She stole a furtive peek at Joe.

"I'd say they each have their attractions," the attorney tossed off as he handed her iced tea in a leaded glass. "Joe, didn't I hear you lived in Baltimore before moving to Kent County? I'm sure you enjoyed the city life while you were there."

"I did. Lived in Fells Point. It was a nice little neighborhood, though certainly not Rittenhouse Square." Joe cleared his throat. "Shall we get started?" He pulled out a pad.

They left the city hours later with more questions for Adrian.

* * *

"You will not believe what happened today!" Lizzie was sitting across from her mother in the Port Anne Yacht Club's dining room that evening, her blue eyes flashing.

Helen raised her eyebrows.

"Adrian walked in on Greg and Tara."

"Walked in on what?"

"What do you think?" Lizzie exclaimed. "He was furious. I was standing outside talking to one of the hand models. He started shouting at Greg, 'Did we hire Tara because you wanted to get in her pants?'"

Helen touched her index finger to her lips. "Keep your voice down."

Lizzie whispered under her breath. "Word spread all over the building." She took a bite of her salad. "Since we're talking about romance, did you have a fun afternoon on Pete's boat?"

Helen made a little wince. "It was wonderful. We had a great time. His boat is beautiful."

Her daughter rolled her eyes at her mother. "I'm sure it is. Seems to me, Pete's pretty gorgeous too. When he'd stop by our house to visit with you and Dad, all my friends would drool. Can you be a little more specific?"

"What is this, Nancy? Digging for dirt? He's very nice. Very handsome. A gentleman." Helen rearranged her utensils on the table. "He asked me what I'd think if he put in an offer on Adrian's house."

Lizzie dropped her fork. "No way." She glanced across the room and lowered her tone to a croak. "No way. What did you say?"

"I told him it would be a great investment but don't do it for me. I wasn't ready."

Lizzie leaned back and groaned. "You didn't. You've got to let go of the Jessica attitude and be more like Agatha. Have some fun."

"Agatha usually gets burned. She's not the best at picking good men, and she's had a string of husbands," Helen mused.

"Does Joe know?" Her daughter made an exasperated face.

"I let it slip. He was shooting daggers."

"Maybe it's what he needs," Lizzie prodded.

"His level of interest isn't the problem. I'm the problem."

Her daughter chewed. "You need a good man in your life."

"Do I? I'm not sure about that."

"You have two of them interested. Stop trying to chase bad guys and pay attention to your own life. Pay attention to the good guys."

Helen didn't answer.

Lizzie pressed on. "You wouldn't have to traipse around with picky buyers if Pete was around. You could turn down creepy houses with smelly basements."

"That's for sure."

"You wouldn't have to worry about cooking."

"Why's that?"

"He'd probably have you out at the best restaurants in Philly every night."

Helen studied her wine glass. "Hmmm. Interesting point. You'd stop giving me eggplant-colored frying pans and expecting me to use them."

Lizzie tilted her head to the side and grinned. "Decide now, and I'll cancel my order for your Instant Pot. They're expensive."

Chapter Thirty-Six

Watson and Trixie were sitting on the windowsill watching for her arrival as Helen unlocked her front door the following night. She tossed down her tote and kicked off her shoes. She was feeling sorry for herself. She'd officially pulled Adrian's house off the market, and rumors were flying. When she'd stopped for coffee, Jean told her someone said Helen was fired because she'd focused on playing detective instead of concentrating on selling her client's house. Adrian wasn't returning her phone calls or texts, sure she was the cause of the police questioning his Fiji purchase. He was right.

Lizzie called her earlier. Greg had torn into her, threatening to reduce her airtime if she didn't get her mother to back off on her probing into Barto Enterprises. Roberto's killer had been found, and he, Tara, and Adrian were launching Barto products like the Flying Pan with a new approach. The tension between Tara and Lizzie was obvious, and they struggled to keep it off the network airwaves. Their show this morning had tanked. The network expected round-the-clock 'best buds' chatter. Greg's last words to her were 'work it out!'"

Pete went silent as a source for more information. She totally understood his caution. One positive, he suggested dinner next weekend.

Lighting candles and turning on music, she wandered from room to room. After pouring a glass of white wine, she changed into pajamas. She served Watson and Trixie their tuna to quiet their pleas. About eight, she started to root through her kitchen pantry for something easy to cook. All these discussions about chefs and good food made the two frozen, low-calorie dinners and a package of uncooked chicken waiting in a bare refrigerator even less appealing than usual. Her cell pinged a new text. My third credit card notice this week. Shouldn't my fraud issues have caught up with the cancellations I filed? Damn, damn, damn.

Roberto's handsome face on the shiny cover of his cookbook stared up from her coffee table. It was waiting to be wrapped. She wanted to drop it off to Olivia this week. She fanned the pages for something easy to cook. 'I know, Agatha. It's very uncharacteristic of us, isn't it?' She turned back to the title page with Roberto's flourish of a signature. Definitely the artist, she thought regretfully. She gazed across the empty kitchen.

She set Olivia's copy aside and pulled out her own. As little as her few cookbooks were put to use, she seemed to dribble any rare drops of butter and oil possible. At the title page, she hesitated. With careful fingers, she traced the autograph, one letter after the other. She shifted the book under the ship lanterns hanging over her island and turned up the beams to their brightest. Her stomach twinged and not from hunger. Reaching for Olivia's, she returned to the title page and set it side by side with hers. How was it both signatures appeared identical? Was that normal?

Her eyes traveled over to her bookcases, seeking two books autographed by the same author. Pulling books out one by one, she landed on two mysteries signed at a book fair last spring. Turning to one title page, then turning to the second, she set them next to each other in the light. Two autographs, similar, but different. One slightly bolder and the second, the same last name written with a sharper slant.

With Nora's prodding, Helen poured herself another glass of wine and began to pace. What do I really know about authors' signatures? Not a lot, she admitted. Opening her laptop, she Googled a search about autographs.

"Well," she declared to her cats. They both raised their heads, their ears twitching. Now she knew how Adrian supplied more signed copies to Calli's shop. Some authors used a device called an autopen which duplicated their signature. Some books could have been signed before Roberto's death and the newest, signed with an autopen. Fans never knew which they received. Reminded her of actors' photographs sent to fans. A perfectly legitimate business practice. Another dead end. She snapped shut his cookbooks, disgusted.

Four in the morning, she smelled smoke. She bolted upright, blinking in the pitch dark. Agatha puffed on a cigarette at the bottom of her bed. Nora, dressed in 1930's satin pajamas, painted her nails. Jane raised her head from her knitting and slowly fastened her clear blue eyes on Helen. Nancy and Jessica gave her expectant stares. 'What in the world do you all want from me?' Exasperated, she threw back the covers and marched into the bathroom for Tylenol and water. She reprimanded her exhausted image in the mirror. 'I drank too much wine last night.'

* * *

Tammi caught her as she jogged to the lighthouse, her voice coming in and out with the weak cell service.

"I'm sorry I let you down," Helen lamented. "I hoped the sale of Riding Cross might free up a nice vacation for you."

"Don't rub it in. Would have been a nice cushion for both of us," her assistant ruminated. "You'll just have to dig up another big fish for us."

"Ha! They don't come along very often. Back to the salt mines." She puffed into the phone as she moved up the trail. "Heard any new gossip around town?"

"Everything from Adrian's restaurants in trouble to you being too much of a snoop. Someone said you need a new slogan."

"Oh? I'm all ears. We've been trying to think of one."

"They said you should call yourself 'not the typical Realtor.'"

Helen groaned. "So now people think I'm crazy."

"We already know you're crazy. We've just been trying to hide it. Are you coming into the office?"

"I guess I don't have a choice. Otherwise, everyone will say I'm hiding out in embarrassment."

"They'll move on with the next piece of local gossip," Tammi philosophized.

"Want to know Jane Marple's philosophy? She says the trouble with gossip is you're never quite sure where it started."

Tammi grunted. "You need a fresh injection of Jessica's persistence."

They hung up. Helen reached a concrete bench next to the lighthouse. She stuck her legs out in front of her and raised her face to the warm sun. 'How could I ever do without Tammi? She's the best. She's right about persistence. This gossip could kill my business if I let it. It's up to me to stop it cold, and quickly.'

* * *

Helen stopped in at Calli's shop on the way into Safe Harbor.

"Hi! Hope you don't mind. I wanted to take a peek at your copies of Roberto's cookbooks. Do you have any of the first two he wrote?"

Calli shuffled through the stacks and pulled out two different covers. "What are you up to?"

She flipped inside and studied the autographs. "I'd like to snap photos of the title pages."

"Of course." The shopkeeper turned to another customer. "Help yourself."

* * *

From Safe Harbor, she texted Joe. **Got any time for me today?**

In office, he responded. **Meeting plumber at my house at 3. Hot water heater leaking.**

She hesitated. **If I bring sandwiches, could I stop by? Or am I rude?** She pasted in a Bitmoji of her lying on the floor in despair. She waited.

Sure. 302 Old Forge Lane. Carriage house before big farmhouse.

She texted back a smiley face.

"Tammi, got a minute?"

"Sure, you need something?" The young woman stuck her head in the door. Labor Day weekend was coming up. She was wearing red, white, and blue earrings glistening with large rhinestones.

"Check these out." Helen pointed at her laptop screen with a bent Twizzler she'd pulled out of her desk drawer.

"What am I looking for?"

"Here are four signatures on Olivia's listing agreement and two on her disclosures. What do you notice?" She sat back and watched her assistant's expression as her eyes traveled from image to image.

She shrugged. "They seem complete to me. I don't see anything missing."

"Would you assume she signed all of them?"

"Yes."

"Would you think it odd each signature is different?"

Tammi looked puzzled. "No. They're all similar enough. My signature never appears exactly the same. Depends on what I'm signing. Or where I am when I sign it."

"Exactly." Helen gave a self-satisfied nod.

"Are you suggesting Olivia didn't sign all these documents?"

"Oh, no. She definitely signed them all."

"What's your point?"

Helen shut down the screen. "Just thinking. Thanks for your help. I'm heading over to Joe's house." She tossed two more Twizzlers into her purse.

"Is that lunch?"

"Don't start. I'll call you tomorrow morning."

"Wait. You're going to his house? That's a new twist. You never told me, how was the sail with Pete?"

Helen laughed. "Sailing with Pete went great. This stop is strictly business."

* * *

Jamestown was a little whistle stop, a few minutes north of Port Anne, and squarely in the midst of Far Hill, known for its horse farms and equestrian competitions. It had a single intersection with a stop sign. A church, now housing a historical society, had served as a school during the 1700s. A white clapboard building, originally the Old Jamestown Store and now an antique shop, sat on another corner with a post office long closed. A potter's field of a hundred unmarked graves ceased operating in the 1950s.

Over the past few years, the land began to attract out-of-the-area builders and exploded with high-end new residential construction. When she asked him last spring where he lived, he'd described his house as a cottage subdivided from its original farm. Being the nosy Realtor she was, Helen checked her multiple listing service before she left the office. It was a carriage house, and he bought it three years ago at a pretty penny. Interesting.

She slowed at a wooden sign set into a grey stone column marking the private drive and turned onto a neat, graveled road about a quarter of a mile long. A Victorian farmhouse came into view first, ornamented with a tall, peaked roof, a turret, and a wide, turn-railed porch. The road split off to the north, gave the house a wide birth, and led up to Joe's. She spotted his black four-by-four and parked.

As was typical, the carriage house was almost as large as the main house, mirroring the architecture with a steep roof, dormer windows, and elaborate scrollwork. With three large wooden doors that could accommodate carriages, horse stables, and equipment, she guessed it's second story used to board staff years ago.

He walked out to greet her in a grey polo shirt and cargo shorts with Rocky happily encircling her as his greeting.

"I'm glad to see you came dressed for the country," he said, pointing at her cotton sweater, jeans, and sandals. He took her laptop from under her arm.

"I'm so short on sleep, I couldn't face putting work clothes on today." She shaded her eyes with her hands and gazed up at the roofline. "You told me you'd bought a cottage. This is more like a barn. What's the history?"

Joe pointed her way through the main doorway. "Came across it four years ago. It's one of the reasons why I decided to leave Baltimore State Troopers. The seller replaced the electrical, plumbing and put on a new roof. I got to finish the inside the way I wanted."

Helen stood back, studying the room layout with living room, kitchen, and eating area open to each other. "No walls."

"I installed the iron staircase up the center. The original was in bad shape. There's two bedrooms and two bathrooms. Used to be a loft and a bunkhouse for farm hands."

She ran her fingertips across the concrete kitchen countertops. The cabinets were made of warm pine. An oversized Viking gas range with big red knobs sat under a stainless range hood. Wood beams pointed toward the loft ceiling.

"Do you use this stove?" Her head jerked back. "It's serious equipment."

He laughed. "Don't be so shocked. Just because I eat pizza at your house doesn't mean I don't like to cook. I just don't get a lot of time to experiment. Too many late nights eating in my car." He gave a resigned shrug.

"Now I'm really embarrassed. Who picked out your furniture? You told me you didn't like women who rearranged your stuff. Did you choose this?" Helen rubbed her hands across a huge, dark brown, leather-tufted couch in front of the stone, open-hearth fireplace.

He handed her a light beer and opened one for himself. "I hate picking furniture and once it's broken in, I never like to replace it. An ex-girlfriend helped me choose this."

"She certainly had good taste." She sank into the sofa and sighed. "Here I pictured you living in a one-bedroom farm cottage with a microwave and a coffee pot."

"Why? Because Robert B. Parker's detective Jesse Stone lives in a decrepit house out on a peninsula with hand-me-downs abandoned by the past tenant? Do I also have to drink twelve-year-old scotch in a bar glass brought from my previous life like him?"

Helen laughed. "You do read mysteries!"

"Of course I do. You've got me reading *Murder in the Vicarage* right now."

"One of my favorites. It's why I got thinking about how chaos helps murderers. You should study Jane's description of the vicarage parlor scene. Lots of people passing around drinks."

"I'm glad you don't decorate like Jane. Too many teacups." He raised his eyebrows at her. "Remember, I have three older sisters checking on me. They like to ship off my nieces and nephews for a few weeks every summer. Kids today are used to conveniences."

"That's for sure," Helen grinned. "Show me your workspace."

He pointed to an oversized oak desk and a worn leather office chair in the corner. Black and white photographs of the Adirondacks were on the long wall in front of it. He pointed out some photos of an old townhouse. "That was my place in Baltimore. It was a pit when I bought it."

"Looks great." Helen's eyes grazed across certificates and diplomas tied into law enforcement, and three shiny commendations lined up next to each other from the Maryland State Police. Above them, a wide navy ribbon hanging from a gilded gold emblem shone from behind the glass. The words "For extraordinary valor in the face of imminent danger" was engraved below. She turned to him. "You were awarded a Governor's Citation and Medal? Why haven't you ever mentioned it to me? That's amazing." She touched his arm. "What happened?"

The detective shrugged. "Another time. Let's break out those sandwiches, and you can tell me what's bothering you." He started pulling plates and napkins from cabinets. "Hungry?"

"Stupid question."

They finished chomping on chips while she opened her laptop and showed him her images of Olivia's signed agreement pages. She pointed out the variations from signature to signature.

"I don't know if any of this is relevant," she started. "I've realized Roberto didn't always autograph his books. Some of them, probably a lot of them, were signed using an autopen."

Joe frowned. "Excuse me?"

"I never knew they existed until last night. The machines are expensive. Big-time authors and actors, and musicians use them to sign photos and posters for fans. It's also legal."

"What got you going down this rabbit hole?"

"After my credit cards were stolen, I had to cancel them. I kept getting notices asking if I'd used them for purchases across the country. It's amazing how fast thieves reuse those cards. Made me think about whether it's possible someone, Adrian or Greg or even Dana, could have used Roberto's autopen machine to sign documents he didn't know they were signing."

"If we want to prosecute someone for forgery, we have to prove one of two things. We have to prove the perpetrator signed for Roberto without his consent, or we'd have to prove they had intent to trick him. I'm assuming Adrian had consent for all kinds of business documents. Be tough to prove otherwise."

"I agree. But why was the company so short of cash? It sounds to me like someone was taking money they shouldn't have."

He stretched out on his couch. "We don't have any proof."

"I think we can find it," she insisted.

"I don't know how. Every time Roberto and Adrian wrote checks, they were paying themselves, or bought goods and services needed to run their business. We even grilled Neal on expenses for their restaurants. Nothing was out of line."

"What are you saying?"

"I'm saying Mariah killed Roberto. Your question is whether someone encouraged her hate and resentment. Drove her to it. If they did, it would be extremely hard to prove it."

She gave a huge sigh of resignation. "My brain is fried. Even my chums are exhausted. Why don't you show me the rest of your house and walk your property before it's too dark? I need to head home."

"Come on." He grabbed her wrist and pulled her to her feet. "I'll show you the rest of the house." They climbed the iron stairs, and she poked her head into the two bedrooms. "Love the colors. Are you sure you chose these on your own?"

He lifted his hands, his expression sheepish. "I told you. I have four sisters."

"And an ex-girlfriend," she said, fluttering her lashes.

"It's almost six. Let's have a drink on the patio before you leave." He brought out a vodka tonic for her and a bourbon for him. She gazed over the hillside.

"This is lovely. I'm happy for you. Here I thought you were such a rolling stone." Twilight took over. Helen slumped into her chair and closed her eyes.

She woke up two hours later on the couch, a blanket tucked around her. The house lights were dim. She tiptoed up the stairs to find Joe sprawled across his bed, snoring. She scrawled a note and left it on his kitchen counter.

CHAPTER THIRTY-SIX

"Thanks for the nap. Talk tomorrow."

Chapter Thirty-Seven

On the way home to Osprey Point, she detoured down the drive of Riding Cross. She couldn't help herself. Adrian had told Joe he'd be in Baltimore for the night. The big house was dark and quiet, its roofline hulking in the moonlight. The bay was quiet, the water shimmering at a distance. Helen quietly crept down the drive to the front door, powered open her windows, and turned off her engine. The silence was interrupted by the squawk of geese down near the docks. The air smelled fresh.

'What do I do?' Her gut told her this was her last chance. She had to check on Adrian's records one more time. Silently, she slipped out of her car and crept toward the front door. Automatic sensors turned on flood lights. She punched in the security code, and the latch released with a metal snap. She slid beyond the entranceway and silently closed the door behind her. How would she explain her entry at this time of night? 'You'll be gone before he's back,' Nancy told her.

She turned on her flashlight on her phone and ran it around the perimeter of the wide front hall. The house seemed larger than ever, cavernous. This was fruitless, she said to herself. If Adrian cheated Roberto, he could hide his records anywhere.

She moved into the first-floor office and searched again. No papers, no transfers, no autopen. She headed up to Roberto's study and then Adrian's bedroom. Quickly, she surveyed the room. His suitcase was on the bed, half full. Fiji? She spotted a ring of keys on his dresser and stashed them in her pocket.

Edging her way back down the stairs, she hesitated at the bottom. She bit her lip to keep them from quivering. She crept down the next stairway to the lower level, her feet soundless on the deep carpet.

Six plush recliners faced a wall-to-wall television screen. "The only thing we're missing is the popcorn," she muttered to herself. She flipped on the lights and glanced around. 'Let's check the wine cellar,' her squad of sleuths urged her. She crossed the room. Pulling out Adrian's ring of keys, she inserted them one by one until the lock on the barn-style door gave way. She opened the door, felt her way down the wall, and flipped a light switch. Bathed in soft light, Roberto's bar glasses glistened against the dark woodwork.

Everything seemed perfectly normal. She swallowed, then tugged on the far door leading to the root cellar. It was as she expected, locked.

Her eyes traveled around the room and back to the door. She fingered the mass of keys from her pocket and tried each one. No, no, no. Her hands shook. Sweat gathered around her armpits. No, no, no, click! Time was ticking. You need to leave, she groaned aloud. The lock slid open. Whew.

Scanning the completely dark room, she spotted a light switch. A light switch in a root cellar?

Helen switched off her cell light to save battery. The room was about fifteen by fifteen with a low ceiling. Goosebumps ran up her arms. The temperature felt chilled. On a far wall, she spotted a thermostat like the one in the wine cellar. 'I'll be damned.'

In the center of the room was a long stainless steel-topped island with overhead lights bright enough to be an operating room. She pulled open a small under-counter refrigerator. Loaded with test tubes and Petri dishes. Some full, some almost empty. Jane had no comment. This was not her expertise. Nora peered over her shoulder. She was a pro at mixology and was delighted to offer her opinion. 'No, Nora, this isn't the right time to mix up a Manhattan,' Helen reprimanded. Her body made a little shiver.

Why did Roberto and Adrian have this room? It mimicked a chemistry laboratory. Her body made another little shiver. Roberto was the chef. He had two beautiful kitchens. This must be Adrian's passion, since he was the chemist who invented the organic coating for their Flying Pans. Perhaps he wanted his own private space to continue experiments on new products. The concrete walls, different from the dirt basement where she'd been attacked, were coated with fresh plaster and painted. The flooring was laminate planking, much like the wine cellar.

Computer printouts and invoices from suppliers and contractors were stacked on a metal desk in the corner. She sat down and flipped through them, careful to keep them in the same order. Taylor Lumber stood out. The first was an invoice for $17,400. The next one requested another $4,750. She ran her fingers down a list of items which added up to correct balances on each. Most of the items were similar, if not identical. Only the quantities changed. "Made perfect sense," she muttered to herself. Each shipment would vary depending on orders needed each week. Instinct told her to snap some photos.

When the police interviewed Adrian and reviewed the company's finances, he said both he and Roberto had to sign all checks leaving the company. They also didn't use check stamps as their signatures. She sorted further down on the pile and found two invoices from another lumberyard, Augustino, with an address of Upper Ferry. She turned to another invoice from a third yard outside of Baltimore. 'That's interesting. I guess they didn't order all their materials from Dottie Taylor like she hoped.'

Pebbled black three-ring binders, each labeled with the year, stood neatly on a shelf above the desk. Helen pulled the latest one and flipped to printouts listing all the vendors alphabetically. She saw Taylor and Augustino listed. She spotted a well-known plumbing supplier on the list. A few spaces down were three more plumbing suppliers. She stopped. She wondered why Barto Enterprises liked using multiple companies to provide the same services. She would think they would have gotten better pricing if they were loyal to one.

She recognized Adrian's handwriting down the pages, neat and tight. He'd checked off each of their payments. 'Writes like a trained scientist. Reminds me of my teachers in college chemistry classes,' she grimaced. 'I hated those classes. I was completely out of my element. I scraped through with a 'C' and never looked back. Give me literature or business any day.'

She studied the name of the lumberyard in Upper Ferry again. Jessica leaned over her shoulder. 'Look them up,' she suggested. Helen pulled her cell out of her pocket and Googled Decoro Lumber. The company description popped up. Hmmm. She studied the list and searched for the three plumbing companies. The first and second came up immediately. The third name was off by two letters. She inputted the name Augustino Lumber. Nothing came up.

She rubbed her temples and stared at the search bar. How could that be? How likely was it Barto was paying invoices for not one but two companies, one plumbing, one electrical, who didn't show up on an online search? She sat down and stared at the cabinet in front of her. The wheels were spinning. Could Adrian be processing bills for fake companies and pocketing the payments? It had to represent thousands and thousands of dollars.

Both partners had to sign all the checks. Could Roberto not have seen these invoices? Did Adrian sign the chef's signature on all the checks intended for these fake companies? Had Roberto discovered Adrian in a forgery scheme? Her head spun. Her heart pounded.

She stood up and moved to a metal cabinet hung in the third corner of the room. Varying-sized bottles and flasks were lined up in neat order from small to large. With shaky hands, Helen reached out and touched a tube in the last row. These were different from the rest of the laboratory glassware. There were only two, both about three inches high, with green rubber stoppers slitted at their tops. She almost dropped one when she recognized them. They were not test tubes. They were used for transporting and preserving live flowers. She gasped.

The shock sent a red flush from her chest, up to her cheeks, and out to her fingertips. Adrian was the one who extracted the Daphne poisonous liquid and put it into the flower tubes delivered by Mariah to the studio! They must have worked together.

Returning to the invoices, she spotted four from Mariah. All paid. A file cabinet to the right held invoices by the name of the recipient. She pulled out a folder on Mariah. Her normal fees for shows were there, going back eighteen months. The fees charged the last six months had jumped by thirty percent. Notations on the invoices said *Consulting.* Why?

Helen sat back and stared at the stone walls. Did Adrian pay her to help him eliminate his partner? Did he realize she was angry and vengeful and had easy access to the set? She may have considered killing Roberto. Being offered money to do it by Adrian would only sweeten the pie for her. He found a way to kill Roberto before he discovered why money was so tight, far beyond his personal gambling debts. With Mariah's help, he styled a perfect murder while avoiding the murder scene.

Helen touched open her cell for the time. It was eleven twenty-six. 'You must find the autopen device,' hissed Agatha. Her exhaustion from earlier was gone, replaced with pure pumping adrenaline.

She pulled a chair over and stood on it to reach the highest shelf. Stretching forward, she shifted a box of folders aside and ran her fingers over the shelf. They touched something metal. She drew out a square device that resembled a very small printer. *Autopen* in bold silver lettering lay across the front.

"Holy sh...t!" She cried out loud, pulling it down and setting it on the island like it was a hot potato. She grabbed her cell and clicked off photos. Gently, she picked up the autopen and placed it back on the shelf, moving the folders back in front. She grabbed the back of the chair and began to step to the floor.

The door of the laboratory swung open, and Adrian stepped in. She jumped a mile.

Chapter Thirty-Eight

"Helen! How did you get in here?" His small eyes behind his glasses were blazing. His expression was apoplectic. He was beyond furious. In disbelief, he took in her movement from the cabinet to the floor.

"Hello, Adrian." She swallowed hard, tucking in her shirt and straightening her hair. "Those buyers have come back. I'm hoping it's not too late for you to accept an offer from them. Did you sign away the house yet?" She struggled to act like this was another ordinary day. She pasted on a meager smile. Who was she kidding?

"Why are you in here?"

She stepped down and put the island between them. "I came down here for one reason. I wanted to confirm this was an unfinished space. Since we were up against a deadline and you were out of town, I decided to check."

"Don't bullsh..t me! Does this buyer even exist? If they did, they couldn't care a crap about this room." He spotted the invoices turned upside down, the piles askew. I warned you and warned you. I should have known better. You wouldn't stop poking your nose where you didn't belong."

She surveyed the room. One door and one small basement window. It was like a tomb, solid and soundless. She swallowed, trying not to panic. Her cell was on the desk. If she could push the panic app she'd just installed, the police would be notified.

"Listen to me. I have good news. I have an offer."

"Where?" He sneered.

"On the seat of my car. Why don't we go upstairs? I'll get it for you?" She started to edge around the island toward the door.

He leaned on the door. "You're not leaving here. Your days are over." He cast about the room with wild eyes. "This is what's going to happen," he paused. "You're going to disappear. The cops won't find you for days. By that time, I'll be safely on a beach."

'Stall for time,' Nancy told her. "You mean the beach in Fiji. Must be beautiful. Why'd you pick Fiji?"

Adrian jerked back. "You're the one who put the police onto my Fiji purchase. I knew it. There's nothing wrong with buying vacation property on the islands, is there?"

"Not at all. Wish I did. 'Course I don't have forged checks as extra income."

He snapped his lips together. "You're crazy. I don't know what you're talking about."

"People have said I'm crazy before, but I don't think so. You bought the Fiji property with embezzled money, didn't you?" Helen pointed to the stack of invoices. "You've been submitting fake invoices to Barto Enterprises for at least the past year. Roberto didn't notice because he never signed the checks. You used his autopen to forge them."

"How could you know about that?"

"I came across some checks dated after he died with his signature on them."

He shrugged. "That was a slip. Didn't dawn on me his signature had to be removed for the bank." Adrian walked over to the cabinet, reached up, and pulled down the little autographing machine. He set it on the island opposite her. "This is amazing." He stroked it gently. "It made forgery easy. I never had to worry about a bad signature giving me away."

"Did Mariah know what you were up to?"

He chuckled. "Mariah was too busy wallowing in her own self-pity. She wanted money. Dana blabbed her nasty mouth and told her Roberto was a gambler in trouble. Mariah came to me and threatened to tell the network he cheated in that contest and about his ties to the Mob. I talked her into revenge instead. She was my answer to getting rid of Roberto. I kept pinching that nerve every time we passed each other at the studio. It didn't take much to get her onboard. I told her I knew a way to make him so sick he'd be fired. She could replace him. I let her think it was all her idea, and I was just providing the Daphne plant to help her do it."

"But he joined Gamblers Anonymous. He was trying to turn himself around. Why didn't you give him time to do that?"

Adrian paced, his hands scrubbing his short beard. "I couldn't. The Mob was starting to send out its henchmen. They'd come into Water Street Bistro or up in Philly or down in Baltimore. They'd sit at the bar and drink. Just their presence was creeping everyone out. Roberto turned into a wreck whenever they walked through the door. Neal was starting to ask questions. Wanted to know why they were hanging around."

"You decided to skim money from Barto Enterprises too." Helen struggled to keep a quiver out of her voice. "His gambling was accelerating. You knew your company was going to implode. You decided you'd better take your share now."

Adrian's face lit up, and he pounded on his chest. "I invented the Flying Pan organic coating! That organic coating was so popular, we couldn't make my cookware fast enough."

"Didn't you get half of the profits from his cookbooks and restaurants?"

"No! He got the lion's share. Everything had his name and his face. I had to do the real work. It was a bad deal I agreed to when we were just starting the business."

She decided to try to show sympathy. "Sounds like you got a raw deal. Weren't you worried his personality would be hard to replace for his fans?"

"He was crumbling under the pressure of gambling debts. I planted the idea of his replacement with Greg months ago. Greg got nervous his golden boy might eventually tank. He agreed we needed a backup plan in case Roberto got sick or disappeared into the bay wearing concrete shoes. We started auditions and came up with Tara."

"Why'd you decide to get rid of him?"

"Ha. He spotted expenses he hadn't authorized. I always got the calls whenever we were late paying contractors. Dottie Taylor screwed that up by calling Roberto directly instead of me. She complained her payments were too far behind. That's when he noticed payments going out to a fake lumberyard."

"Who decided to sell Riding Cross?"

"I encouraged him. He could get out from Mob threats, and we could start over, clean. He hated to sell, but he'd tasted the thrill and recognition of opening more and more restaurants. They won out. I was glad. I didn't believe he'd ever get past his gambling addiction. He was destroying everything I built."

"You built?"

"I built! A chef can be hired. A brilliant mind cannot." He shouted. She stepped back. She'd pushed him too hard.

"With him gone, were you ditching the company for the islands?"

"I thought, with Greg's help at the studio and Neal's help with the restaurants, I could keep the business going. If it started to turn sour, then I'd clean out the till and skip the country. Most of the money is already in foreign bank accounts."

"Did Mariah regret killing Roberto?"

"No. But I was furious when she cozied up with Dana and met with you and Lizzie. I couldn't trust her any longer."

Her eyes opened wide, and she stepped back. "Mariah didn't commit suicide, did she? You killed her."

Adrian burst out in cold laughter, his face twisted. "I'm a scientist. I knew she was taking Loroxide. All I had to do was stop in for a visit and ply her with more pills mixed in vodka. The mix was deadly. She was drunk when I coaxed her to write her note. I hung around until she was gone and then planted the drugs."

She gulped. "You placed the flower tube next to the note to be sure she got pinned for Roberto's murder."

He chuckled. "Worked like a charm. The cops thought his murder was solved." He stopped, then started to move closer to her. "But you kept digging around. Why?"

Helen's eyes bore into him. "I couldn't believe Mariah cared so little about Lizzie. I kept thinking there was more to his killing."

He swung his head from side to side. "That was a miscalculation on my part. Lizzie was a problem for her. We knew she was allergic to coconut, so I convinced Mariah that we'd alter the ingredients for that day's recipe because Lizzie wouldn't eat it. As far as I was concerned, if something happened to her, it was just the cost of doing business." He gave an indifferent shrug.

Helen's eyes blazed. "You sent Rory to threaten me, didn't you?"

"I was sure you'd back down after he roughed you up. He's halfway to Arizona by now. The question is, how do I get rid of you?"

She backed away from the island and toward the desk. Her phone was her last chance. Joe was probably fast asleep. Would his police station tell him she'd sent them an alarm? 'At this stage, I'll take anyone's help,' she prayed.

Darting to the desk, she grabbed the phone. Adrian leaped forward, and the two of them struggled for it. She pushed the new alarm app on her home screen before he could stop her. She lunged toward the door, shoved it open, and managed to get halfway across the wine cellar.

Adrian was right behind her. Enraged, he grabbed her, striking her across the face. The cut from Rory broke open with the impact. Blood streamed down her cheek and onto her shirt. She dropped to her knees and fell back against a rack of wine bottles. He tore her cell phone out of her hands. She bit down on his arm. With a yowl, he grabbed her shirt, twisting her silver chain across her neck, strangling her. The chain broke loose as she was gasping for breath.

Coughing, she scrambled to her feet, but he was too quick. With a chokehold, he dragged her back into the laboratory and shoved her onto the chair. Helen gasped for air as he rooted through a nearby drawer and pulled out a roll of wide yellow tape. Holding her down, he tied her wrists behind her onto the back of the chair.

Panting, he touched his own bloodied arm. "I'll be back."

He flicked off the lights and slammed the door shut. The lock clicked behind him.

* * *

Helen's head lolled forward. She inhaled, desperately trying to control the pounding of her heart which roared in her ears. She blinked, but the utter cave of a room didn't offer the slightest chink of daylight. She felt utterly blinded. She rubbed her chin against her neck, and tears started to seep down her cheeks. Her talisman, Andy's ring, was gone, and it made her feel utterly, completely abandoned.

Sniffling, she caught herself up short. Jessica, her stalwart widow, reprimanded her. Get ahold of yourself. She took a few gulps. What was Adrian doing, she wondered? Most likely packing a bag and ordering a flight out of the country.

From the depths of the house, she could hear a doorbell. Murmurs. Distant voices. Her heart raced. Joe? She wiggled her feet. If she was lucky, Adrian would leave her and go. She called out. Her voice only reverberated within the hidden, impenetrable room. More conversations. Rustling from room to room. Then total quiet. Where did they all go?

She called out, still nothing, then footsteps. The latch turned, and the soft light from the wine room pierced her dark.

The door opened and shut before the lights flipped back on. She blinked, trying to adjust her eyes to the stark change. Her heart dropped, realizing it was Adrian. Where were the police?

He grinned. In fresh clothes and a shaven face, he came across the room towards her. A handgun was tucked into his belt.

"Sorry to disappoint you. They're gone. I told them I came home to an empty house. The fools."

Helen swallowed. "My car?"

"I moved it into an old stable on the back of the property. I'll be long gone before they come back again."

He turned and reached into the little refrigerator and picked out a glass tapered flask with clear liquid and a stopper. Holding it up to the light, he nodded, satisfied. "Just enough to take care of you. How fortunate." He walked to the cabinet and pulled out a small beaker.

Helen strained on the tape. "Adrian, leave me here. You don't need to kill me."

He straightened his shoulders and simpered, pleased with himself. "I do need to kill you. You forced me to go to plan B. I thought I'd be here much longer, running my company as lead man. You've taken that away from me."

Her eyes were transfixed on his slender, neat fingers as he carefully swished the clear liquid around in the flask. He pulled out its rubber stopper and poured the liquid into the beaker.

She rocked back and forth as he approached her.

His eyes bore in. "Sit still! I'm looking forward to seeing a Ricket's Grin on your face. It's what you deserve."

Footsteps trampled across the kitchen above them and down the stairs. He stared up at the ceiling and listened. More running, more shouting. The laboratory doorknob rattled.

"Adrian! It's McAlister! Open the door now!" More rustling from the other side.

"Adrian! Open it now, or I'll shoot it open."

Adrian grabbed her hair and yanked her head back. Clamping her mouth shut, she tore her head away. The deadly liquid splashed across her face.

Seconds passed. A blast at the handle and the door broke open, banging on the wall aside it.

Adrian stood behind Helen with one hand on the beaker and the other holding his revolver. "Don't come in! I'll kill her!" His face was livid.

Joe stood in the doorway, the darker wine room outlining his body and the stark laboratory lights forcing him to squint as he tried to focus. Helen twisted, dropping her head down toward the table edge.

Adrian raised his gun to pull the trigger.

Joe was faster. He pulled off two shots, hitting his shoulder and arm. Adrian dropped to the floor.

Chapter Thirty-Nine

Her phone rang about noon the following morning. It looked like spam, and she ignored it. She'd slept in after an endless night in the Sheriff's Office interview room after Adrian's capture. Moments later, a voice mail popped up with a ding.

"Helen, this is Scott Harris. I'm in Port Anne. Thought I'd come take a little tour of Osprey Point and check in on you. Give me a call."

She leaned back and closed her eyes. She swore they were bleeding. Her wrists ached. What in the world did big ego Scott Harris want?

Groaning, she sat up in bed and dialed. "Scott, Helen Morrisey returning your call."

"I met with McAlister's squad this morning for a recap on the Barto and Manley murders. If you're home, I'd like to stop in and see you before I head back to Baltimore."

Helen hesitated. "I'm easily ten minutes out of town and, frankly, exhausted." She paused again. "Could we talk now? It's been a long twenty-four hours. Or schedule another time?"

"Of course." He sounded disappointed. "How are you feeling? Get any sleep?"

"A little. I'm a bit bruised but relieved this investigation is over."

The S.A. chuckled. "I did try to warn you." He sounded smug.

She bristled. "You did. I guess we all have to go with our own instincts."

"I've concluded you are an interesting woman. In some respects, you remind me of myself."

"Really? In what way?"

"You strike me as being rather fearless."

She sighed. "I'm really not. Not at all. I'm sure you work with women reporters and detectives that don't always take your advice."

"They're different. It's their job. Often, they regret it later."

"Do you prefer working with women that are more compliant?"

He gave a little uneasy laugh. "You misunderstand me. I was only concerned."

"This case forced me to be protective. A good friend of mine taught me there can be evil hidden in people. Not everyone, just a few."

"Are we talking about McAlister?"

She smiled to herself. "Actually, a wise woman by the name of Jane. Let's leave it at that."

"Helen," he paused. "I'm struck by the idea we could be an unusual duo. Has that occurred to you?"

Helen looked at the phone and then returned it to her ear. She was sure she could feel his smug charm oozing over the call. "I can't say I have. I...." She bit her tongue, thinking of Joe and Shawn, who both had to work with his office. She inhaled and let out a slow breath. "Scott, thank you. I appreciate your call. Can I wish you good luck with your press conference today? I'm sure, with your level of experience, you'll make the most of it."

His laugh was hollow. She knew he wasn't sure how to accept her offside compliment. "We'll talk again."

Hopefully not, Helen thought.

* * *

Under Shawn and Lizzie's stern orders, Helen had been assigned to her desk at Safe Harbor all the following week. She accused Tammi of attaching a GPS tracker to her Mini. Her personal drill sergeant kept a close eye on her. Walking down to Jean's for coffee was her big adventure for the day.

"I'll be right back. I want to check in on Dottie Taylor."

Tammi gave her a wave.

* * *

Dottie was in the back room, chewing on a sandwich, when Helen dropped by. She got up and gave her a huge hug.

"You beat me to it. I was going to stop by this afternoon. The attorney handling Barto Enterprises contacted me this morning."

"Really!"

"They're going to release half of what they owe me in about ten days. I'll get the rest after Riding Cross is sold."

"That's great news."

"You have no idea. How are you doing?" The yard owner looked her up and down.

"Right now, Shawn and Lizzie have me under lockdown. They're intent on keeping me out of any more trouble."

"Tell them, 'good luck with that.' The Barto attorney asked about you. Wanted to know your reputation as a real estate agent."

Helen groaned. "What did you tell him?"

"I told him there's no one better."

"Thank you for that." She smiled. "Let's hope he'll send me some business." She gave Dottie a wave. The fat cat on the counter gave her a slow blink and a cat grin as she passed by.

* * *

Back in the office, she complained about her confinement to Tammi. "The only benefit of being glued to this chair is I've finished creating the program for Kent County Board of Realtors. We're calling it 'Work Smart, Work Safe.' Shawn's speaking for the district attorney's office. Joe and Rick will demonstrate safety tactics. The Realtors who'd been attacked are talking about their experiences and lessons learned. I'm hopeful we have a strong turnout." Her green eyes were bright. "If this goes well, we'll probably offer it all over the state."

Her cell rang. It was Shawn.

"I've got good news for you." He sounded pleased. "Baltimore police picked up the man who attacked those real estate agents."

"That's such great news! The entire community will be relieved. How did you find him?"

"An agent down here got a suspicious request to show a property and called their local police. They staked out the house, then brought him in for questioning."

"Does Joe know?"

"We talked a few minutes ago. He'll be talking to the press later today." Shawn's cell clicked. "I've got another call. See you tonight."

Her cell rang again. "Helen Morrisey."

"This is Stuart Hirsch from Hirsch and Leeds. We're overseeing the disposition of property for Barto Enterprises."

She crossed her fingers. "How can I help you, Stuart?"

"You may not have heard. The restaurants and all product lines are being sold to a conglomerate based in Miami. The restaurant managers will continue to run their locations."

"Does this mean Neal will remain general manager?"

"Exactly. According to our numbers, he's doing well, even with all that's happened."

"I'm glad for him."

Stuart cleared his throat. "From all I've read and heard, you were unusually involved in the Barto case. You were representing Roberto and Adrian on the sale of Riding Cross?"

"Yes, that's right. We had a buyer who was very interested in the property. That cooled when liens were filed, and Adrian was arrested."

"Understood. We also heard you market yourself as," he paused and shifted papers. "Not your typical Realtor," he read.

She issued a little gasp. "I'm not sure it's my official description."

He returned a little chuckle. "With the help of your county district attorney's office, we believe we can resolve the debts hindering a sale. I don't need to tell you, banks don't like holding onto property. The party owed, who remains nameless, is willing to cooperate with the state and the bank, giving us a short window to sell. We would like you to resume negotiations with that buyer. If they are no longer interested, then you'll need to remarket, but quickly. Would this be acceptable to you?"

Helen sat down in her desk chair with a thud.

"Um. Very acceptable. When can I begin work?"

"I'll send your paperwork this afternoon."

It was her turn to clear her throat. "Thank you, Stuart. I'm excited to be working with you."

"The same to you, Mrs. Morrisey." He clicked off.

"Tammi!" She stood up and shouted. "Tammi!"

She rushed into the room. "For heaven's sake, are you all right? Now what's happening?"

Helen clasped Tammi's hands. "Get on the phone. Call Till Travel."

"Where are you going?"

"Not me! You and Kayla. I want you to tell them your trip to Disney World is back on!"

Tammi's Labor Day red, white, and blue earrings swung wildly side to side. "Why?"

"Because we're going to sell Riding Cross. When we lost the listing, I was so upset. I had your trip planned. I've wanted to treat you for ages. You deserve it. Give me a hug and go call Kayla!"

Chapter Forty

The sailor in her dreaded September and the end of summer. Already the talk at Port Anne Yacht Club and the local marinas shifted as people planned their last overnight cruises for the fall season down the bay. The sun was setting a little earlier each evening. Chatter turned toward November and preparations for pulling boats for the winter. She loved being out on the water in the late fall but hated talk about winterizing and dry docking.

She decided to gather a small celebratory contingent together for a picnic dinner and a sail on *Persuasion*. It was a full crew, convening on the dock. It was going to be a full moon, perfect.

Joe helped her ready her boat. It was about six o'clock when Lizzie came down the pier, a huge L.L.Bean tote bag over her shoulder.

"What in the world do you have in here?" laughed Joe as he hauled it onboard, pretending to strain. Lizzie, smiling as if the world was right again, clutched onto a lifeline and stepped in. Minutes later, Tammi, little Kayla, and Susan climbed on.

"How was your trip, partner?" Helen greeted Susan, exchanging big hugs. "I feel like you've been gone for ages."

Susan, always dressed perfectly for every occasion, made a little twirl to show off her sailing jacket and matching, blue-striped boat shoes. "Great vacation. Days on the beach and nights at the tiki bar."

"As it should be. I'm glad. You're back just in time to take over for me next week."

Susan grinned. "I'm ready."

245

Little Kayla handed up her Disney backpack. "Aunt Helen, Mommy bought me my own Minnie backpack for our trip next month. Isn't it pretty?"

"It sure is! I can't wait to see all the pictures after your trip."

Glancing up, she spotted Shawn and Olivia. He was carrying her big canvas bag and a beer cooler on his shoulders.

"Ahoy! If you think I'm no longer under the thumb of my high school principal, think again," he laughed as tiny Olivia tapped his arm and directed him to hand up her treats.

"Looks like we've enough food and drink to cruise for a week, not an evening," Helen shouted. "Now that I've got my experienced crew aboard, let's shove off."

Shawn tossed up the stern lines from the dock while Lizzie fended off the bow. Tammi tucked her daughter down below in the V-berth with a book and some snacks.

Once everyone was settled, Olivia spoke up. "Who's going to fill us in on all the bits and pieces of Roberto's murder investigation? What led you to Mariah and Adrian?"

"When Roberto was killed," Helen began, "I never dreamed Mariah, who seemed a direct descendant from the Woodstock generation, would hurt anyone. She was so quirky and perky the Sunday we first met. Adrian was smart to fuel her hidden anger. He became desperate to end his partnership. He recognized her longstanding grievance against Roberto and pushed her into revenge."

Susan spoke up. "Why would he choose to poison Roberto in the middle of the studio? There are so many people there twenty-four seven."

"I credit Jane Marple for helping us there. She was key. She believed murder in the midst of chaos provided much more diversion than choosing time alone with a victim. Sure enough, the police were swamped with suspects. I suggested to Joe motive plus opportunity plus chaos equals the perfect crime." She counted them off on three fingers. "What could create more confusion than a crime in the middle of Roberto's live studio kitchen?"

She sipped on her wine. "The challenge was finding a motive strong enough to inspire murder. Mariah was turned down for the new chef job.

Dana was hemorrhaging money in lost sales because his popularity was cutting into her fan base."

"Adrian and Greg appeared to be least likely," Joe added. "They had so much riding on Roberto's success. The Mob was another possibility. They're not patient people, and they wanted their money. Roberto was feeling their pressure to pay up, and soon. He was out of time. I just didn't believe a poisoning was Mob style. It wasn't a fit."

"Mariah told Dana about the thugs threatening him in the parking lot after a show. Dana decided to make his life even more miserable by talking her into leaving a threatening note he'd assume came from the Mob. I'd say Dana was regretful later. It placed her back into the middle of the investigation."

"Did Roberto really cheat Mariah out of a big New York City chef contest?" Olivia asked.

Joe passed another beer to Shawn. "He did. She pointed us in the right direction with her newspaper clippings. It took some digging, but we found two former students who confirmed her story. They walked in on him as he was hovering over her dishes just before the final judging. When she tasted them, she knew they'd been ruined."

"Adrian made a mistake by removing those photos from Roberto's office," Helen explained. "At first, we thought he removed the photos at the casino to keep Roberto's debts to the Mob quiet. That made sense since he was protecting Barto Enterprises from bad press. Then I remembered advice from my Detection Club."

"Mom," Shawn protested.

She wasn't deterred. "They told me I shouldn't concentrate on the obvious. The photo of him winning a contest that launched his career was much more important. It took us ages to recognize Mariah in the background."

Tammi spoke up. "What were you searching for the night Adrian caught you?"

She eyed Joe. "It started with the autographed cookbooks. We couldn't find anything in the Barto accounts that seemed out of line. I started wondering why all Roberto's signatures appeared identical. When I found out famous people sometimes used an autopen, I wondered if Adrian used one to sign checks without Roberto's knowledge."

Helen turned toward her son. "I realize I should have never gone back to Riding Cross by myself. I was afraid he was about to disappear on us. It bothered me that I never saw the inside of the root cellar, and I decided I couldn't leave until I tried one more time. That's how I found his chemistry lab and the fake invoices. I recognized the tubes right away. You can thank Pete Askins for that. He'd sent me flowers the week before. I realized Adrian extracted the poisonous fluid from the Daphne plants and provided it to Mariah. It was the perfect foil. She deposited the fluid into Roberto's recipe while Adrian was miles away."

"Where's he now?" asked Shawn.

"He's in Kent County Hospital under guard," Joe said. "I shot him in the shoulder as he aimed his gun. He'll be transferred to a state prison in a few more days, on trial for murder, embezzlement, and forgery. When we patted him down, he had Roberto's electronic signature card for operating the autopen in his wallet."

Helen grimaced, "I dread testifying. This trial will generate a flurry of entertainment since Roberto was such a famous victim. I wish Port Anne's notoriety could return to boating, crabbing, and good restaurants."

"Don't worry," Lizzie spoke up. "ShopTV will be working overtime to focus their shoppers on shopping. Roberto's kitchen is already demolished, and a new, even fancier one is under construction." She chuckled. "Dana's delighted."

Lizzie hugged her mother. "Thank you for never giving up on seeking the truth. I'm back selling my happy products and leaving the law in Joe and Shawn's hands."

Helen returned the hug. "A momma bear will always come to the defense of her cubs."

"Is that a Jane-ism?" asked Olivia.

She laughed. "No, that's a Helen-ism."

"Are you sure you want to stay in real estate after this?"

Helen nodded. "I still believe most people are inherently good. Right, Shawn?"

He smiled. "Yes, you're right, but could you curb your tendency to cross paths with the bad? I'd like to see you give your Detection Club a long rest."

His mother responded, squeezing his hand.

Lizzie smiled her famous smile. "That's good because Alison Davies and her husband invited you to the grand opening of their B&B. Since you sold them the house, you'll have their financial loss on your head if they don't succeed."

"Isn't that house supposed to be haunted?" Susan spoke up.

"Oh no!" the group chorused.

* * *

It was after ten when the party decided to say goodnight.

Helen and Joe closed up the boat, then sat on the edge of the bow for one last gaze at the night sky. Egrets were lined up along a row of pilings in the dark.

"You never told me why you came back to Riding Cross after searching the first time?" she prompted him.

He sighed. "We had a squad and searched every room, every closet. Nothing. No sign of you. So, we left. I was frantic. Rick and I decided to drive to your house and check it out. We searched around. I knew right away you never made it home."

"How did you know?"

"No microwave dinner in the trash?" He smiled. "No empty wine glass on the counter?"

"Very funny, You think you are so clever." She gave him a little push.

"I am clever," he grinned back. "We went back to Riding Cross and sat at the top of the hill. I started thinking about your conversation with Adrian about the floor plans. It reminded me of the crawl space downstairs. Rick and I went back inside. No sign of Adrian when we called out. We ran down to the wine cellar. That's when I spotted this."

He reached into his pocket and pulled out her silver chain with Andy's ring dangling from it."

Her eyes widened. "My wedding band!" Tears sprang to her eyes. "How did you find it?"

"It had skidded under the wine rack closest to the laboratory door. No one spotted it the first time we'd searched. As soon as I saw it, I knew the crawl space door had to lead to you."

"Thank God you did!" she exclaimed.

"I prayed when I shot off the lock you weren't right near the door. It was a terrible decision."

"Not any more than for me. I was terrified when you stepped inside. You were outlined in the light behind you. Adrian's eyes were accustomed to the laboratory lights. I knew you were blinded. You saved my life," she said.

"You saved yourself by ducking. I prayed I'd hit him, not you, as I took my shots."

Joe pulled her in tight against him and leaned against a rail. "How's Pete?"

"Pete?" She smiled. "Pete is Pete. He's smart and handsome and successful and charming."

He studied her face in the pale light. "That's a lot of 'ands.' Where is he tonight?"

"He's out of town on business. He sent me Godiva chocolates yesterday."

"Chocolates?"

"I think he decided, given the way Roberto was murdered, flowers might not be appropriate right now." She grinned in the dark, her eyes teasing.

"Hmmm. Not sure how I feel about that. I don't think he plans to give up on you easily."

Helen twirled her chain around her fingers. "I'm not sure how I feel about any of this."

Joe watched the ring catch the moonlight. "What's your club say about dating?"

She smiled. "Five women, five opinions. No help at all."

"As long as you tell me I've got a better shot."

She shrugged. "I *might* be leaning toward men a little more rugged, a little more curious, a little more Nick Charles."

"Not Jesse Stone?"

"Oh, him too," she said.

Acknowledgements

How do I thank all those that embraced my debut mystery, *Murder in the Master*, and helped turn it into a multiple award-winner? Who do I thank that helped Helen plunge into her second mystery in *Killer in the Kitchen* and come out victorious again?

I'll start with my husband, John, who put up with my abandoning him for days on end as I headed up to my study. So thankful to my beta readers: My daughter, Meghan, provided me with expert advice on home shopping networks and how they worked. My son, John, the law enforcement expert, kept my officers on task even as my sleuths disrupted their days and nights. Their willingness to be my sounding board provided me clarity as I worked through a manuscript full of red herrings and a range of characters. Another thank you to a good friend and Syracuse University roommate, Patricia Hennigan, who cheered me on while sharpening her copy-checking pencil.

Thank you to the librarians of Cecil County Maryland Library System who offered me sanctuary whenever I needed an alternative writing retreat. There is nothing like walking through the doors of a library to remind us how the world of books is such a wide and inspirational one. If you haven't wandered among the stacks recently, I urge you, stop in. Digital versions of books may be handy, but they will never replace this sensory delight.

My appreciation for all those hard-working people in the real estate profession. I hope, like Helen, they become more safety conscious.

Thank you to Shawn Reilly Simmons, my publisher at Level Best Books, for her talented editorial advice, chef experience, and tenacity. To Dawn Dowdle of Blue Ridge Literary Agency, I am grateful for her patience as she guided me along.

Which leads me to thanking you, the encouraging friends and newly found fans, who quickly turned pages, rooted for my heroine, and passed on their recommendations to others.

Now, it's time, my friends, to pull up the covers, turn on your nightlight, and give a little shiver of anticipation. The hunt is on, and the wicked will soon be exposed!

Judy L. Murray

About the Author

Judy L. Murray is an Independent Publisher Silver Medalist, a Silver Falchion Award Winner, and an Agatha Award Nominee for Best First Novel with *Murder in the Master – A Chesapeake Bay Mystery. Killer in the Kitchen* is second in the series. A Philadelphia real estate broker and restoration addict, Judy has worked with enough delusional sellers, jittery buyers, testy contractors, and diva agents to fill her head with back-office insight and truth versus gossip. She began her professional writing career, after graduating in newspaper journalism from the S.I. Newhouse School at Syracuse University, as a reporter and magazine columnist. She holds a Master's in Business from Penn State University. She lives atop a cliff on the Chesapeake Bay with her husband. They're buffeted by winds in winter and invaded by family and dogs in summer. Judy is a member of Sisters in Crime Chesapeake Chapter and Mystery Writers of America. Sign up for her newsletter at www.judylmurraymysteries.com to learn more.

SOCIAL MEDIA HANDLES:
  https://www.facebook.com/judymurray4
  https://twitter.com/judylmurray

https://www.instagram.com/judylmurraymysterywriter/
https://www.linkedin.com/in/murrayjudy/

AUTHOR WEBSITE:
www.judylmurraymysteries.com

Also by Judy L. Murray

Murder in the Master – A Chesapeake Bay Mystery